W9-CBO-130

The
Time
Chamber

A Novel

ADAM BLOOD

Copyright © 2015 Adam Blood
All rights reserved
First Edition

Fulton Books, Inc.
Meadville, PA

First originally published by Fulton Books 2015

ISBN 978-1-63338-083-7 (paperback)
ISBN 978-1-63338-084-4 (digital)

Printed in the United States of America

To John and Shea, for encouraging me and believing when
I did not believe in myself. Of all the words to follow, none
have the impact of the three you told me: "Go for it."

To Jack, Art, and Nikki, for never letting me hold myself back.

Chapter 1

If hell had a sound, it would be an alarm clock. It would be a loud, screeching alarm clock that fills the brains of whomever it can reach. Within every howl and chilling shriek, one can hear the oncoming volley of demands and deadlines. The grating noise would be the sound of a lifetime of labor painfully trying to fit itself into too small of a timeframe. Its loud chimes only serve as a reminder of another day of too much work and not enough hours.

When I finally tried to silence this small instrument of evil, my hand came crashing down on the alarm clock like a sledgehammer. As my eyes fully focused, the scene around me was the natural habitat of the North American workaholic. My small one-bedroom apartment was flooded with dirty laundry, fast-food wrappers, and rolled-up balls of paper where my ideas had gone to die. The sink was overflowing with dirty dishes, and my overworked coffee maker almost seemed to beg for a merciful cleaning. The image in the bathroom mirror was not much better. My hair had grown long and disheveled, my face was haggard and unshaven, and the dark circles beneath my eyes had started to become a mainstay around the leathery bags caused by overwork and fatigue. I looked as though I had died weeks ago, and yet my body continued to walk around upright, still growing hair and underachieving.

The next stop in the apartment was my laptop. I couldn't recall exactly what hour I had gone to sleep, but I knew that the one thing I could always rely upon was my almost religious practice of saving my work before stepping away from the desk. The document on my word processor was sitting open with a timestamp that read, "Last saved February 22, 4:27 a.m." That was less than three hours before, which meant I had only gotten about two hours of sleep in the last two days. What waited for me on the screen sent chills up my spine. The failed attempt at an all-nighter, trying to write a research paper and a column, had led to several hours of scrapping together an idea, writing a few words, getting frustrated, then hitting delete. Pursuing my master's in communication with an emphasis in journalism while working as a columnist for a young Chicago news magazine had made nights with little or no sleep all too common.

When I looked at the screen, all that waited for me was an incomplete, fragmented sentence that started with nothing and went directly to nowhere. I grimaced at the sight of this abuse of the written word, and then with a quick highlight and one click of the backspace key, my nightmare incarnate sat waiting for me.

It was the abysmal blank screen. This was what I often referred to as that large empty white space where all my brilliance should go. As an undergraduate and a writer for the school newspaper, I used to be able to fill up entire pages at a time with articles and compositions. In the two weeks leading up to that particular morning, I couldn't put a sentence together. It was only my second semester of grad school, and I had been working at the Falcon for less than a year. Slowly but surely, meeting even the simplest of deadlines had become an insurmountable task. That was where I found myself that morning, constantly behind with a week's worth of work that was woefully behind schedule.

I had a meeting with Dr. Karzeck, my research-methods professor, at eight o'clock, and it was quickly approaching seven thirty. I walked past my kitchen table and pulled off one of the chairs what I haphazardly decided was the cleanest shirt in my apartment. I buried my nose in the shirt, trying to determine if it was acceptable to wear. The fatigue was so severe that I could barely see straight. This logic would dictate that I should put little or no trust into my olfactory senses. But nonetheless, the shirt passed the smell test, and I quickly draped it around my shoulders, buttoned it up, and then tucked it into wrinkled slacks that went through an equally unscientific test of cleanliness. This was the most energy I could possibly allocate to my appearance that morning as I gathered whatever necessary items I needed and vacated my apartment.

Right outside my apartment building was a small newsstand that normally supplied my morning cup of coffee. The antiquated coffee pot made a dark bitter sludge, but it was consumable and gave me my needed dosage of caffeine. I had gotten used to drinking it black, not necessarily because of some decision to give up cream and sugar, but more because the constant state of hurry and exhaustion left me too impatient to add them.

Immediately after paying for my coffee, I sent a quick text message to Trish, who was more than likely in the middle of opening shop at the bookstore. This text was nothing more than a quick hello, as she had grown accustomed to me being unavailable during long and overbooked days. The walk to campus to meet Dr. Karzeck was just over six blocks, which I had come to measure as one cup of less-than-satisfactory newsstand coffee. On that particular morning, my thoughts during the walk were all haunted by one singular image: the blank screen.

The blank screen came to represent everything that was standing in my way. As the deadlines mounted and I fell further and further behind, the endless white abyss felt more and more impassible.

The meeting I was approaching was intended to discuss a paper for the research methods class. I had signed up for this course because I knew the semester-long project was a paper that could be easily converted into a thesis prospectus. My constantly multitasking mind was intrigued at the idea of a course that would put me ahead of the game for graduate work for the next two semesters. Having already taken the graduate-level theories course the semester before, I could have used this course to choose my theoretical perspective, select my methodology, and make great strides toward completing the long and often tedious review of literature. Of course, all ideas that would help this endeavor turn into written work had been led like lambs into slaughter into the deep, abysmal, blank screen.

So there I was, walking like the living dead toward a meeting that would undoubtedly end in yet another disappointment. Many of my classmates were already ten or even fifteen pages into their paper, whereas I, the former crown jewel of the journalism department, was struggling to put together a single sentence.

As I drew closer and closer to campus, I started to review exactly what I had accomplished leading up to that morning. I had already chosen the theoretical setting and had somewhat narrowed down the context in which I would write my paper, but I was still lacking a clear hypothesis. There were at least twenty articles that sat waiting on my flash drive, as at some point I ran a search and saved every scholarly article that seemed to fit my topic area to be read at a later date. This meant that only reading and writing stood in the way of progressing through my graduate work. "If not for all this reading and writing nonsense," I thought aloud, "school would be cakewalk."

At some point, I grew careless as my mind was wandering, and the door to a diner on the way to campus flew open, colliding with my forehead and knocking me to the ground. As I tried to brace myself, I could feel the cold, abrasive concrete tear against the palm of my hand. This sharp pain then combined with the feeling of my coffee spilling all over my chest and stomach, scalding me and staining my shirt, which was questionably clean to begin with. As I rose to my feet, a man in his late sixties stood looking down at me, his mouth was hanging wide open. He said, "I'm sorry, I didn't even see you there."

"It's okay," I grunted while trying to regain my feet. "I should have been paying better attention." I could tell that this man was about to continue his apology, but I was already in a hurry and couldn't slow down, so I gave him a quick pat on the back and went along my way. A quick glance over my shoulder found him standing in the middle of the sidewalk with his eyes locked on me. His face had a remorseful, embarrassed gaze, and through the dull roar of passersby, I could have sworn I heard him shout "Sorry about the shirt, Eric." Was that even possible? I had never seen this man before, so how could he know my name? By that point, I was positive that my sleep-deprived brain was playing tricks on me.

Finally, I arrived on campus and quickly made my way toward Dr. Karzeck's office. Eight o'clock, the scheduled time for our meeting, was quickly approaching. As I climbed the stairs, my thoughts then began to center on Dr. Karzeck. He had been my mentor since my freshman year of college. His sterling recommendation had helped me obtain my job as a journalist, and it was his guidance that led me to pursue a master's degree. His influence was present in every word I wrote, and knowing that I was about to egregiously disappoint him was more agonizing than the exhaustion that held me down that morning.

As I walked into the office suite, Alice, the office professional, looked almost startled by my appearance. She was the one that students and professors alike would normally approach with any concerns or inquiries. Her job involved aiding faculty with everything from ordering office supplies to submitting final grades. Her demeanor was that mix of friendliness and sarcasm that came from a genuinely caring person who has weathered many years of tedious requests from professors and frustrated inquiries from confused students.

In the several years that I had attended classes at the University of Chicago, she and I had developed something of a rapport. In the few days that I had been hiding from Dr. Karzeck, my appearance had taken a drastic turn for the worse, or as Alice put it, I looked like I had "been hit by a bus full of homeless people." Finally, he arrived, hurried but with an ever-willing ear to listen to a young aspiring journalist. I followed him into his office and, with his prompting, took a seat in front of his desk.

"How's work at the Falcon?" he asked.

I couldn't bring myself to tell him that that my underperformance in the classroom was carrying over into the columns that I wrote. The Falcon was the perfect job for me, and he knew it. It was a new, upstart journal with an ambitious editor that was looking for young talent. They wanted people who were skilled, hungry, and ready to take on the world. Dr. Karzeck thought I would fit the bill, and at the time he gave his recommendation, there was no reason for him to believe otherwise. I decided that although I couldn't be completely honest, my conscience and pride would at least allow ambiguity.

"Oh," I began, "you know how it goes. I write. They edit. I revise. They publish."

He responded with a grin, "Well, at least that last part is happening for you. How's the paper going?"

"Well, as you know, I've selected a theory to guide my research."

"Yes, I'm aware."

"I've also compiled many readings for a review of literature."

"Several weeks ago."

"So now I'm in the process of writing."

"Yes, you are in the process of writing, as you so put it, but let me ask you, how much have you actually written?"

At this point, I could no longer skirt the issue. I knew his patience was running thin, and I couldn't bring myself to be dishonest with someone whom I respected so much. "Not a word," I replied while burying my face in my skinned and dirty palms.

"Eric, I know you have everything it takes to become a talented journalist, and beyond that, you're one of the best minds in our graduate program. However, you seem to be backsliding at an alarming rate. You used to have every single assignment in on time, even early, but this project you've started is now falling farther and farther behind. It's only going to be a matter of months before you have to put together a thesis committee, and I don't know if I'd be able to support you if I can't depend on your ability to meet the deadline."

"Dr. Karzeck, I understand. This isn't like me. It just seems as though school and work are starting to catch up with me, and when I try to sit down and write, nothing comes out."

"Eric, the writing for you has never been the issue. The only thing that is standing in your way at this point is you. Like you've said, you've gathered the readings and you've even narrowed the focus of your research. From this point, the paper will begin to write itself if you let it. I will tell you rather candidly that my patience is near its limits. I'd like to see something on my desk this week. And if I don't, you may want to consider whether or not grad school is really the right place for you, and by the way, what's on your shirt?"

"Um, I spilled coffee on my way to your office this morning." My response had such a tone of embarrassment that I was almost mumbling. His stance, although justifiable, was somewhat surprising. As an undergraduate, I had grown used to being the golden child of the entire journalism department. This grad-school thing was his idea. I was convinced I could get the job I wanted without a master's degree, and I'm not even really sure why I was writing a thesis in the first place. Nonetheless, when I told him I would write one, he put a lot of time into mentoring and guiding me; and here I was, unshaved, smelling like stale coffee and death, and I finding new and creative ways to screw the proverbial pooch on every single project.

I was even pretty well respected throughout the whole college of arts and humanities. Every professor who had me in his class during my undergrad knew that I could meet a deadline and that I produced quality work. Dr. Karzeck's criticism, which had the very sound of an ultimatum, was the first I had ever heard that I couldn't cut it in the classroom. His words formed a rock at the pit of my stomach, made all the more noticeable by the fact that I had ingested nothing but caffeine for the last God knows how long.

I left Dr. Karzeck's office around eight twenty, and as I was leaving the office suite, it felt as though every nearby sound was miles away. I was in such a state of fatigue and disarray that every sensation, the glow of the fluorescent lights, the sound of the running printer, and the smell of the industrial cleaner used in the carpet, all faded into a sort of dull aura that filled my senses. Alice offered some parting remark, which, knowing Alice, could've ranged anywhere from words of kindness to playful sarcastic commentary. Nonetheless, I gave her an unresponsive grunt, trying to force some sort of grin while my glazed eyes stared off at nothing.

The Falcon building was almost three miles from campus, and I had nowhere near the patience or energy to make that walk, so I stopped at the nearby bus stop. The bus barely halted as I, along with a few other commuters, climbed aboard. Some people view riding the bus as a chance to take in all the sights of a bustling city. Not me. All the buildings, the cars, and the symphony of sights and sounds seemed to blur together into a dull urban backdrop underneath an endless gray sky. I used to view this large city with such wide-eyed mysticism, finding excitement in countless details that jumped to grasp my attention. That was before I took on the lifestyle of perpetual fatigue. People could have been dancing in the street, and I wouldn't have batted an eye. I was preoccupied, stressed, and on the verge of outright depression.

When I found a seat on the bus, it took everything I had to keep from nodding off. In this effort to stay awake, I found myself trying to make small talk with Trish via text message. On days like that, it felt like Trish was all that kept me from walking into traffic.

We had been together almost two years. I had met her in an elective course during my junior year as an undergraduate. She was hoping to become a high school English teacher, and I was a young aspiring journalist. She was without a doubt the most beautiful girl I had ever seen, with an intellect that I could only hope to keep up with. To this day, I can't fathom why she agreed to go on a date with me, but from then on, we were inseparable.

Then she got the phone call. Only two weeks after we graduated, her father died of a massive heart attack. He owned a small bookstore downtown and was by far the most well-read man on the planet. My hopes to be a journalist and my love for the written word were probably the main reason that Trish and her father accepted me. Since I had lost my father when I was thirteen, Trish's dad quietly filled the role of mentor, the male role model that I had been missing through a large part of my life. When Trish lost her father, the following weeks were filled with nights where I held her while she cried until her eyes turned a deep, dark red. I don't own a single shirt that didn't at one time wear her tears on one shoulder or another. Nonetheless, Trish pulled through with a resilience and inner strength that astounded me beyond words. (This, by the way, isn't the easiest thing to do to a journalist.)

The few months that followed were an absolute whirlwind. Trish took over her father's bookstore along with her two younger sisters while I started my job at the Falcon and received word of my acceptance into the master's program. Trish put all of her passion and energy into her new pet project, and because of this, the bookstore flourished. Meanwhile, I was in a summer transition between graduation and grad school, so I focused solely on writing columns. Rick, my editor, frequently commented that he could make a completely separate publication based solely on my writing. I often worked from home or even sat and wrote in the back room of Trish's bookstore, then sent my column submissions to Rick via email. I was quickly heralded as the up-and-coming poster child of the Falcon. When grad school started, the quantity and quality of my work slowly began to decline. The workload doubled, so did the pressure, and I felt myself beginning to buckle.

These trends led me to where I was on that particular morning, red-eyed, exhausted, and in a rush to get to work so that I could more than likely get a tongue-lashing from my boss. The nearest bus stop was about three blocks away from my destination, and I was already running late, so I picked up a fairly brisk pace to avoid keeping Rick waiting any longer than absolutely necessary. I was in a frenzied rush. While walking, I began rustling through my brown leather courier bag, trying to separate the papers from school from the ones from work. My bag also shared the kind of disarray that was consistent with the rest of my life, as the complete lack of organization was accentuated by a thick lining of several crumpled to-do lists with few, if any, items crossed out. I was walking so fast and in such a state of distraction that the other people on the sidewalk seemed a blur to me. No sight or sound really registered as they all blended into the dull buzz that had been filling my mind all morning.

After turning the corner within half a block of the Falcon, I couldn't help but think about how the building had looked when I first took the job as columnist. The fourteen-story structure stood like a tower of opportunity, with sunlight reflecting off the windows and seeming to smile down upon me. Rick, my newfound mentor and boss, was looking to hire aspiring, professional young journalists who would be pushed harder than the average staff writer but, in turn, would be paid a higher salary. The application process showed that I was entering into what would become a coveted and prestigious group, as the news magazine was only in the second year of its existence. Thus, I felt as though I was a standard-setting member of an elite staff, and the building took the form of a portal into a long and successful career.

This stood in striking contrast with the image of the menacing structure that stood before me that morning. Although the structure itself hadn't changed, its entire countenance seemed dark and contorted. The light reflecting off the windows seemed like scornful, disappointed eyes that followed my every step. Behind the doors to that building, the death of my career as a journalist seemed to lurk in every corner. The morning from hell wasn't even half over.

It always seems like on mornings such as that one, the one person you'd like to see the least ends up being the person with whom you end up sharing an elevator. In this case it was Jim Bersntandt. He stood next to me and looked at me out of the corner of his eye. He was a heavyset, balding man whose every attempt at pleasantry came with a pompous, arrogant smirk. Berstandt was the Food and Dining contributor to the Falcon, who would write reviews of the Chicago restaurants that were supposed to add some regional allure to our journalistic endeavor. Before working for the Falcon, he was a rather successful chef and restaurateur who looked down on this position at the Falcon as if it were some sort of cushy retirement job. He seldom passed up the opportunity to point out that this was my first job out of college.

"Hey, sport," he shouted. He also never passed up the opportunity to give me some sort of condescending name to highlight my youth and lack of experience. If I was referred to as Tiger, Sport, Champ, or Rookie one more time, I knew it would lead to me throwing him down a flight of stairs. Disregarding my rather obvious cringe at his greeting, he continued, "You look a little worse for wear, and what's that on your shirt?"

I couldn't contain myself, as his pompous demeanor demanded all the sarcasm I could muster. "Funny thing happened this morning. I left a copy of our last issue open in front of my coffee machine. It read a few lines of your last restaurant review and just started to vomit all over me."

For a moment, I found my retort somewhat witty. I liked the idea of granting personification to my coffee machine and suggesting that ole Jimbo Bernstandt's writing could make it nauseous. Bernstandt's nostrils began to flare as he quickly snapped, "Well, you sure look like hell. I hope the real world isn't too much for you." With that, the elevator door opened, and he waddled his portly frame away from me and took a seat at his desk.

As I walked into the office suite, which was arranged like a bullpen newsroom with several desks grouped in small clusters, I was greeted by Marcus, my closest friend in the office. He and I immediately hit it off when I took the job at the Falcon. After playing only a few years in the NFL, which were tragically shortened by injury, he came to our small magazine with a credibility connected to a sportswriter who had actually been on the field at the highest level. This served as a great complement to his charismatic and humorous personality. I truly believe that if his football career hadn't been ended by injury, his persona alone would've made him the second coming of Deion Sanders.

Marcus came to my desk with that usual lighthearted, confident swagger that could make you believe he had just leapt out of a magazine advertisement for cologne or athletic wear. He was cool in a way I never thought I could be, as though his walk almost demanded theme music. "Hey, man, what dumpster did you wake up in this morning, and what's that on your shirt?"

Unable to construct a normal explanation, I shot up from my desk and started yelling, "Okay everyone, I get it! I'm drenched in coffee, and I look like shit!" In retrospect I can admit that sure, I probably overreacted, but a high degree of stress paired with a lack of sleep is a fairly common formula for a violently irrational response. Marcus appeared to be slightly taken aback, but his positivity and enthusiasm was always contagious. After a brief, awkward pause, we both shared a halfhearted laugh while he sat down beside my desk.

"Seriously, man," he started, "you look like hell, and the boss looks pissed." As he said this, he nodded his head toward Rick, who was sitting in his office with the door open, staring straight at me. This led Marcus to elaborate. "He looks like he's about to kick your ass."

I tried to appear relaxed. "Is anyone in the office betting on me?"

"Nobody's that stupid." Marcus's tone had shifted to one so dark and gravely serious that it almost gave me a cold sweat.

"Well, twenty bucks says I come out alive. I may be unemployed, but at least I'll be alive."

"We can only hope."

"When I end up waiting tables, be sure to come see me and don't stiff me on the tip." I shuffled away from my desk and onward to Rick's office, my mouth hanging slightly open with a dazed look of fatigue.

Rick sat at his desk, not even making eye contact. His hunched posture was almost indicative of the workload he carried on a daily basis. The Falcon was his brainchild, his pet project. Thus, any shortcoming or inefficiency affected him on a deeply personal level.

Rick clearly looked annoyed. At one edge of his desk I saw a wrinkled set of papers sitting stapled together under a coffee mug. I quickly realized that at the top of the stack sat my most recent column submission. Rick picked up his coffee mug and tossed the draft of the column in my lap. He then sat down at his desk and began loudly slurping his coffee. His mannerisms suggested that he was beyond irritated, and his eyes almost refused to meet mine. A quick glance at my submission gave immediate insight into the reason for his frustration. Even a passing glance could catch several awkward sentences, and further examination would find several erroneous claims and fluffy pontification with no real substance. I might as well have written it in crayon. What was almost worse than the woeful deficiencies in the writing was the condition of the paper itself. The jagged crumpled edges were accentuated by a large brown circle from Rick's coffee mug and a noticeable stain that appeared to be mustard. This suggested that my most recent endeavor was such a failure that Rick would rather eat off of it than read it again.

"Are there problems with what I wrote?" I asked in a soft tone of voice.

Rick glared at me as if the mere question was not only a waste of his time but also an insult to his intelligence. Rick started. "It's garbage. I would've given my usual suggestions and revisions, but in order to cover all the flaws there would've been more red ink than black."

I had submitted this work three days earlier, hoping to get it approved early so that I could focus my attention solely on the research paper for Dr. Karzeck. After a few months of too much work and not enough sleep, my column submissions became a half-hearted regurgitation of whatever I could throw together. "Well, I admit that my work has been declining lately."

"Not just declining, Eric, but doing so at a rate so catastrophic that it could only compare to the Hindenburg or the Titanic." (That was harsh but not altogether inaccurate, and at least Rick never let his anger get in the way of a good analogy.) "You used to give me four or five well-polished diamonds every week. How you went from that to this steamy pile of shit is beyond me. The only reason I haven't canned you yet is because I've seen your true capabilities." Rick paused for a second; he knew that last part would get to me. He was like the parent who knew just when to use the word *disappointed* instead of *angry* for true dramatic effect. Before I could even utter a retort in my self-defense, he continued, "We are set to print on Wednesday, and today is Monday. I want to see a rewrite on my desk tomorrow."

He and I both knew this sort of task would be near impossible, partly because we had both been unfortunate enough to have read my column. At that particular moment, like Hyde transforming into Jekyll, his tone shifted from irate boss to one of a fatherly mentor. "I know you have a lot on your plate, but you probably should question how much you can really handle. It may be time to ask yourself if something is going to give. We print in two days. Before you put your work on my desk, ask yourself if it's really something you would be willing to put your name on."

With that, I exited Rick's office, carrying a dazed, disoriented gait that could only be compared to that of a punch-drunk fighter who was being led from the ring after getting knocked flat on his face. The buzz that had been filling my head all morning was replaced by a staggering feeling of dozens of pairs of eyes burning into me. Everyone in the office had stopped dead in their tracks. They were all staring at me as if wondering what was going to happen next. They must have been expecting me to break into tears or storm angrily out of the building. Besides, no one was able to hear the conversation in Rick's office, so they couldn't be sure if I was even still employed by the Falcon.

I felt an odd urge to say something, considering all eyes were on me. I never had been the theatrical type, but for some reason, I had this odd urge to put on some sort of show. However, my fatigued brain couldn't put together much, so I just spouted out whatever I could come up with. "Is there any coffee left?"

With that, most of my coworkers went back to whatever they were doing. I heard a few sighs, as if a few of my loyal colleagues were disappointed that they didn't get to see an elaborate melodrama play out before their eyes. As the activity in the bullpen resumed, the dull roar of whispers filled the room. The decline in the quality of my work hadn't exactly gone unnoticed. As a matter of fact, I had almost gotten used to avoiding the water cooler altogether, as I had grown tired of having every conversation come to a screeching halt as soon as I was within earshot.

After sitting at my desk for about three hours, trying to make sense out of my sorry excuse for a column, I realized I wasn't going to get any meaningful work done with eyes on me and the passing gossip of the office that nobody thought I could hear. I slowly began to gather what I could find on the desk and pile it into my courier bag. Any method or reason in my packing quickly disintegrated, as I started grabbing whatever sat on my desk and shoving it into the small piece of luggage. The last item on the desk was the coffee thermos that I kept forgetting to bring home with me. I tossed it into the main compartment of my bag along with all the various papers, and then I pulled the zipper closed to pack it all together. Once I had gotten only a few steps away from my desk, it occurred to me that not only was the thermos open, but it contained at least two inches of standing, stale, week-old coffee, which was proceeding to seep into all my of my papers and belongings. Coffee, my one saving grace on the long and tiring mornings, was adding insult to injury at every turn. I had been through several bad days in the past, but the coffee was an interesting touch.

Chapter 2

After a few hours of working from home, the number of words on the page was only slightly longer than it had been when I left the Falcon office. I was beginning to feel as though no matter where I went, my inadequacy was going to follow me. Several failed attempts at revising my column led me to the equally painful conclusion that I simply needed to go back to the drawing board and start from scratch. This presented a problem; apparently, the white space had been waiting for me all day. I would write a word, a sentence, or even a paragraph, and then begin to second guess myself. I would then highlight, hit Backspace, and there was the blank white abyss staring back at me. I knew that this decision to start over could possibly result in a better column, but the downside was that it was going to take more time, and the deadline to get my work on Rick's desk was the next morning, approaching faster with each passing unproductive hour.

Finally, I looked up to check my phone. Trish had sent me a text over an hour before, but on days like this, my communication dwindled as time went on. I felt as though her usual patience deserved more than a text message. Besides, after the day from hell, if anything was going to help me, it was going to be hearing Trish's voice. Just as I was about to call her, I heard a knock at my door.

"Hey. I haven't heard from you all day."

With everything that had happened that day, I had forgotten that this was the night she would stop to see me on her way home from yoga class. On many nights, she would have stayed at my apartment, but she had gotten used to me telling her that I was too busy. I knew she was concerned, to say the least. But seeing her was possibly the only positive moment of a long and taxing day that was still nowhere near over.

I tried to hide the obvious exhaustion that affected everything from my posture to my tone of voice. "Hey. How was work?"

Trish's concern had exceeded her willingness to engage in small talk. "It was okay, except for spending most of my day wondering whether or not my boyfriend was going to call me back." Trish was not, by any stretch of the imagination, a demanding or controlling partner. She understood that I was busy and that sometimes the many demands of being a student and a journalist made me inaccessible. But today, the overwhelming lack of contact caused her to be exceedingly concerned.

I knew she deserved some explanation, so I quickly responded, "I know and I'm sorry. It was a long one."

"What happened?"

I had absolutely no idea how to begin answering this question. I didn't want to tell her that I was underperforming at the Falcon and then there was the woeful inadequacy of my graduate work. She knew I was struggling in putting together my research paper, but she just didn't know to what degree. Perhaps it was my pride, or it could have just been that I wanted the love of my life to be proud of me, but I didn't want to tell her I was on the verge of complete professional and academic failure. I decided maybe I could get away with being ambiguous. "Well, a lot of things happened today."

"Such as…" Trish saw right through me, almost as though she was reminding me that being ambiguous didn't, and never would, work with her. She knew me too well.

"Oh, Rick had some problems with my column, so I need to do some work on that, and I had a meeting with Dr. Karzeck about the research paper."

"How's that going?" Trish asked in reference to the paper. "Have you made some progress?"

"Well, I've… Okay no. Absolutely none. One word would be a breakthrough."

I had always been transparent with Trish, but in this instance, the blunt honesty was almost a surprise for both of us. I couldn't believe how quickly this confession came out of my mouth. One confession turned into another, and the next thing I knew, I was telling Trish everything. The defunct article, the rewrite, the blank screen, I let it all flow, while Trish sat listening with absolute patience and empathy.

Finally, Trish interjected. "What do you think is standing in your way?"

I hadn't really thought about what my biggest obstacle was, but when asked, it immediately came to mind. Running on very little sleep, I was, if anything, too tired to beat around the bush. "I just don't want to let anyone down, especially you."

"What does this have to do with letting me down?"

I always felt as though my pursuits—the publications, the credentials, the education—were not only my personal goals but an attempt to prove that I was worth Trish's time. Deep within myself, I always felt like she was out of my league, like she settled, and I really had to prove I was worth it. "Trish, you deserve a success, and that's what I want to be."

Trish seemed almost shocked by this notion. "Eric, I fell for you when we were undergraduates. Your passion and work ethic is what first impressed me about you. You don't have to prove anything to me. I just want you around more."

I felt my heart sink. I knew that somewhere along the way, all my efforts to become a success had led me to neglect our relationship. Although this took top priority in my heart and mind, my daily efforts would suggest that it was an afterthought. I knew that something had to give, I just wasn't sure what. After a long pause, I responded, "I know, Trish, and I'm sorry. Once I get past these deadlines, I will be able to be more attentive."

"Eric, we both know that there are going to be other deadlines after this one. I know how hard you work, and that's something I truly love about you. But this all gets harder when you're never around and you don't answer my calls."

"I know, Trish, and I'll do better."

Trish gave a slight smile to show her support and understanding. "I'm going home, Eric. I know you have a lot on your plate right now, and I'm here for you whenever you need me."

We embraced, and I didn't want to let go. I felt as though I had someone with whom to share my burden. After a long kiss, Trish told me she would call in the morning to see how I was doing. By this time, Trish knew she shouldn't bother to bring up the idea of me getting sleep, because she could only hear the phrase "I'll sleep when it's done" so many times before the whole effort became futile. As Trish left and the door closed behind her, I felt the entire world fall back on my shoulders. I was alone in a dirty apartment. It was just me and the deadlines.

As I closed the door, it felt as though the walls were closing in around me. When this day began, I was simply tired and overworked. Somehow, over the course of twelve hours, it was brought to my attention that I was a disappointment as a student, a floundering journalist, and worst of all, a neglectful boyfriend.

A quick glance at the clock revealed that it was close to midnight. I needed a moment to breathe and collect my thoughts. About half a block away from my apartment sat a twenty-four hour convenience store. I walked there to buy a Red Bull. Right outside the store was a small bench where I sat for a moment. I had to figure out what my next step would be. I would put all my remaining energy into writing my column and get it on Rick's desk by 8:00 a.m. I would scrape together whatever I could from my several failed attempts at finishing this godforsaken project and try to turn it into something acceptable.

If one thing was certain, I knew sleep wasn't an option. If I even tried to power nap, I knew that I would sleep through the alarm, through the deadline, and right out of my job at the Falcon. When this reality came to mind, it was accompanied by the recognition that this little planning session was little more than a sophisticated form of stalling. Trying to gather whatever enthusiasm or motivation I could muster, it took everything I had to put one foot in front of the other as I pushed back toward my apartment.

Just as I got to my door, a voice from the sidewalk called out to me. "Excuse me, sir, could I trouble you for a glass of water?" The voice belonged to a man who appeared to be at least sixty years old. His face was haggard, poorly shaven, and elongated with fatigue. His slacks and sport coat were wrinkled, with a worn, brown leather briefcase that seemed to hang lifelessly at his side.

Good God, I thought. *It's my future.* This guy looks tired, gaunt, and overworked. He's me in forty years. Along with the startled feeling, there was some sense of familiarity; I could have sworn I had seen his face before.

After only a moments delay, he asked again, "All I need is glass of water. I promise you, I mean you no harm."

Every possible concern raced through my mind. *I'm sure this man had passed at least one drinking fountain on the way home from wherever the hell he came from.* There were several bars a few blocks away from here, most of which didn't charge for water, so why did he feel the need to ask a complete stranger for some? Nonetheless, I was rather convinced that he was harmless, and his request was relatively simple. If he was going to kill me, at least it would get me out of this column rewrite. And if his intent was to rob my filthy apartment, he was in for a serious disappointment. He would have to sift through seas of garbage and clutter before finding that I had hardly anything of any particular value. Besides, my grad-school mentor wanted brilliance, my boss wanted a rewrite, and my girlfriend wanted the man of her dreams back. This guy wanted water. What could it hurt?

I went as far as to up the ante on this man's rather simple request and invited him into my apartment. There is a point where fatigue erodes judgment and emotional inhibitors to the point that you become a bleeding heart, and this was more than likely what compelled me to respond with such a degree of magnanimity. This too was a sophisticated form of stalling before getting back to work, but at least it carried with it a degree of kindness or philanthropy. I found what had to be the last clean glass in my apartment and even got some ice from the freezer. The man ravenously guzzled the water, as though the dark Chicago street he had just traversed was the middle of the Sahara Desert.

When he finished the drink, he thanked me profusely. As he was talking, I discreetly glanced at my watch. It was twelve forty-five, and my column still hadn't gone anywhere. Just as I was about to end this bizarre encounter, the old man preempted me.

"Thank you so much for you kindness, Eric. I would like to offer you something in exchange. It would be the least I could do for knocking you over and scalding you with coffee this morning."

That was where I had seen him before! Despite being questioned by at least three different people about the coffee on my shirt, getting sucker-punched by a diner door had seemed to fade completely out of my memory. "I appreciate that, but—" I stopped midsentence. Wait a minute. How did this old man know my name? In our brief exchange, we had shared absolutely no introduction. I quickly began to question the conclusion that he was harmless before once again his words interrupted my thoughts.

"Don't worry about how I know your name. I also know you're on a deadline, which makes this inconvenience to which I have subjected you all the more kind."

"Wait. Who are you?"

"That is also unimportant. For the sake of putting a name to a face, you can just call me Michael."

"That was my father's name. It also happens to be my middle name."

"I'm aware."

At this point, I was perplexed but altogether too tired to even try to piece these circumstances together. Thus, I didn't even utter a question about how he knew these details. Maybe he was a past acquaintance or someone who knew my family. For some reason, I felt as though I could trust this man. This inexplicable sense of security was counteracted by the uneasy feeling you get when someone seems to know you intimately and you can't even summon up a name. I quickly responded, "I appreciate it, but that's not necessary. I have a lot of work to do."

"I promise, this will take less than ten minutes. As a matter of fact, feel free to set a timer. After ten minutes, I'll be on my way."

I paused for a moment to consider Michael's proposal. In an instant, it became clear. All this time spent burning the candle at both ends had undoubtedly taken at least a few years off my life, and I had wasted several hours chasing my tail on this project, so I quickly decided to give in to his request. After all, another ten minutes would be just a drop in the proverbial ocean of wasted time. Just to play along, I switched to the timer function on my digital watch.

In an attempted display of gamesmanship, I took the watch off and put it on the table, turning the face toward him while pressing the Start button.

Michael seemed completely unaffected by the time constraint that had just been placed upon him. He slowly rose from his chair, sidestepping the mess of my apartment. "I believe this calls for some music," he suggested with a smile, "so could you play something?" I scrambled, caught somewhat off guard by this request, and pressed the Play button on my CD player. As I was did so, it occurred to me that I hadn't relaxed and listened to music for so long that I couldn't recall what CD was in the small, modest stereo system. I quickly ascertained that our music for the moment was the Rolling Stones, as "Paint it Black" began to reverberate off the walls of my apartment.

Michael's eyes lit up, seeming to affirm my taste in music. Almost dancing around my relatively small apartment, he cleared some dirty laundry and rolled up papers. This action led me to the recognition that this thirsty, eccentric old man had done more cleaning in my own apartment than I had in the last few weeks. In doing so, he created an open, barren space no more than five feet wide. By this time, my guest's demeanor shifted from weary wanderer to one that was charismatic and full of energy. He seemed like some off-kilter combination of a cheesy used-car salesman and a second-rate magician building suspense for his next allusion. His eyes met mine with a sense of mysticism and grandeur that left me stunned and oddly intrigued.

"You know," he declared, almost shouting with enthusiasm, "you're a smart kid with all the creativity in the world, but there aren't enough hours in the day. I think I have a solution."

Along with the music, I could hear the sounds of a crowded city right outside my window. Although it was rather late, I could still pick out the noise of car alarms and traffic, along with the intermittent howls of drunks as they staggered home. I glanced at the small digital time display on my cable box, which could always be depended upon for accuracy. It was 12:57 a.m. The timer on my watch showed that Michael was little more than one minute into his rather flamboyant demonstration. He reached down into his briefcase and pulled out a bizarre metal object no more than fifteen inches long and no wider than a baseball bat. In the middle of this small apparatus was a glowing blue orb that appeared to be some sort of button.

The wanderer turned showman then kneeled down, pushed the blue button, and shouted, "An answer to all your problems!"

The Rolling Stones were the most prevalent sound in my ears, as the voice of Mick Jagger howled against the chorus of noises that created a dull roar in the auditory backdrop. "I see a red door, and I want to paint it..." Those were the words that seemed to echo through the room as Michael pushed the small blue button. He pushed it with such a degree of resolve that one would think he was launching a missile. Everything in the room seemed eerily unaffected with one glaring exception. A white door stood in the middle of my living room floor, with a freestanding frame attached to no walls or ceiling. The pure, clean white door was in striking contrast to the surrounding filth and disarray of my apartment.

Leaning against the door frame, Michael stood with an inviting smile, almost whispering, "Open the door, Eric."

Without as much as a word, I stepped forward and put my hand on the silver metallic doorknob. The moment he had pushed the button, this overwhelming feeling had struck me. As my trembling hand wrapped around the doorknob, my mind was finally able to identify what that feeling was. It was stillness. The sound of the music, the low hum of the refrigerator, the grumbling of the heating system, and the racket of the city right outside the window were all suddenly enshrouded in a silence that could make the hair on the back of my neck stand at attention.

As I stepped through the door, the eerie silence became even more unsettling, and the world around me seemed to pause. The door led into what seemed like a new home, with pure and perfectly clean white walls.

"I've equipped it with a few things I think you might need," Michael said with a grin. "You can work, sleep, exercise, or whatever else you feel like you've needed to do."

I couldn't believe that such a perfect inner sanctum was now accessible through a door that wasn't in my apartment a few moments before. I began to explore the new living space. It had a fully functional office area, a king-sized bed, a kitchen, and a bathroom. All of these were lavish, the kind I hoped to one day have in some sort of palatial home if my career took off in an astronomical way. The workout space featured every piece of weight equipment I could ever want, as well as a treadmill and an exercise bike. It looked less like a home gym and more like a high-end health club that some would spend hundreds of dollars a month to join.

The office was also grandiose and spacious. I explored with wide-eyed enthusiasm as I leaned over and turned on the computer, which was alarmingly similar to my laptop. Next to the desk there was a table with a printer/copier and various other office essentials, such as a stapler, a three-hole punch, Post-It notes and a spacious dry-erase board mounted on the wall. There was also a wide, deep cabinet, which I quickly inventoried. It held several reams of paper, many boxes of G-2 pens (my favorites), highlighters, extra ink cartridges, and a few legal pads. On the top of the cabinet rested an ornate coffee station with a Kuerig single-cup coffeemaker, a sealed sugar pot, and a small tub of french vanilla coffee creamer (also my favorite). It was a far cry from the makeshift office space I had thrown together in my apartment. Instead, it seemed as though a committee of cubicle-dwelling workaholics had gathered to gathered the perfect office space.

After admiring my new inner sanctum, my attention shifted back to Michael, who was leaning against the desk with a proud, patient grin.

"It's all yours!" he began with an excited shout. "You can knock out that rewrite, finish your schoolwork, and even shed a few of those pounds you've put on from all these months you've spent tethered to a desk."

His listing of tasks brought my mind back to all the work I had to finish over the next few days. The new work and living space could grant me some convenience, and perhaps even a renewed sense of enthusiasm, but the deadlines were still the main problem. As long as I had those time constraints breathing down my neck, I would still be haunted by the clock and, worst of all, the blank white screen.

As if he was reading my mind, Michael chimed in. "This isn't even the best part."

"There's more?" I was almost gasping with disbelief. "You've almost doubled the size of my living space."

"Well, Eric, I think you could use more than just some improved housing. For me to show you the best part, we're going to have to step back through the door. Before we do, how long do you think we have been in here?"

"I don't know. I left the timer on the table. We must have been in here at least fifteen minutes." It occurred to me that we had well exceeded the ten-minute limitation that we both agreed upon. I didn't care, and apparently, neither did he.

"Sure," he responded. "Fifteen minutes sounds good. Keep that in mind when we go back through the door." He put his hand on my shoulder and led me out through the door.

As we stepped back into the familiar, dirty surroundings of my apartment, the absence of sound became suddenly apparent once again. In the new living space, the silence seemed consistent because the walls were solid and white with no windows. But in the cluttered mess of my apartment, the silence was completely unsettling.

Then it happened. Michael pulled closed the isolated white door, and everything seemed to start back up again. When I looked at the clock, it was still 12:57 a.m., and the timer showed that only a few minutes had elapsed. The background noise had returned, and within it, the sounds of the Rolling Stones came blasting back into my ears as the song resumed on the exact same line, "Black. No colors anymore I want them to turn black."

I was completely astounded. How had absolutely no time elapsed on either clock? How could the music continue on the exact same lyric after several minutes? Once again, I was left with more questions than answers, but before my mind could even put together an inquiry, Michael interjected.

"That's right, Eric. No matter how much time you spend behind that door, no more than one second will elapse out here. You can work, sleep, or whatever you need, and when you come back through this door, the world will resume right back from the moment you left. This isn't just a new work space—it's a time chamber."

It then occurred to me that the white door that had stood before me just moments before was gone, as though it had evaporated upon closure. In its place sat the small metallic devise that Michael retrieved from his briefcase. "How is this possible?"

"What you are about to gain is an incredible blessing. I think questions such as 'how' are better left unanswered."

"And it's just mine?"

"You bet. It is yours for as long as you decide you need it. However, there are a few rules."

"Such as?"

"First, you and only you can enter the time chamber. You are not allowed to take anyone else with you."

I shrugged. "Okay, that sounds easy enough. What else?"

"Well, you were chosen to receive this blessing because I feel that you can use it to make a particular difference. I can't tell you what this difference is or how you are going to get there. Those decisions are up to you. However, because you have been specifically chosen for this, no one else can know about it. So the very existence of this chamber must be kept in absolute secrecy."

"So don't let anyone in and don't tell anyone. That sounds fair." I had this odd urge to conceal my excitement. Although I was still in a state of stunned disbelief, the very notion of this gift made me feel like a kid on Christmas morning. I also felt the need to fire away any question I possibly could. "What about the refrigerator? The treadmill?"

"What about them?"

"Well, how do they receive electricity?"

"Eric, the chamber generates its own power and water. Besides, I'm giving you the power to freeze time and you're asking about the utility bills?"

"True." He had me there. I was oddly embarrassed. For all the work I had put into becoming a journalist, I certainly seemed to be having trouble coming up with the important questions.

"It's all right, my friend. I can imagine that this is a lot to wrap your mind around."

"So while in this chamber, time stands still?"

"Well, sort of. When you walk through the chamber door, you exit time. No matter how many hours, days, or even weeks you decide to spend inside the chamber, once you step back through the door, you reenter this time as we know it at the exact same second. So as far as you're concerned, yes, time effectually freezes."

"What, then, do you expect me to do with this?"

"Eric, I don't doubt for a moment that you can do incredible things when time is no longer limited for you. How you decide to use it is up to you."

"How long do I get to keep it?"

Michael grimaced as the foolishness of yet another overly sim-plistic question set in. "Think about that one for a second. Does the question of how long really matter when what I'm giving you is the gift of unlimited time?"

"I guess you have a point there."

"To answer your question, you can keep the time chamber as long as you'd like. If you decide at some point you no longer want it or need it, well let's just say we'll cross that bridge when we get to it. In the meantime, you have a rewrite to finish and a research assign-ment that is well overdue. Plus, take some advice from an older man. Trish loves you. Spend some time with her." With that, Michael began to walk toward the door. Right before he made his exit, he left one parting remark. "One more thing. With or without the chamber, there is still no tragedy in this world greater than wasted time."

I had absolutely no idea what to say. I didn't know whether to follow him with more questions, to thank him, or to doubt whether anything that had just occurred was even possible. Nonetheless, my newfound friend made his humble and quiet exit, leaving behind the small contraption that could give me the opportunity to bend time to my will. I had to test it.

It was 1:08 a.m., and if by chance the machine didn't once again make the clock freeze, I would still have about six hours to finish my rewrite before I had to get back to the Falcon. My experiment was a little simplistic, but it would be enough to tell me what I needed to know.

I used a small piece of duct tape to affix about five feet of string to a glass that I left sitting on the edge of my kitchen counter. I then kneeled down and let one hand hover over the little blue button while my free hand clutched the other end of the string. After a count of three, I pulled the string just enough to make the glass tip over slowly and fall off the counter. Only a split second after the glass began its descent, I pushed the little blue button. As the button was pushed, there was once again an overwhelming silence to match the staggering stillness. All the sounds I had grown so accustomed to hearing and taking for granted, the hum of the refrigerator, the dull murmur of the heating system, and the harmony of winds and traffic outside my window, all came to a staggering halt.

I looked over and saw the glass sitting suspended a few inches off the counter, frozen in midfall, frozen in time. A quick glance in the other direction revealed the same freestanding white door staring back at me. The clock on the cable box showed that it was still 1:08 a.m. Once again, I had frozen the hands on the clock. A huge wave of excitement and relief crashed over me. At that point, time no longer felt as though it was breathing down my neck. I felt prepared. I felt invincible. I was ready to work.

After reentering the time chamber, I couldn't help but explore my new domain. A quick appraisal of my work and living space left me almost giddy with enthusiasm. I took a quick peek through the door back into my apartment and found nothing but the same frozen silence. The glass was still resting in midfall as though an invisible hand was holding it up against the pull of gravity. I couldn't help but let out an almost frenzied chuckle. Besides, who could hear me?

As I sat down at the desk in the chamber and turned on the computer, a sense of focus began to run down my spine. My eyes widened. I reached into my pocket and withdrew the flash drive that contained all my documents from school and work. As I began working on my column rewrite, the focus cut through my fatigue and took the form of an adrenaline rush. My hands started flying across the keyboard. The ideas were jumping from my mind to my hands to the page almost as fast as I could conceptualize them. Words formed paragraphs, and paragraphs became pages. The words I once struggled to find were now roaring as though they were a river with no dam of stress and pressure to hold them back.

It didn't take long before I had to stop myself for fear of my little column becoming a book. *A book*, I thought. There's an idea. I had always thought about writing a book of some sort but never wanted to dedicate that much time to a project that could ultimately fail so easily. Sitting in the quiet recesses of the time chamber, it all seemed possible, and that fear of failure had completely subsided. What would I write? Fiction? Nonfiction? A novel? A series of novels? Why not dream big?

I quickly stopped myself from further exploring the notion of a literary career because I could feel my focus beginning to fade. My column not only was finished, but I gave it a full review with revisions, then a second, then a third. As I read through it for the last time, it felt as though I was going to be able to put yet another polished diamond on Rick's desk for the first time in far too long. As the column finished printing, the hum of the printer became the only sound that echoed off the time chamber walls. The rewrite was only a small item on my already overgrown to-do list, but all the same, it was still an obstacle that I was able to overcome.

With my first task finished, I stepped back into my apartment, and thus, back into a world controlled by the ticking clock. The digital time display on my cable box still read 1:08 a.m. and the glass was still sitting, suspended in midair. I had been working in the time chamber the equivalent of several hours, but the world was waiting at rest as though I hadn't even moved. As I pulled the door to the chamber closed, the sounds of the world around me once again came screeching back. Otherwise commonplace, unnoticeable noises became almost deafening. This chorus of noises was joined by the sound of the glass shattering as it crashed onto my kitchen floor. In the excited construction of my experiment, it never occurred to me that a piece of glassware would be sacrificed in the process of testing my hypothesis.

I then realized that being back on schedule was actually a fore-seeable and achievable goal. Thinking through the next several tasks that lay ahead no longer felt like planning my ultimate demise. I had a new lease on my future. With this sense of great relief, another sensation came crashing into the forefront of my mind. I had been running on an absolute adrenaline rush from the moment Michael gave me the time chamber. Once I had finally taken to step outside a moment and catch my breath, the fatigue seemed to bull rush me from behind.

This was where the image of the time-chamber bed became the only one at the forefront of my attention. I knew that I could go into the time chamber and rest as long as I needed without fear of sleep-ing through meetings or deadlines. After I pulled my weight up the stairs and back into my apartment, I almost stumbled through the door and crawled back to the tiny blue apparatus. The time-chamber bed seemed to welcome me, and I laughed as the urge to set an alarm passed through my mind. What waited before me was the magical amount of rest—enough. As I reclined back and put my head on the pillow, I thought to myself, *If I go to sleep right now, I can wake up whenever.*

Chapter 3

When I awoke in the time chamber, a comfortable grin darted across my face with the recognition that I could continue to snooze as long as I pleased. After finally coming to the conclusion that I was well-rested and energized, I stepped out through the door. This left me feeling somewhat disoriented, as such a long sleep was followed by the conditioned response to expect daylight through my apartment windows. However, when no daylight was there to greet me, I stood idle in my apartment, having to reorient myself to my surroundings. It was roughly two o'clock in the morning, just as it had been before I laid myself down to rest within the chamber.

The first sensation that struck me was a general feeling of disgust. The filth and disarray of my apartment stood in stark contrast to the cleanliness and order of the chamber. Before a plan could fully crystalize in my head, I was in a flurry of movement from one side of my humble dwelling to another. While load after load of laundry spun through my washing machine and dryer, I washed the dishes and gathered all the small wads of rolled up paper to be taken to the trash. Next, I vacuumed the carpet and ran a mop across the small patch of linoleum in my meager kitchen space. Before I finally stopped to catch my breath, it was 5:00 a.m. All my dishes were clean, my books and papers were neatly organized, and the laundry and trash were gone from the floor. It then occurred to me that my home was the closest to spotlessly clean it had been since I moved in.

Satisfied with what I had accomplished, I quickly came to the conclusion that I needed even more of a head start. With this in mind, I gathered a few materials for a couple of projects and some exercise clothes, packed them all in a backpack, and then quickly retreated back into the time chamber. The feeling of having all the time I needed brought me a sense of focus unlike anything I had ever felt before. First, I plugged my flash drive into the office area's desktop computer. I then grabbed a legal pad to jot down any ideas or thoughts that would emerge from my work.

Next, I pulled open the numerous files containing the long and often difficult to read articles I needed for my research paper. Finally, my hands reached deep into my backpack to pull out two books. One was a style guide that would be used to ensure the proper format for my paper, and the other was a used book on how to speak Italian that I had bought on a whim a long time ago. I purchased the second book about a month after Trish and I started dating, hoping to impress her by learning a new language. From that point on, the book began to collect dust while I hid behind the excuse of "When am I going to have the time to do that?" With these items sitting neatly on my desk, the initial preparation was complete, galvanizing the resolve that now almost anything was within my own personal realm of accomplishment.

My next decision was to determine exactly how I should multitask with no time restrictions. No longer would I be constrained to trying to complete several tasks at the same time. Instead, each project, each endeavor, and every word I wrote would receive my undivided attention until I could no longer retain focus. I would work on a task as long as I could keep my momentum and then shift to another endeavor as soon as I felt I was getting stuck or distracted. I didn't put much thought into this method because if my work was slow, what did it matter? Finally having the time and energy to produce quality work and focus on the details gave me a newfound sense of pride and confidence even though I had not yet really accomplished anything.

I began my work by printing article after article to use for my research paper. The next step was to thoroughly read each article, highlight whatever I found noteworthy, and leave any necessary comments in the side margins. My inner nerd was being fed by no longer having to check the clock. Whenever the research grew tedious, I would switch to giving myself a small impromptu Italian lesson. Once I had learned past my capability to remember, I would search the internet to spur some column ideas, which quickly led to my fingers flying across the keyboard like they had before, churning out draft after draft of several different column submissions. I remembered one of my professors in an intro-to-journalism class telling me that there were stories everywhere if I was willing to take the time to dig. Now I had that time, and I would leave no stone unturned.

The glory of this ever-shifting approach, as I quickly found out, was that each time I switched to a different task, I was able to approach it with a newfound vigor and focus. Plus, I could return to each project with fresh eyes and ideas that would almost immediately present themselves while my propensity to find and eradicate errors was sharpened. Once a haggard and defeated underachiever, I worked like a finely tuned, incredibly precise champion of productivity.

Before long, I was several pages into my research paper, I had two column submissions (in addition to the rewrite), and the small book on Italian had two chapters littered with dog-eared pages and margins made black from my notes. If this was the kind of efficiency the time chamber could produce, then the immediate conclusion was that no task could be deemed insurmountable. I no longer stood with deadlines looming above me, but instead I could test the very limits of my intellect and ability. I wanted to learn, to create, to take the world by storm, but all at once my focus shifted once again.

My eyes quickly glanced over to the exercise equipment on the other side of the time chamber. No longer were the hours on the clock going to serve as an excuse to overlook my physical health. I hadn't had both the time and energy to work out in who knows how long, and I wasn't going to let this opportunity pass me by. First came a quick warm-up on the treadmill, followed by as intense a weightlifting routine as I could muster. There was absolutely no reason or logic to my workout, but I didn't care. I tried every possible exercise that I could recall from fitness magazines or sports movies. If I looked silly or like I didn't know what I was doing, it didn't matter because no one was there to see me. I could even loudly grunt while lifting an otherwise unimpressive amount of weight. After all, I was the strongest person in the gym, even if this came by virtue of being the only person in the gym. Finally, I ran a little over a mile on the treadmill before realizing exactly how much endurance I had lost from several months of little or no exercise.

With my apartment clean, my work back on schedule, and a completed workout, my next priority was my appearance. I was already drenched with sweat, which logically dictated that I was in need of a shower, so why not use the time advantage to get a good trim and shave? The one area of the time chamber I had not really explored was the bathroom. Although I had used it once or twice during my work sessions, I never stopped to inventory its contents. This large, luxurious bathroom came stocked with every toiletry and grooming item that I could dream of, including an electric trimmer that I used to thin out my sideburns and clean up my neck and hairline. Covered in sweat and loose hair, I took a long, hot shower, which seemed to wash away the life of stress and frustration that had me feeling filthy for far too long. Next, I stood before the mirror and gave well-overdue attention to each and every detail, shaving and combing my hair with the slow, deliberate precision that comes only to those with all the time they need.

Looking, and more importantly, feeling, like a new man, I walked back to the desk in the chamber office space. Each of my new column submissions had been fully revised and edited several times, so I hit Print. My rewrite was complete, as was the work for the next week. In that moment, a sudden and euphoric sensation overcame me—I was, for the first time in far too long, ahead of schedule. For many, this feeling brings with it the comfort of free time. In light of my new time chamber, this benefit had lost at least some of its luster. Nonetheless, I felt once again in control of my own life. Moreover, I could close the door on the days of constant disappointment and underachievement. No longer would I be called onto the proverbial hot seat by Rick or Dr. Karzeck for another tongue-lashing.

As I gathered my papers, got dressed, and was about to exit the apartment, I was stuck by two last-minute decisions. The first was to grab my car keys. My mind was racing with ideas for what I hoped to accomplish that day. I didn't want long walks or dances with public transit to interfere with any plans that might come to mind. The second decision was to conceal the small chamber device in my courier bag so that I could use it to manipulate the clock at any time and at any place throughout the day. Remembering the two promises I had made to Michael, namely the oath of secrecy, I put thorough and deliberate effort into concealing this small contraption.

On the inside of my courier bag sat a zipper compartment just large enough to hold the device, and this pocket would be completely hidden from view. When I slipped my new secret weapon into this compartment, I was surprised at how little weight it actually added to the bag. After I actuated the two decisions, I swiftly exited my apartment, possibly more prepared to face the day than I had ever been before in my life.

My first stop was a florist's shop, following an idea that came to me at the spur of the moment while getting into my car. It was only 6:00 a.m., and finding a flower shop that was open at such an early hour seemed to be another one of the many strokes of good fortune that followed me at every single turn. I had the florist arrange a rather grandiose bouquet of two dozen lilies and a card that simply read, "Dinner tonight?" This spur-of-the-moment decision was growing into a rather elaborate plan, which I was making up with each and every passing step. With my new purchase in the passenger seat of my car, I proceeded to Trish's bookstore.

When I walked in, the bookstore employees, two girls that Trish hired herself both did a double take as I approached the front counter. They, like almost everyone else, had grown accustomed to seeing me in my more disheveled form. I must have appeared as a completely different person. Downplaying their astonishment, I playfully asked to see the owner of the store. One of the giggling young ladies dashed to the back room.

Before she saw what was waiting for her, I watched Trish rush to the front. Her young employee must have intended to help me surprise her, saying something to the effect of "Someone would like to see you," without alluding to who that someone was. Because of this, I could tell from Trish's mannerisms and facial expressions that she was expecting anything from a walk-in solicitor to a disgruntled customer. When she emerged from the corridor, the surprise was evident in her entire countenance. She stopped dead in her tracks and her eyes widened. Before she could utter a single word, a smile shot across my rested and freshly shaven face, and I slid the flowers toward her across the large granite counter.

"Hey, there!" Her voice had a high pitch of excitement and enthusiasm that further widened the smile on my face.

As her gaze shifted from me to the gift, I could almost detect joyful tears begin to well up in her eyes. For Trish, this kind of overt display of emotion was exceptionally uncommon, so this response was rather telling of how our relationship had been strained over the last few months. She had been so patient and supportive, while I had become more and more distracted. In the downward spiral I had been following the previous few months, it didn't occur to me how much she quietly yearned for some sign of affection or reassurance. Thus, this small gesture proved so meaningful that it elicited a rather uncommon emotional response.

Realizing that she was starting to crack her own veneer of professional stoicism, she quickly changed the subject, but the smile upon her face couldn't contain itself. "Don't you have to get your work on Rick's desk this morning?"

"Our meeting is an hour from now, and after I leave here, I'll be on my way to the Falcon."

"Is the rewrite finished?"

"Oh yeah. I kicked its ass, if I do say so myself." This small boast came out just as my lips curled into a coy, playful grin.

"And you came all this way to see me?"

"Of course. But that's not all. You free tonight?"

"What'd you have in mind?"

"Dinner at my place?" I quickly realized that this verbal request made the card on the flowers rather redundant, but I doubted that she would mind any more than I did.

"I'd love to!" Another pang of affection shot across her face. "Can I speak with you in private?"

"Sure thing."

She gestured toward a back room, wherein sat her small, makeshift office space for keeping the books and handling many of the clerical tasks of the business. She walked in first, and once I was inside, she abruptly pushed the door shut behind me, closing us into a space where we were the only inhabitants. She threw her arms around me, and her lips pressed against mine with an intense, affectionate urgency. Whatever she was holding back for the sake of propriety at the front desk was now unleashed in one passionate embrace. Once she pulled back, I leaned back against the door with a deer-in-the-headlights look of astonishment on my face.

"I don't know what you've done since I saw you last night," she said with a playful smile on her face, "but I like it. Looking forward to tonight."

As she walked me back toward the front of the bookstore, it took everything I had to pull my gaze from her and watch where I was going. I even tripped over my own feet and ran headfirst into the door while making my exit. My gaze was fixed on her like that of a hormonal high school freshman who was catching his first glimpse of the prom queen. She looked back with a warm smile that suggested that somewhere deep within her she knew the kind intoxicating hold she could put on me with just the right amount of affection. I was about to write my own new success story, and it felt all the better having her in my corner.

Chapter 4

My next stop was the Falcon office. I parked my car in a freestanding lot about two blocks away and marched the rest of the brief journey with an assertive, confident bounce in my step. It was an unseasonably warm and sunny February day, and the light seemed to smile off the windows onto me once again. I had stood before this building only twenty-four hours earlier, but because of the time chamber, it felt as though I had been gone for a long weekend. The building no longer seemed dark and menacing, haunted with deadlines and disappointments. Instead, its bright lights appeared to beckon me as I was looking back at the structure like a conquering hero about to claim his spoils.

My confident march continued straight from the elevator toward Rick's office. Occasionally, I caught a double take from my coworkers, as the shock value of the abrupt change in my appearance seemed to follow me everywhere I went. Through the crack in Rick's door, I could see that someone was sitting in front of his desk. This visitor was more than likely an advertiser or solicitor making some sort of pitch, as Rick seemed impatient and ready to get on to his work. I loudly and violently threw the door open and tossed my rewrite, along with the two new column submissions, on to Rick's desk. "Here's the rewrite," I shouted, "and two other possible columns. Run what you like, toss what you don't."

Rick was obviously flabbergasted by this startling entrance, and his surprise was only exacerbated by the fact that I was standing there a few minutes early, with the striking enthusiasm and assertiveness that I wore with the chip on my shoulder when I first took the job at the Falcon. He stuttered as he tried to annunciate some sort of response, "Wait, are you telling me you finished the rewrite *and* you wrote two new columns?"

"Yes, sir." My response came with a matter-of-fact sort of blank facial expression that suggested that this sort of newfound productivity was just par for the course. "I also have another column idea that I'm putting together. It will either be on your desk or in your email tomorrow morning."

"You'll get it to me tomorrow, as in the day after today?" Rick carefully chose the wording of his question and paired it with a slow rate of speech as a means to explicitly express his disbelief.

"Yes, sir. Tomorrow. That's the day after today, and two days after yesterday. I hope you like what I've written so far, and I'm sorry for interrupting, whatever it is this gentleman was discussing with you."

The visitor sat just as confused as Rick. He could tell that what was going on was something of an anomaly, even if he didn't know why. I didn't really regret interrupting, nor did I actually have an idea for my next column. I came in to make a splash, and the promise of the new column only added to the effect. Because of the time chamber, a promise to have completed a task tomorrow or even within the next hour was the equivalent of saying, "I'll do something someday." The next column was just a drop in the proverbial ocean of tasks I was zealous to complete, and the self-imposed deadline wasn't even a concern.

When I stepped out of Rick's office, there was a stunned silence, combined with the unsettling sensation of dozens of pairs of eyes fixed on me, just as they had been yesterday, but for an entirely different reason. The sudden silence was so discernible that I thought for a moment I had accidentally triggered the time-chamber device hidden deep within the courier bag that hung at my side. I glanced over my shoulder, expecting the white door to have materialized right behind me. The dull hum of the printer broke this silence, which brought my attention to the fact that although time hadn't frozen, everyone in the office was stopped dead in their tracks and all eyes were on me. I had given these people a show that more than compensated for the lackluster performance I had put on the morning before.

I then began to make a grandiose exit, with an upbeat gait and an imperturbable grin that could only be worn by an unshakable juggernaut. I stood as a powerhouse that could overcome any demand or deadline. Adding yet another level of victory to my display, I noticed Jim Bernstandt, sitting red-faced over a submission for food and dining that was littered with comments and corrections from Rick's red pen. Everyone in the office made note of Rick's low-tech method of giving feedback, as his red ink gave us all flashbacks of our high school English teachers. Although it wasn't the most time-effective editing method, we respected the old school commitment to quality. Plus, his elaborate personal attention galvanized our belief that he was a wonderful leader and editor. The only one who didn't respect this practice was Bernstandt, who believed that everything he said and wrote was gospel truth and that no one, not even Rick, could make his submissions any better.

As he sat there with grumblings of frustration under his breath, I couldn't help but add insult to his injury. "Hey, Jimbo," I shouted. "Why the long chubby face?" I knew this would strike a nerve. The young hotshot fresh out of college was not only referring to him by a bastardization of his first name but was also making a reference to his weight.

"I'm fine," he snapped. "Just making some changes to my article for food and dining."

I could tell that he was irritated, which motivated me to push the issue even further. "Well, if you're having some trouble with Rick's suggestions, anyone in the office would be happy to explain the big words to you. If that is too challenging, just remember that you're the food and dining guy, and nobody reads your shit anyway." I then grinned, patted him on the chest in a gesture to consummate the condescension, and strolled away with a dull murmur of snickers in my wake. Stephen, the quiet PR guy who seldom spoke or even made eye contact with anyone, looked up from desk to let out a muffled chuckle. My rebirth in the Falcon office was complete, and thus, I went along my way.

My next stop was the office where I would stop by to set up yet another appointment with Dr. Karzeck. The drive from the Falcon building to campus was accentuated by the feeling of triumph that I carried with me from one place to another. I drove with the windows rolled down and my music blaring for the world to hear. There was a visitor parking lot right next to the building that housed the communication department, so I spent the extra five dollars to park my car there for the day. I was in such an excellent mood that I was going to spare no indulgence, small or large, and the convenience of the short walk only widened the smile on my face.

Of all the people who reveled in my sudden change in appearance, the best reaction came from Alice, the same office professional who told me the day before that my appearance looked like a bus full of homeless people had run me over. When most people simply turned their heads or raised their eyebrows, Alice convulsed with surprise as though I had walked through the office door naked with my hair on fire. I asked her if Dr. Karzeck was in his office, and she sarcastically inquired if my change in appearance came about because I was about to ask him on a date. I simply laughed as she gestured toward his office.

Dr. Karzeck, who was in the middle of grading papers and answering student emails, contained his otherwise easily observed state of surprise. His eyebrows raised only slightly from behind his reading glasses. I handed him my new research paper, which by then was over fifteen pages long, and he told me he would read it as soon as he could. Dr. Karzeck was not the most easily impressed man in the world, so even the reserved display of affirmation spoke volumes. As I was just about to walk away from his office, he held his palm over the phone, muffling the conversation I had inadvertently interrupted, and whispered, "Well done, Eric. I knew you had this in you. I'll read it over, and you'll be on to your prospectus in no time."

This little bit of affirmation only fueled the fire that had been lit beneath me due to the time chamber. I raced from the communication building to the library, where I was going to gather several books. No longer was my reading list going to collect dust in hopes that someday I would have the time for leisure reading. I also was picking out a few additional readings for my soon-to-be prospectus, based on the assumption that Dr. Karzeck would approve my preliminary work and I would need to create a larger review of literature. I knew that I had ample sources for the research paper I had just submitted to Dr. Karzeck, but I also knew that many more were going to be required if I were to turn that research paper into a proper review of lit for a thesis. I was starting to get that feeling that most grad students describe when the thesis idea finally begins to crystalize itself, making enthusiasm begin to flow alongside the adrenaline in my bloodstream. Next thing I knew, I had ten books under my arm. Five were for my personal reading list, and the other five were to go into my thesis. As I was checking out, the librarian was kind enough to offer me a large paper sack. She suggested that I wouldn't be able to read all these works and have them in before the due date. "Challenge accepted," I replied.

With the heavy bags of books in one hand and my courier bag in the other, I was headed out of the library and back toward my car. On my way out, I noticed a group of students all huddled around a table. They were obviously some sort of study group preparing for an exam. As I strolled closer, I was able to ascertain from their muffled conversation that they were accounting students who were struggling and anxious about the upcoming test. I stood at a distance where they couldn't tell I was listening to their conversation, and from there, I was able to determine that the subject that was causing the struggle was depreciation, which I knew little about except its laypersons definition and that it was an accounting term. This gave me an idea.

I slipped out away from the study area and went into the men's restroom. After checking to ensure that I was the only one in the room, I pulled the chamber device out from its safe hiding place in my courier bag and quickly pushed the little blue button. I pulled up the computer inside the chamber and searched everything I could find about depreciation, including resources and quizzes for accounting students. I then gave myself a lengthy self-study course on the topic and then thought out ways I could describe the subject and answer any possible questions. Once I finished, I quickly exited the chamber, returned the device to its safe and concealed pocket, and left the bathroom. The students were still at the table, scratching their heads with their faces contorted with confusion.

"Excuse me," I interrupted, "is the depreciation section stumping you?"

"You have no idea." One of them was rather vocal with his frustration. "I'm going to bomb this test."

As I slid into conversation with this group, I started to recall everything that I had just taught myself. "The first major step in calculating the depreciation expense is to determine which method is being used. Whether it's straight line, declining balance, double declining balance, or sum of the year's use, the method of depreciation will go a long way to help you determine what the expense is going to be." The first line was intended to simply get their heads swimming with the terms and make it sound like I was some sort of expert. Next, I slowly explained each of these terms to the confused students, dazzling them with my newfound knowledge without divulging into how insufficient my expertise really was.

"Did you get a degree in accounting?" one of them asked at the end of my impromptu lecture.

"Nope," I responded, "my degree is in journalism."

As I departed from the group, I left blank faces of astounded confusion in my wake. This inspired an idea for the column that I had promised Rick just hours before, although at the time I had no clue what I was actually going to write about. Once I got into my car, I jotted a few to-do items down in a notebook for my next work session in the time chamber and then left myself a quick note of only three words, "Next column: Renaissance." I was then off to the grocery store.

While purchasing groceries, I pulled out my phone and searched the internet for the best recipes for chicken parmesan, Trish's favorite meal. I bought all the necessary ingredients, meanwhile getting all the rations I needed to stock both my apartment and the time chamber for a long haul. No longer was I going to force myself to subsist on whatever I could purchase quickly in between jobs. I now had the luxury of having enough time to truly take care of myself. Although never fancying myself to be a health fanatic, my grocery cart would have suggested I was, as it was quickly filled with lean meats, vegetables, and vitamin supplements. If it looked healthy, I bought it. Every purchase came in twos, as I was now shopping for two entirely separate lives, one inside the chamber and the other in the world of the ticking clock. I then paid the cashier what had to be the largest grocery purchase I had ever made and then continued back to my apartment.

When I arrived home, I was almost startled at the newfound cleanliness of my home. Nonetheless, with a speed and precision that was becoming somewhat familiar to me, I quickly sorted my groceries and put them into their respective places, both in my apartment and in the time chamber. Stepping in and out of the chamber door gave me a somewhat uneasy feeling because time had frozen and unfrozen so many times. Had I been sorting groceries for several minutes or several hours? It didn't really matter, but I took note of how easily I could become disoriented if I used the chamber without a clear purpose.

In the case of that afternoon, the purpose of the chamber was to be yet another crash course. This time I wasn't teaching myself about depreciation for a cheap parlor trick in front of confused college students; I was teaching myself how to make chicken parmesan for a date that I wanted to be absolutely perfect. The first time I attempted to prepare the dish, it came out somewhat bland, so I double-checked the recipes on the time-chamber computer. After three attempts, I was pleased with the product I was finally able to produce. Feeling satisfied and ready for the evening, I exited the time chamber and feverishly started preparing the dinner for my date with Trish. While the dish was in the oven, I shaved for the second time in less than twenty-four hours, and put on some of my freshly cleaned clothes.

As I was finishing the preparation of the chicken parmesan, I acted in full recognition of the fact that the rehearsal was over and the show was about to begin. Although I had put the equivalent of several hours into learning how to make Trish's favorite dinner, this specific preparation was the only one that mattered. I put an intense amount of attention into every single detail, lighting candles and setting the table. Although the idea of the candlelit dinner was somewhat cliché, it would serve as a demonstration of the effort that I had

long neglected in our relationship. Trish had been patient and understanding as my academic and professional endeavors drew time and
energy away from the relationship. Tonight I would begin returning
the favor.

As I prepared the dinner, sensations from our first date came
to mind. Although I had almost gotten used to the idea of unlimited time, the idea of a countdown to Trish's arrival was definitely
intriguing. I thought about how the hours would crawl by when I
was looking forward to a date with her and then how an hour could
feel like seconds when I was in her company. This feeling gave me
a completely new perspective in light of what I had gained from the
time chamber. The ability to fit days' and nights' worth of progress
into a single second completely changed the way I viewed time. It
occurred to me that time was not merely a measurement but a sense.
It was a sense that was much different from those such as sight and
sound. Much like the human body has several nerve endings that
relate messages to the brain about the body's position relative to the
ground, there was a also a sense of how much time had elapsed, and
mine was suddenly more alert than ever.

A quick glance at the clock showed that it was 6:05 p.m. This
meant that Trish's arrival was only fifty-five minutes away; it might
as well have been an eternity. A few minutes later, I received a text
message from her: "Hey, babe. I got home later than expected. I could
use more time to get ready. How's 7:30 p.m.?" I responded almost
instantly, saying the extra half hour was no big deal. In reality, I felt
as though I was about to explode with anxiety. Once again, she had
been so patient with me that I really couldn't complain about thirty
minutes. But then again, it seemed much longer to me since we last
saw each other than it probably did to her.

I slowed down the process of preparing the dinner, meanwhile
taking any steps I could to ensure the apartment was presentable. I
was beyond determined that the evening was going to be impres-

sive. The minutes seemed to crawl by as I looked into every possible detail. I vacuumed the floor (again), cleaned the wine glasses, and even shined my shoes. While I completed each of these tasks, my main focus was trying to keep my eyes off the clock. This was all but impossible, as I felt like this unassuming timepiece had eyes that burned into me while my back was turned.

When Trish finally arrived at my door, I immediately saw the end result of thirty extra minutes of preparation. She looked as stunning as ever, wearing a purple dress that she always knew could get my attention. As she stepped into my apartment, her facial expression was one of surprise. The order and cleanliness of my home served as a striking contrast to the filth and disarray that had stood in its place only a day before. On the coffee table, sitting alone, was a printed document almost demanding attention. It was the research paper, the very mention of which had been enough to immediately put me in a bad mood only twenty-four hours before. In striking contrast, I stood over it smiling with pride at what I had just accomplished.

Trish quickly picked it up and started thumbing through the pages with absolute awe. After a few brief seconds, her eyes met mine. "Eric, what is this?"

"It's my paper for Dr. Karzeck."

"Did you make progress?"

"More than that—it's finished. I left a copy with Dr. Karzeck this morning."

"Wait, just last night you were struggling to write your first paragraph. Now it's done. How does that happen?"

I knew I couldn't tell her about the chamber. I was rather flippant when I agreed to Michael's oath of secrecy, not realizing the attacks of conscience it would cause me. This was a huge secret, and that alone made me feel dishonest. However, I quickly justified this with the conclusion that a half-truth was somehow more morally sound than an absolute lie. I responded, "Well, after our conversation last night, I decided to pull myself together. I guess in doing so, I regained my focus." There was nothing untrue about that statement; I just omitted the details about *what* pulled me together and *how* I regained my focus. I was doing the best I could to give just enough information to satisfy her curiosity while keeping the chamber a secret. This was when I came to the conclusion that if one does not have the luxury of being completely honest, the poor but ready substitute is ambiguity.

Over dinner, we immediately rediscovered what we loved about each other's company. We laughed and told stories, and as the conversation grew deeper, the hours started flying by. I couldn't care less what time it was, but Trish, on the other hand, was still limited by the world of the ticking clock. Not long after midnight, she volunteered to start washing dishes. As she washed and I rinsed and dried, without exchanging a word, we both decided that we didn't really care if the dishes got clean. As we retired to the bedroom, I discretely set my alarm for 4:30 a.m., knowing that Trish could sleep through almost any commotion I could cause. The next morning, just as predicted, the alarm went off, pulling me into consciousness while leaving Trish largely undisturbed. Although it pained me to get out of bed while she was still there, I knew I could make a great impression with the aid of the time chamber.

I quickly changed into a workout outfit and then gathered the clothes I was going to wear that day. I decided that I should activate the chamber behind a closed and locked bathroom door, just to be sure that I could constantly keep the device concealed. I went into the chamber, laid down for a little extra sleep, and then put myself through yet another strenuous workout. After that, as well as a shower and my new grooming routine, I was awake, alert, and once again ambitious to face the day. I put a little extra effort into my appearance, for I knew that I would be the first thing Trish saw when she awoke. My attire was not as impressive as the day before, but still showed a noticeable degree of effort and preparation. I wore a pair of slacks and a purple button-up shirt. I knew that Trish loved this shirt since purple was her favorite color. Thus, the shirt would be a small but excellent detail for the morning I had envisioned.

After I felt as though I had a head start on the day, I stepped out of the chamber and back into the bathroom of my apartment. It was still only 4:30 a.m., and although I had been awake for the equivalent of several hours, the day was still well in its infancy. I wrapped the device in a towel and hid it, sandwiched between other towels, in my rather small linen closet. I then quickly started moving back and forth across my kitchen, brewing coffee, scrambling eggs, and frying bacon. Trish would have to be awake around five thirty to get ready to work at the bookstore, and as her wake-up time drew closer, I had a flash of creativity. The small cutting board on the top of my kitchen cabinet would be the perfect size for a tray for breakfast in bed. The breakfast, the added effort, and the extra attention to my appearance all combined into what felt like a sudden bid for some sort of "boyfriend of the year" award.

As I awoke Trish, her breakfast was waiting on the bedside table. Eggs, bacon, toast, orange juice and coffee all combined into some sort of thank you for all the support Trish had given me over the past several months. As Trish woke up, she seemed surprised by all this extra effort, and her astonishment was readily apparent on her face. "Are you going to eat with me?" Trish asked with a warm smile on her face.

"Sure thing!" I dashed into the kitchen and filled a plate with the leftover breakfast. After pouring myself another cup of coffee, I went back into the bedroom. Sitting in a complete state of awe, Trish looked up in between sips of coffee. "All right, Mr. Wonderful," she asked, "what's going on?"

"What do you mean?" I was trying to act confused, knowing that doing so wasn't going to work with Trish. That was one mixed blessing of our relationship. I knew from the start that since I was otherwise an average guy, the one and only way I was going to attract a girl like Trish was because of my intellect. While this fact brought me a great sense of pride, it also meant that I could never really get away with playing stupid.

"Well, Eric," Trish answered, seemingly searching for words, "you haven't been this attentive for months. I've always known you to be a caring boyfriend, but the last few months you were going downhill. I mean, yesterday, I could hardly get you to answer your phone, and now I'm getting breakfast in bed."

"Well, I realized that work and school have gotten in the way and I haven't been paying you much attention. I decided to stop making excuses and give you the treatment and effort you deserve." I was really hoping that this explanation would stop the questions.

"It's not just that, Eric." It quickly became obvious that these questions were only the beginning. "It's everything. Yesterday your apartment was a hell hole, and now it's immaculate. You've gotten so much work done, and you look... well, you look incredible."

As her inquiry shifted from my work habits to my appearance, it seemed as though she was able to distract herself, as her tone morphed from one of suspicion to one that demonstrated some sort of renewed physical attraction. Although this small recognition of my new and improved appearance was flattering, I knew that she would not be so easily distracted for very long.

"Well, babe." I was beginning to conjure up an explanation. "When you left here last night, I was frustrated, and as hard as I tried, I couldn't find a way to get anything accomplished. Then I heard the pop."

"The what?"

"The pop! What, you didn't hear it? The sound should have been deafening."

"I don't know what you're talking about."

"There was a loud pop. It was the sound of me pulling my head out of my ass."

Trish couldn't help but laugh. I knew that my self-effacing sense of humor always endeared her to me. However, I also knew that I couldn't keep playing clueless. She could see right through it. The problem was that I still couldn't be completely honest, either.

"Trish," I added, "I just came to the realization that I needed to take control. I let myself run on the hamster wheel for far too long, and I made our relationship suffer. I just couldn't do that anymore. So I buckled down and just started getting things done. If you hadn't been there for me through all of this, I don't know if I'd have gotten half this far."

Although it seemed that she had her doubts, she began to back off her inquiry mode once again. I quietly concluded that she just wanted to enjoy the rebirth of her loving and caring boyfriend. For Trish, it had to feel as though she was getting me back. She looked at me with a sense of wide-eyed disbelief. Beyond this, her eyes seemed like she truly missed me. When I was buried in my work, there was a sense of desperation in her eyes that I never saw until I took the time to stop and take notice. With the prison bars of my work and stress no longer between us, her eyes seemed to lock on and follow me. There was a shared feeling that a storm had just passed and now we could look to the road that lay before us with a spirit of both security and ambition.

Although I shared the same excitement, I saw this newfound energy as an empowering force that would help me embrace something more meaningful and timeless. The last twenty-four hours, which really seemed much longer to me, were marked by a complete personal metamorphosis, a spontaneous evolution sparked by my ability to bend time to my will. Although it felt amazing to stomp over the obstacles that once plagued us, that wasn't what mattered to me at that particular moment. I had enjoyed immense personal victories, but what meant more was that I had someone with whom to share these successes. Although I was the one who put these storms into our relationship, I felt the unique opportunity to put the wind at our backs again.

After our breakfast was over, Trish gathered her clothes and started getting ready for work. She always kept a second set of makeup and her various toiletries in my apartment. In the mess of my prior lifestyle, these items had been pushed to the back of my bathroom cabinet, hidden by clutter and dirty towels. As a result of my cleaning spree, they sat neatly and affectionately organized, suggesting that my apartment was just as much her home as it was mine. As she got ready, I simply stood in the doorway, giving her my full attention and almost hanging on her every word.

After she kissed me good-bye for the day and walked out the door, I was once again left alone in my apartment. For a moment, my mind began to gravitate around all that had occurred in the last twenty-four hours of real time. All the burdens that were once looming over my head had crumbled in one fell swoop. I was no longer up against the deadlines. Instead, the only things that could stand in my way were my own physical and mental limitations. I went to the bathroom and withdrew the time chamber apparatus from its hiding place and pushed the small blue button. The overwhelming stillness and silence was no longer unsettling; it was a familiar part of my routine. I was no longer getting caught up in my new incredible power. Instead, I was preparing for the long haul ahead. After a little bit of cardio and a long, relaxing reading session, I sat down to write the column that I had promised Rick. This was where the idea from the library came flashing across my memory. I thought about the students who were left dumbfounded at my knowledge of an accounting concept because my undergraduate degree was in journalism. This paired with my new plans to learn languages, to read more, and to learn.

I used those events from the library as inspiration for a column that criticized the modern college student. I wrote about how students only learn what is necessary to get them a degree. I questioned when the connection between a college degree and a career led to the loss of a true love of learning. At the end, I made an appeal to the rebirth of Renaissance learning, hoping that the students would, in the words of Mark Twain, "not let their schooling get in the way of their education." While I revised the column, I felt as though this work was far better than my last few submissions. There was a liberating feeling that came with working without any concerns for when I would have to stop, with no phone calls or interruptions and no background noise to demand my attention. I could pour myself into whatever task to which I devoted my energy. I could live, breathe, and work in the moment, digging further into my own untapped potential. I then stepped out of the chamber and once again into my apartment. I had fit a full day into my morning, and that wasn't good enough. I was no longer satisfied simply by how much more time I had at my disposal. Instead, I was hungry to see what I could become.

Chapter 5

It was roughly 7:00 a.m. when Trish left my apartment, and the trip to the chamber made it feel like the middle of the afternoon, so I stepped outside to sit on a bench and acclimate myself to the time. It is truly amazing what one can overlook while rushing to one place or another. The world buzzed by me in a frenzy of activity, as I just sat back and took in every detail. I watched as people scuffled by, such as the visibly irritated businessman yelling into his cell phone. Another was a delivery boy on a bicycle who seemed to be in such a hurry that he barely avoided running over other pedestrians. However, the one who entertained me the most was the young woman in the sophisticated black skirted suit who managed to break both of her high-heeled shoes within one block of her scurry, loudly yelling "Shit!" in a high-pitched screech as each long stem cracked and separated itself from the rest of the shoe.

For each of these people, I found myself conjuring up some sort of story. I imagined what their families were like, if they had any. I wondered if they had even heard of the Falcon news magazine and, if so, if they had ever happened to read any of my columns. These details, once lost in a blurred-gray frenzy of rush and stress, now presented themselves so vividly that they leapt out to assault my senses. It then occurred to me that I was sitting on the very same bench that I had used to stall under the guise of a planning session just moments before Michael wandered into my life and gave me the rare gift that would forever change the way I viewed time and the world around me.

It was that moment, that glass of water, and that brief but meaningful exchange with Michael that brought me to where I was on this particular morning, finding so much entertainment in witnessing the acts of strangers. What if *they* had what I had? What if *their* precious minutes and hours suddenly came to know absolutely no limits? What if I hadn't happened to wander out onto the street at that precise moment? The what-if questions alone were enough to make my head spin, and yet they seemed to all be coalescing and driving toward some sort of deeper conclusion, although such a revelation stood just outside my reach. Nonetheless, I let this deeper philosophical inquiry rest for the moment as I returned to my apartment.

I pondered the day that lay before me with a childlike thirst for adventure and conquest. I would begin with yet another triumphant return to the Falcon office. I had a freshly printed column that I felt deserved to be delivered in person. I had no intention of quietly pushing my writing through the rather passive, less glorious e-mail submission. I would then sit at my desk and bask in the glow of once again being the golden child of the office. But what would I do after that?

It was Wednesday, which meant that Trish would be unavailable that evening. Wednesday nights were always blocked off for her to have an almost sacred girl time with her sisters. This ritual was established only a few weeks after their father passed away, and from then on, the weekly ritual galvanized their bond to the point that they became closer than ever before. For a moment, I wondered whether my little surprise visit, the flowers, and the dinner date were going to come up in the plethora of topics that Trish blithely and ambiguously referred to as girl talk. As that question received its well-deserved degree of consideration, I resolved that from that point on, if I were to come up in their conversations, I would give Trish nothing to report but stories of extra attention and acts of romance. The flowers and the dinner were just the beginning, as the ideas for a lifelong series of little surprises came spinning forward with intricate detail.

I would have to stop by the Falcon building to drop off my new column idea to Rick. This meant that I had about two hours' worth of obligations and then the rest of the day was at my disposal. If it were up to me, I would have spent that evening with Trish, but I knew that Wednesday nights were for girl time, and I wasn't going to do anything to wreck that. From what Trish told me, they would often all meet at one of their homes to watch movies and talk about anything but their work at the bookstore. While the television would show some sappy movie about Matthew McConaughey miraculously turning his life around to win the love of some girl, the three sisters would talk about their love lives or yoga or whatever the hell women talk about when men aren't around. Although it pleased me to see that Trish had this ritual, the fact remained that it left me without a date for the evening. Thus, I would have almost the entire day to myself.

When I finally did arrive at the Falcon building, I leisurely strolled into the elevator from the lobby. Only seconds after the doors closed, they reopened as Rick joined me on the elevator from the second floor. It was at this moment that it occurred to me that I never took the time to figure out what else was in this building. I knew how to find anything and everything on the fourteenth floor, but the remaining twenty floors were a mystery that I had never taken the time to investigate. As Rick extended a finger to push the button marked "14," he immediately pulled it back as he detected the glow of the small white square. He put his hand in his pocket and then began to engage in his awkward version of small talk.

"Hey Eric, how's it going?"

"I'm good. How are you doing?"

"Great. Hey—" Just as he was about to shift from the greeting, some sort of idea or remembrance shot across his face. "Actually, I needed to talk with you."

"What's up?" I carried a tone that showed my interest in his input, but otherwise no additional tone of concern or worry presented itself in my voice.

"Have you heard of a man named William Gastineux?"

"Yeah," I replied, although it did take me a moment to actually register who he was talking about. As soon as my mind could pull the information from its interior filing system, my response continued. "He's the real-estate investor turned venture capitalist from New York who took up residence here in Chicago and turned around about half a dozen businesses. What about him?"

"He's hosting this black tie affair next week, you know, one of those god-awful fundraisers. I hate going to them, but he and I are acquaintances, and my wife will never pass up an opportunity to buy a new dress."

"Well, that sounds like fun." I had yet to ascertain what any of this had to with me.

"Well, it is fun the first couple of times. Once you've been to about a hundred of them, they all start to look alike, and next thing you know, you're bored out of your mind."

I must have looked puzzled by that point. Rick was a successful and influential figure, with a fairly stellar career as a financial journalist before he ventured out on his own to start the Falcon. I, on the other hand, was just some young, hopeful columnist in his first year of grad school. What was leading Rick to believe that I was somehow on my way to a future of hobnobbing with wealthy, influential people in a slew of grandiose fundraisers?

"I guess I'd need to go to one to know."

"Mr. Gastineux wants you to be there. He sought me out and told me to personally give you an invitation."

That puzzled me even further. Not only was some wealthy entrepreneur I had never met seeming to go out of his way to invite me to a fundraiser, but he was also willing to use my boss as some sort of errand boy. Oddly enough, Rick didn't seem to mind. In fact, it seemed to excite him. He reached into his shirt pocket to hand me a small engraved envelope with my name. "Eric McHayden plus one," it read. While I was thrilled to see my name in those gold embossed letters, the "plus one" was what really tickled my imagination. Trish and I were not the type to go on grandiose and ostentatious dates, but this was a great opportunity to show off for her. This was the kind of date that said, "Guess what, sweetheart? Your boyfriend is a somebody." And besides, I knew, albeit from only one experience, that she looked stunning in an evening gown.

"I'll be there!" I responded, trying to conceal my excitement. With what had just occurred, I had forgotten the very reason that I came all this way. I was supposed to give Rick a copy of my new column. Of course, I could have simply sent it to him as an attachment in an email, but with the work and creative thinking I had expended in its creation, that just seemed like some odd sort of blasphemy. I felt as though my work deserved to be exchanged the old-fashioned way, that I should print it off myself and hand it to my editor in person. Besides, I now had the time to actually come into the office and really immerse myself in the goings-on at my workplace. Just as the elevator door opened, I declared, "Oh yeah, I almost forgot. I have a column for you, as promised yesterday."

Rick chuckled while patting me on the arm, "Of course you do."

As the two large heavy doors slid open, I could feel the whirring buzz of activity from our fourteenth-floor office suite begin to surround me. It felt as though I was moving in slow motion, as if everyone else in the office was in some sort of hurry and I was not. Of course, they all had things to accomplish on a time frame that would forever be shorter than mine. I found humorous the number of times I could spot one of my coworkers stopping to check his watch or glance up at the clock. I couldn't care less what time it was if I tried. Was it noon? What did it matter? I knew that it was only getting close to 10:00 a.m., which meant everybody in the room was trying to wrap up one task or another as the lunch break drew closer.

I looked around the room, hoping to find Marcus. When my shifty-eyed search didn't find him, I asked Lauren, our intern, where he was. She told me that he was off on an interview. Even though I was surrounded by sounds and faces, the absence of my closest friend made the office seem somewhat lonely. Then Stephen, the shy PR guy, caught my attention. From where I was standing, I could only see his forehead, as the rest of his rather small, sickly figure was hidden by his desktop computer. His eyes glanced up over the top of the monitor, and when they met mine, he quickly shot back out of view, making him all too similar to a turtle taking refuge deep within its shell. As I bounded toward his desk, I tried to be as friendly as I could in striking up a conversation.

"Hello, Stephen. How are you doing?"

"Um... hi." He seemed almost startled that someone had even taken the time to notice him. "Things are all good here. We're getting a lot of good feedback on our social networking platforms, and I believe the last staff meeting indicated that subscriptions have increased. Also, search engines are showing an increase in hits on the subjects we are writing about, which to me suggests that—"

"I get it man. We're doing well." It was somewhat sad that it seemed he was only used to being spoken to when he was expected to give a report on the status of the Falcon. "I was really asking how you are doing."

"Well, um, I'm doing okay, I guess."

"Awesome. Did you do anything fun over the weekend?" The weekend question was always a last resort, right up there with the weather for last-ditch conversation topics.

"Not really. I helped my cousin put together a TV stand Friday night and spent my Saturday and Sunday working on a few of my hobbies."

"Hobbies? Like what?"

"Oh, they really aren't exciting."

"Come on, you can tell me."

"Well, I always have enjoyed writing poetry, and I've played guitar since I was a little kid, so every now and then I, well, I—"

"You're a songwriter."

"I wouldn't go that far." He began to blush and stare awkwardly at the floor. As he tried to change the topic of conversation, the next word on his tongue froze as if an invisible hand had come and clutched his throat. His eyes shifted quickly to the other side of the room.

I scanned the bullpen area to see what had caught Stephen's attention. Lauren, the new intern, was reentering the room. I started to glance back and forth, shifting my weight to where I could easily view both Stephen and Lauren. His eyes seemed to follow her as she loaded paper into a printer and then continued to buzz about the office.

Lauren had been working at the Falcon for a little over two months. Her acceptance into the internship came during my pre-time-chamber life of disarray and underperformance (I must have been terribly welcoming.) The most regrettable reality of her internship was that a few of the writers, namely Bernstandt, treated her like little more than an assistant, making her do rather inglorious and remedial jobs that were both belittling and degrading. She was a junior at the University of Chicago and, much like Stephen, was so quiet that hardly anyone seemed to know her. Since Stephen seldom drew attention to himself, I doubt that anyone had previously noticed his infatuation with her. I instantly decided that our conversation had a new direction.

"Stephen, we should hang out some time. Have you met my girlfriend?"

"I think I've seen her come in once or twice."

"Well, maybe we could all go out some time. Maybe you could ask Lauren?"

"Oh, I don't think she'd want to go with me."

"What makes you say that?"

"I'm sure she has a boyfriend or something."

"Do you know that for sure?"

"No, but I'm sure a girl like her would have a date any night she wants one. Why would she want to go with the PR guy nobody talks to?"

"You never know until you try." I tried to sound as encouraging as possible. Just then, I saw Marcus come bounding back into the office. Apparently it was a quick interview.

Marcus' walk carried that kind of confident strut that made him the envy of almost any man in the office. When he approached, we shared small talk about the interview and what he was planning to write for next week's printing. I made sure to stand in a way that included Stephen in our lighthearted banter. If our one-on-one exchange made him appear startled and nervous, then what was the beginning of a group conversation made him almost freeze up in terror. Nonetheless, I continued my efforts to make him feel welcome as I would repeatedly shoot him a grin or ask him a question to give him the sense of inclusion. As the idle small talk started to dwindle down, an idea came to mind.

"You know," I said, "we hardly ever go out and hang like coworkers."

Marcus looked at me strangely; he and I had gone out for drinks on several occasions, but I was referring to a larger "we" than simply Marcus and me. "What did you have in mind?" Marcus asked.

"I was thinking we'd hang out at Fritz's bar tonight. We'll get anyone from the office who wants to go, and we'd all go have a few drinks together." I then shot my glance over to Stephen. "You should come!"

"Umm, okay, yeah. What's the name of the bar?"

"It's Fritz's. It's that hole in the wall sports bar a couple blocks from here."

"What time?" Marcus asked.

"Let's plan on seven o'clock and ask anyone in the office."

I knew that Rick wouldn't attend because he religiously took his wife out to dinner on Wednesday nights after the Falcon was printed and distributed. It was his way of taking his mind off of the magazine and actually having a life outside the office, if that was even possible. I also knew that Bernstandt wouldn't attend because he was the kind of arrogant schmuck who looked down his nose at everyone else in the office. Neither of these realities bothered me. I enjoyed Rick's company but understood both his Wednesday night ritual and the ever-present professional barrier between him and the people who worked under him. And Bernstandt, well, I was glad he wouldn't attend because I would've rather slammed my manly bits in a sliding glass door than spend any more time with him than I absolutely had to.

I went on to ask a few of my coworkers if they would like to attend the evening's festivities, making a deliberate, separate effort to invite Lauren. I felt this compulsion to make sure that she and Stephen got the opportunity to speak to one another in a strictly social setting away from the office. For some reason, the conversation with Stephen, where I noted his attraction to her, made me think of all the nerves and anxiety I felt when I first asked Trish out on a date and how I wished that I had some sort of wing man to establish a setting and give me some sort of guidance in my bumbling attempts to win her affection. Lauren agreed to attend, and that was enough for the day. I had plans for my evening, and the rest of the afternoon was at my disposal.

With my affairs for work in order, I headed next to have lunch with Trish, who was probably working away at the bookstore, answering questions and running inventory. I stopped by a small bistro and picked up some sandwiches for us and then took the fastest route I knew back to her work. This drive was much less leisurely as I raced back to see her. Even though I was driving faster and taking a route with less stoplights, it amazed me how a trip seems longer when filled with excitement about the destination.

Once I arrived at the back of the bookstore, we had our usual lunchtime conversation and yet another passionate backroom exchange. She had complained that the computer inventory system had been giving them problems all morning and that no one in the office could figure out exactly what was causing the problem. This gave me an idea that was somewhat similar to the parlor trick I had pulled in front of the confused accounting students not long before. Once she stepped out of the room, I opened up the backroom computer just long enough to figure out what sort of inventory program was being used, and then my next step was to pull the time-chamber device from my courier bag and activate it in the solitude behind the closed backroom door.

With the walls of frozen time surrounding me, I then put myself through a crash course on the ins and outs of the IRT 3700 inventory system, learning everything I could absorb about its major functions, typical troubleshooting practices, and even unique functions and features that would take some degree of research to identify. Much like

I had done during the crash course on depreciation, I made sure that the necessary information was readily available at the forefront of my memory.

With that, I made a quick exit from the chamber and found myself once again alone in the back room of the bookstore, where I immediately hid the chamber device deep within my courier bag. I then sat down at Trish's computer and began putting my newfound knowledge to the test. My hands moved with a quick and deliberate precision as I was able to find, diagnose, and then resolve the problem in no time. All of this occurred before Trish returned from answering a phone call.

"I fixed the inventory system," I called out from behind the computer monitor.

"You what?"

"I fixed it. There was a problem with the connection between the inventory system back here and the sales computers at the front desk. Thus, the computer didn't know which items had been sold and removed from the shelves. I fixed it, and now it should be able to give you a more updated inventory list."

After the initial astonishment subsided, Trish reached over my shoulder and began to push button after button, apparently testing my assertion that the inventory system was indeed brought back to proper working order. Once I had completed talking Trish through what went wrong with the inventory system (admittedly, I was showing off), I kissed her good-bye and told her about my plans for the evening. Once I left the bookstore, it occurred to me that it was roughly one in the afternoon, and my plans to meet up with my coworkers wouldn't take place until seven that evening, so I was left to decide what I would do with the rest of my afternoon. And then it occurred to me—not a damn thing.

Chapter 6

My afternoon of leisure, which would be capped off by an evening carousing with my coworkers, began at a humble video rental store that sat on the route between Trish's bookstore and my apartment. Once inside, I didn't particularly care how long it took me to make a selection, as I casually breezed up and down the aisles and browsed the wide array of films. After what felt like a good twenty minutes or so of searching, I finally decided on an old action flick starring Sylvester Stallone. Those kinds of white knuckle, gunfight, and explosion films were always my favorite as a kid, so I was somewhat surprised to come across a midnineties Stallone movie that I hadn't seen before. As I checked out, I added on my favorite indulgence—popcorn and a Coke. With the movie and snacks in hand, I returned to my apartment.

A few small preparations, such as pulling the curtains closed over the windows and microwaving popcorn, helped convert the living room space of my apartment into a makeshift movie theater. Before long, I was able to relax and lose myself in a Stallone-driven symphony of explosions, gunfights, and the almost obligatory high-speed chase. After the movie ended, once the villain was slain and the world was safe again, I felt all at once ready to get back to work.

It was roughly 5:00 p.m. when the movie ended, which meant that any project I wanted to start would've had to be halted midway if not for the use of the time chamber. After yet another gathering of clothes and materials, followed by a quick push of the little blue button, I was off to the races. Once again pivoting from one project to another, columns started to flow out of me. If I wasn't writing a column, I was reading a book. If I lost momentum on either of those two tasks, I would work on my Italian. When I got tired of working on these projects, I would leave my desk and get some exercise in the chamber's workout area. I was constantly moving, constantly hungry for more, and it didn't take long before I had four completed columns, I had read two books, I had almost doubled my Italian vocabulary, and I had exercised my body to the point of exhaustion.

I realized that although my time knew no limits, my body did, as my stomach rumbled for a warm meal and my eyes grew heavy from lack of sleep. I didn't take much time to rest, and the finished products on the chamber desk suggested that I had been at work for what could have been ten hours or more. I knew that this hunger and fatigue would get the best of me, but before they did, I began to cook a large meal from the rations that seemed to call out to me from the chamber's refrigerator. I marinated chicken and put it in a baking pan with some vegetables, while remembering that I had some microwavable mashed potatoes, the kind that you buy in the freezer section, which would go well with the meal I was preparing. After eating my fill, the next step was to take another long, hot shower. From the looks of the thick stubble that had begun to darken my jaw line and the smell of my clothes as I pulled them off, I must have been at work for an exceptionally long time. "Look at me go," I said to myself. "I even manage to fit a good day of work into the afternoon I meant to set aside to do nothing."

The shower was so hot and relaxing that I almost felt myself nod off under the hot stream. It took everything I had to pull myself out of the enclosure to dry off and shave. Once I had completed this, I trudged out of the chamber's bathroom and sat down at the foot of the bed. My hands moved almost autonomously from my brain as they pulled the third book off the large stack I had rented from the library, as if my mind had developed some sort of preconditioned urge to keep working and reading even when I had resigned myself to getting some rest. The book was *The Idiot* by Dostoyevsky, and as soon as I pulled it open, the musty smell of the pages began to fill my nostrils. Before I could even finish reading the first page, I drifted off into a deep restful sleep.

When I awoke, the immediate logical questions arose, most of which were the conditioned ones about what time it was or how long I had been asleep. Although the chamber was becoming more and more familiar, waking up in the chamber bed was all too similar to being jolted awake in a hotel bedroom, only to be met with the disorienting feeling that asks, "Where am I?" I then laughed at the recognition that I had fallen asleep still wet from the shower wearing nothing but a towel. Before I gathered my belongings to exit the chamber, I printed my new writing and put some gel in my hair. Once outside the chamber, when the feeling of a good night's sleep collided with the fact that it was still just five o'clock in the evening, I readied myself for a long overdue evening of drinking and socializing with my friends from the Falcon.

I could tell immediately from my time of departure that I would arrive at least an hour early, and that brought me comfort. Being in the kind of suspended isolation that the chamber provided really unveiled to me the inherent need for the presence of other people. I was willing to work the long hours, but the solitude was enough to drive a man crazy. Besides, I had gotten an exceptional amount of work done, so I felt that the evening deserved considerable celebration. I would treat myself to one of Fritz's delectable buffalo-chicken sandwiches, maybe crack a joke or two with the bartender, and would be at least two drinks in before my coworkers arrived. I was by no means a shy person, but it was truly amazing how a serving or two of liquid courage could turn me into an outright social butterfly.

Fritz's bar and grill was relatively quiet, except for a small dinner crowd in the restaurant area. It was 5:30 p.m. on a Wednesday night, not necessarily the typical time when one would really expect a large social scene. I ordered the buffalo-chicken sandwich, realizing that since I had awakened in the time chamber less than an hour or so before after the equivalent of a long night's sleep, this would be the substitute for my "breakfast of champions." The first two beers went down rather quickly as they cut through the heat the sandwich left in my mouth. Then just as the bartender took my plate and I was about to order a third drink, I felt someone come up behind me to take a seat at my immediate left.

"You're looking better."

Before the familiarity of the voice could truly register, my head turned so quickly that it looked like an owl impression. It was Michael.

"Hey!" I couldn't suppress my surprise. "How are you?"

"I'm pretty good, but not taking the world by storm, like somebody who shall remain nameless. It sure looks like you're back to your old tricks."

My lips curled up into a smile that could only exist for the concealment of secrets. "What can I say? I've had some great help."

Michael's grin reciprocated my own as his finger raised to his lips in mum's-the-word sort of gesture. "And I see you're putting it to good use"

"Yes, I used it"—I made a long pause to suggest that the item in question deserved some sort of reverence—"just before I came here."

"Good for you," Michael replied. Our tone suggested that we were speaking in some kind of code, like two thieves planning a heist in broad daylight while trying to avoid suspicion. "Well, keep putting it to good use, and I'm sure things will come together quite nicely."

"I do have some questions."

"Those can be answered later. In the meantime, keep up the good work and know that I'm cheering for you. Remember, no greater crime than wasted time."

Our conversation then turned to small talk, and for some unearthly reason, I felt unable to ask him any questions about his personal life. It then occurred to me that at every turn in our conversation, he would change the subject to whatever inconsequential matter he could, be it the sports highlights on the barroom TV or how such a hole in the wall could have such a great scotch selection.

The conversation went on for about thirty minutes, and Michael began his exit, once again leaving me with more questions than answers. It struck me as odd, but what could I do? My first instinct was to chase him out of the bar yelling, "Magic man, tell me your secrets!" However, I knew that this would cause at least a small scene. Thus, I stood dumbfounded, just as I had been the night he left the small metallic device in my apartment. As he was leaving, he passed by yet another patron who carried with him an equal and yet opposite surprise. This second visitor was Rick, who I had assumed would rather avoid an evening drinking with the Falcon staff.

"Rick? I didn't think you would come."

"Well, I thought I'd make an appearance." Rick carried a fidgety demeanor that always suggested that his mind was on the next task. "Also," he continued, "I wanted to remind you that we have our staff meeting tomorrow morning." He could somehow immediately tell that I had forgotten. Our staff meetings occurred on a biweekly basis and were mandatory for everyone who worked at the Falcon.

"Anything interesting?" My inquiry hinted at suspicion as to why Rick would go out of his way to remind me about a staff meeting.

"Nothing groundbreaking. I just wanted to make sure you remembered."

"Okay." I could tell that Rick hadn't come all this way to a social function he would otherwise avoid just to bust my chops about some staff meeting. The only other thing that stood out in my mind was this surprise invitation to the fundraising event. "Oh yeah, and about this Gastineux thing." I could tell that I had started to ask the right question, but Rick wasn't going to just spell anything out to me.

"What about it?" Rick was going to make me do most of the work of the conversation.

"Well, of all the people who he could invite, why did he go out of his way to get an invitation to one of your columnists?"

"Eric"—his pause felt like it went on for hours, and I could tell that he was choosing his words very carefully—"I'll be honest. When I first hired you, I really felt like I had found something, and I may have bragged about you to him. Then you fell into this slump. All of a sudden, I didn't have a reason to brag anymore. Do you know when Gastineux gave me the invitation to pass along to you?"

This question was abrupt and, for the moment, struck me as something of a non sequitur, for I couldn't tell what it had to do with the "slump" to which Rick was referring.

"When?"

"He gave it to me two months ago, but by then, you had stopped giving me the two or three well-polished diamond columns per week. Hell, you were barely turning in one column a week, and those were, well—"

"I know." Those words came out of my mouth so quickly that I was startled at the sound. It was as though a dark, ugly creature named ego had been lurking in the back of my mind and had come roaring out, unable to handle even the slightest of criticisms.

Despite the rude and startling interruption, Rick continued. "Anyway, two days ago, you walk into my office, looking like a completely different person, and you turn in something that looked like the work of the Eric McHayden I had envisioned when I first hired you. Then came these last three submissions you've put on my desk. Eric, they're incredible. They're original, insightful, and something close to innovative."

His words began to really have a profound effect. I was aware that I had been falling behind in almost every aspect of life before the chamber, but I didn't realize exactly how far I had fallen. I felt as though I had pulled myself out of a pit, only to understand how deep it was by looking down from its mouth. Had I really gone from being a bragging right to an absolute embarrassment? Was the abyss of my once-impending failure truly that deep?

At some point in his narrative, Rick realized that his gestures were becoming somewhat grandiose, so he reined himself in as smoothly as he could and brought the story to a close. "It was after I read those columns that I regained confidence in you, so the next logical step was to pass along the invitation."

Although it was intriguing to hear the story of my rebirth through the words of someone else, Rick hadn't really answered the question. "I get it, Rick," I responded. "You had spoken well of me, and you didn't want me to appear as some sort of embarrassment." (At this point, I'll note that it takes a special kind of arrogance to speak with this kind of blunt honesty. Maybe it was the alcohol talking.) I continued. "I'm still a little confused. Why does Gastineux want me there?"

Rick considered my question for a moment, then formulated the best response he was willing to give. "Mr. Gastineux is nearing the end of a long, almost prolific career. He's made more than enough money to make sure that his grandchildren's grandchildren will be set for life, barring catastrophe. A few years ago, he came to the conclusion that he should have someone write his biography. He's the type that has reached such a pinnacle of success that now he just thinks about things like legacies. I think he may be considering asking you to do it."

This idea sent chills of excitement up my spine. "Do you really think so?"

"Hell if I know. Maybe he's just so tired of hearing me brag about you that he just has to find out for himself."

With that, we both shared a good laugh, and then I noticed that Marcus and a few other Falcon employees were coming into the bar. As everyone was filing in, it didn't take long until the party was in full swing. I drank that evening at a pace that could only be compared to the way my life was moving, pummeling forward, only to answer to a call for more. Before the voice of reason could set in, beers turned into mixed drinks, and mixed drinks into shots.

At one moment, while another drink was barreling toward my lips, Marcus's hand stopped the glass just short of my mouth in an ultimately futile, concerned gesture. "Hey man," he said with a slight slur, "we have a staff meeting tomorrow morning. Don't you think you ought to slow down?"

"It's okay," I retorted with a drunken slur to my speech that far eclipsed Marcus's. "I have a plan."

I had a plan all right. After coaxing my coworkers into more drinks than they probably needed, I began the stagger of about four blocks back to my apartment. At some point, I stopped by a convenience store to buy a six pack of cheap beer, which I consumed in the solitude of my apartment. "Anyone who thinks drinking alone is a problem doesn't know what good company I am," I must have said that to myself at some point. The last few hours of the evening were all a blur, which was all right because of the "plan" I so enigmatically alluded to at the bar. I had used my time chamber for a wide array of purposes, but that evening was the first night that it served as a hangover-recovery device. Of course, there was nothing about the chamber that could help a long night of drinking run its course, except for its ability to block out natural daylight. On the other hand, the fact that I could fit an indefinite amount of time into a single second meant that I could sleep for the equivalent of hours, or even days, and step out only a moment later good as new. Telling this story in retrospect, I must say that I am proud that such creativity came to me in such a drunken stupor.

I awoke in the time chamber unable to recount the events after I left the bar. Later on, I would retrace the steps of those two hours or so in a manner that made me feel like Bradley Cooper or Zack Galifianakis in one of the *Hangover* films. Luckily, my detective work would recover that I ravenously drank six beers by myself in the safe confines of my apartment before retreating into the chamber to pass out. When I awoke in the chamber, I was sprawled across the bed in my underwear, and waiting for me was a note on the bedside table with only two words: flying pants. What on earth did that mean?

A quick shot of pain in my forehead told me that I was not yet ready to solve such a mystery, and I retreated back to under the covers for more restorative sleep. When I arose once again, I felt refreshed and ready to face the day. Still in my undergarments, I climbed on the treadmill and ran just enough to sweat out the remaining alcohol. Throughout the run, my mind kept trying to make sense out of the message and what in the world I meant by the words "flying pants." This question plagued me through my morning routine, which I carried out in the time-chamber bathroom. As I exited the chamber freshly groomed with a towel around my waist, the answer came to me with the first glimpse into my apartment.

As I stepped back into the world of the ticking clock, the first sight that came to greet me before I allowed time to resume was the sight of my jeans sitting frozen in midair. Apparently, "drunk me" had decided to recreate the falling glass experiment from the night

I received the chamber. Except this time, the experiment took the form of throwing my pants in the air and pushing the little blue button while they were still floating just below the ceiling. Drunk me found this so hilarious that he left a note that would allow sober me to enjoy the tomfoolery the next morning. Admittedly, I had a good laugh while rolling my eyes and pulling the chamber door closed, allowing time to unfreeze and my pants to fall lifelessly onto my apartment floor. Within those pants I found the receipt from the convenience store, which helped my investigation of those hazy two hours that were lost to blackout drunkenness.

Since it was still roughly 3:00 a.m., I found myself pacing from one side of the apartment to another. In those dark, still hours of the morning, I was a pent-up ball of energy just trying to pass the time until the rest of the world awoke to greet me. For some inexplicable reason, Michael's words, "No crime like wasted time," began to resonate. After these words echoed across my memory, my ears felt as though they were filled with a thousand voices, all screaming, "More." A quick estimation concluded that my total day's work, the combined demands of the Falcon and grad school, would only take about three hours a day or so out of my schedule.

Because of the chamber, the tasks that used to eat away days and nights had come to account only for a small portion of my day in the real world. What about the rest of it? I knew that I could enjoy the luxury of doing what I wanted when I wanted, and from that point on, considerable portions of my time in the world of the ticking clock would be set aside for time with Trish, but that still left heaping intervals of time available without a clear purpose. I needed something, or some things, to build.

In an easily overlooked corner of my apartment sat a dusty, old basketball that had belonged to me since I was ten years old. It was a redundant joke among my friends that I might have had a wonderful career on the basketball court had I not tragically grown up to be short and absolutely devoid of athleticism. What stuck out to me from those sweat-drenched memories from the junior high basketball team was the striking imbalance in the time allocation. For what equates to only a few short hours of actual game time, a player will spend days' and weeks' worth of practice time running drills, lifting weights, conditioning, and shooting. I then began thinking about endeavors, both professional and personal, in terms of practice time and game time. The practice time was the hours that I could put in completely by myself, and the game time existed in the hours that I would have to interface with other people. The Falcon was a great starting point, because although I spent some time in the office or out in the field trying to get an interview (game time), most of my work was done alone in front of a computer (practice time). I laughed at the old adage that for college students, an hour in the classroom should have at least two hours of study time. For this analogy, that meant that college carried a two to one ratio of practice time to game time.

Before long, a legal pad on my coffee table had at least two pages of ideas. I started Google-searching some of these possible endeavors, and then a curious eye started to push the cursor toward the Google news function. What struck me was not really the headlines. Instead, I started noticing the intricate detail from some of the news websites. Just for some basis of comparison, I pulled up the Falcon website, which I think I had only looked at once before while applying for the job. A grimace contorted my face in response to what came up to greet me. The site served as little more than a means to purchase a subscription, with brief biographies for each of the contributors. The site was also so out of date that I had no biography, which not only gave me some degree of concern as to the image this obsolete, barren website was creating, but also pricked my ego at the fact that I was missing out on the recognition. Immediately my thoughts shifted back toward all of the columns that didn't get printed and how on an almost daily basis I would hear several of my coworkers come up with ideas for pieces that would get pushed by the wayside.

The more I observed the stunning detail of some of the news sources, the more I lamented the woeful inadequacy of Falcon.com. But at the same time, major opportunities for the growth and development of our little enterprise started to flare up and swirl around the creative part of my brain. Of course, if I could get these ideas together and the Falcon would be the better for it, these suggestions would lead to yet another round of praise from my coworkers.

I'd love to be able to say that I was just trying to help the business, as if this motivation came from the altruistic notions of a selfless team player, but that just wouldn't be the truth. Sure, I wanted to see the Falcon succeed, but that was only a small fraction of my motivation. It had only been a few days since I had stormed reborn into Rick's office with a rewrite and new columns, and the high from that little shot of recognition was well worn off. Thus, this little brainstorm was about getting credit. In addition to being the golden boy columnist, I wanted to be the idea guy who proved himself crucial to the success of the whole magazine. With every idea I wrote down, I imagined how it would sound when I said it, and I envisioned the praise from my peers.

Before I knew it, 8:00 a.m. began to flash on the cable-box time display, and it was time to begin my commute to the Falcon office. I arrived a little early to bring up my idea to Rick, and he told me that it would have to wait until the next staff meeting, which was two weeks away. He then added that he wanted me to gather as much information as I could and lay out my ideas in a presentation to the entire staff. Although this delay was in many ways like dangling meat in front of a hungry wolf, I welcomed the opportunity to look further into the ideas that hadn't existed only five hours before. If asked, I wouldn't be able to recall anything else that was said at that morning's staff meeting because my mind was too busy dancing with ideas—big ideas.

Chapter 7

Once the staff meeting was over, I started to scurry from one side of the office to another, intending to ask various writers and contributors about some of their ideas for our woefully defunct website. I started with Marcus, knowing that a friendly audience for my plan would be enough to give me at least the feeling of momentum. I was also oddly curious as to what his daily workload entailed. Because I only spent one to two hours a day at the office, I didn't have the foggiest idea what our lone sports writer did on a daily basis. After a few short minutes, he was able to quickly dazzle me with the amount of work he would do. He was truly a walking encyclopedia of the Chicago sports scene, never missing a game in any sport and easily ready to rattle off what was going on for each of our city's beloved teams. He could tell me the name of every professional athlete in Chicago, meanwhile firing away a wealth of information about statistics, recent injuries, and salary negotiations.

After a few moments of astounded silence, I asked him, "Do you ever feel like all that is kind of a waste?"

"How so?" The tone of his question indicated that he didn't know whether to be offended or not. Immediately I recognized that the question could have been worded with a little more tact.

"Well," I responded with an underlying apology in my tone, "you compile all this information, and at most you get two or three articles out to print." I could quickly ascertain that he hadn't really thought about it that way before, and that an unexpected wave of frustration was coming over him, not toward me, but toward what I had just pointed out.

"Ya know," he started while leaning in, "you've got a point there. If we had more print space, I'd cover every game for every team."

"Why does it have to be about print space?" I asked in a tone that suggested I was really confused. At some point that morning, I had become committed to the expansion of the Falcon's website, and I desperately wanted Marcus's support, more than I was willing to admit. Thus, this rather redundant question was my way of leading him to believe that it was his idea as much as it was mine.

"Eric, we both know that we all can't have everything we write make it to print. Hell, you should know better than anyone. Ever since you had your little comeback, you've been putting in a bunch of columns every week, and just like me, you only get one or two of them in each issue." His tone was speeding up and getting louder with every word. I could almost see the dots of his idea, which was actually my idea, starting to connect by the look on his face.

Once it became evident that a plan was coming together, I started to relentlessly turn the screws even further. "You're right. I mean, if everything we wrote made to print, the Falcon would look more like a phonebook than a news magazine." We both had a little chuckle at this image before I continued to guide the conversation. "At the same time, there has to be some outlet for the rest of our work. Have you seen our website?"

"Ha!" Marcus's laugh was almost startling, but I could tell that I wasn't alone in my chagrin toward the deficiency of our online presence. "Our website is so old the picture of Bernstandt still has hair."

We both had a good laugh at that one, as Bernstandt's receding hairline was a recurring joke among those who were aware that good ole Jim was an insufferable jackass. The fact that he tried to hide his hair loss with a hideous comb-over gave us even more ammunition.

Once the laughter subsided, Marcus came to the first obvious question. "Do you think Rick would let us publish some of our stuff online? I mean, the man is old school." With this, he gestured down toward an article that had been printed and edited by Rick himself. The article was covered in Rick's old-fashioned red-ink corrections. Those constant red corrections always carried a little bit of nostalgia along with their constructive criticism.

It didn't take much reassurance to make Marcus my compatriot in the website expansion, and our next recruit, based on my recommendation, was Stephen. I knew that our website was a major reflection of our image, so at first I found it somewhat puzzling that our public-relations guy was never tasked with its maintenance and development. Apparently, Rick had a technical-support employee long before I even worked at the Falcon. Stephen also told me that this would-be computer-whiz kid was lazy, constantly late, and there was at least one allegation that he was trying to hack employee emails. Not long after the creation of this position, Rick had fired this underachiever, never replaced him, and the website was inexplicably allowed to fall by the wayside. It didn't take long to ascertain that Stephen lamented the website's deficiencies, but he was too shy and nervous to voice his concerns. Normally afraid of direct eye contact and silent, Stephen lit up with ideas, and it became apparent that we were definitely onto something. We decided that we would spend the next two weeks collecting input from the staff, and my two newfound partners unanimously decided that I would be the one to present our suggestions at the staff meeting.

I left the Falcon office with a combination of adrenaline, satisfaction, and ambition coursing through my veins. The one thing I wanted more than anything was to see Trish. A quick text message set up a date for that evening, and I knew that the afternoon would crawl by as I waited to see her. Since we had last been together, I had managed to achieve what felt like a year's worth of progress and ideas, along with one good drunken evening, so a lovesick pang struck my heart with every moment I allowed my mind to wander. The plan for that night was that I was going to pick her up at her apartment at six, and on the way back to my place, we would get pizza and rent a movie. This rendezvous was rather simplistic compared to the grandiose dinner from two nights before, but this could be easily compensated by a great many things I had to discuss with her. Between the banquet invitation and the possibly that I might be selected to write the biography of William Gastineux, I simply couldn't wait to talk to her.

That text to Trish, however, was far from my last order of business. My first call was to a boutique dress shop on Chicago's Magnificent Mile. I had heard Trish mention this store on several occasions but knew that she had never actually bought one of their dresses she so desired because of the rather exorbitant price tag. After searching the web to find the phone number for the dress shop, a press of the Call button put me on the line with a rather mousey employee. My request was rather simple: I would have Trish come in within the next few days, she could buy any dress she liked, and I would pick up the bill.

My next call was to the Grand Royale Spa, a palatial fortress of relaxation that sat in uptown Chicago. I told them that on Saturday, I would be surprising my girlfriend with a full day at their establishment, and my orders followed the same tone of my call to the dress shop—Trish would get whatever she wanted, and I would be more than willing to pick up the tab. Finally, I wanted to make the evening of the fundraiser a little more extravagant, so my final phone call was to a limousine service, arranging to have a car take us to and from the event. In the back of my mind, I knew that every arrangement was somewhat ostentatious, but I didn't particularly care. I had spent so much time working in the preceding months that I hadn't really taken any time to spend money on myself. Thus, the money was just going to sit in my bank account anyway, and I felt that the occasion justified the expense.

Once these preparations were completed, I returned home. I was still several hours away from my date with Trish, and I didn't want to elongate this time any further, so the chamber device would have to sit waiting in my courier bag. I pulled out my notebook and began to review ideas about other possible endeavors. The first one that really called out to me was the notion of writing a book. I had loved writing since I was a teenager but never considered a literary career, feeling that journalism was a much better fit for me. Having a chamber that not only froze time but also shut out all distractions made the notion of a long writing project seem all the more achievable. This was not the only career avenue that presented itself to me. I felt that completion of grad school had been reduced from a major obstacle to a minor stepping stone, so a career in academia appeared beyond plausible, and the sound of "Dr. Eric McHayden" just rang too beautifully to ignore.

I began searching the web for PhD programs in the Chicago area. Teaching seemed like an ideal use of the game time to practice time decision criteria. I knew that for teachers, every hour in front of the class room would be dwarfed by several more hours of lesson planning and grading. If I could get a course load of two or three classes, the chamber would allow me to fit what would otherwise be a full-time career painlessly into my schedule as if it were just some idle hobby. If I could arrange to teach these courses online, that would further skew the practice time to game time ratio in my favor.

At one point or another, I began to consider the trepidation one puts into deciding on a new career. A quick conclusion was that most of the go-no-go decisions were based on simple time allocation. I then began to wonder how many great books were never written because the would-be author feared putting that much time into a project that could so quickly end in rejection. I also wondered how many other pursuits, professional and personal, one would forego for fear of it all being "wasted time." In those deep questions, my ambition became galvanized by a sense of resolve. My mother had always told me, sometimes in a chiding tone and others in congratulatory praise, that "to whom much is given much is expected." What had been given to me was the chance to bend time to my will, and thus the expectation was that I would do something meaningful. I was obligated by the call to go for it, whatever "it" might be.

The hours crawled by as I expected they would before it was time to get in my car and pick up Trish. Even the drive from my apartment to hers went by slowly. It seemed as though the red lights knew that I was about to explode with excitement. Since those red lights were bored from just watching traffic all day, they found some sick, morbid entertainment in glowing red to prolong the agony of my impatience. During this long drive, I was once again confronted by my only complaint with the fact that my hours had magically become longer than everyone else's—I missed her.

I must have lived and died a thousand times in the moments between my knock on the door and Trish's coming to answer it. As the door opened and she stepped into my line of view, her smile, stunning and gorgeous in every detail, lit a fire at the core of my being. Her clothes, although purchased off the rack at some discount store, the result of her long-ingrained habits to save money, accentuated every inch of her figure without the need to be tight-fitting or revealing. It was Trish's constant practice to dress modestly, but I was convinced that she could wear burlap bags from head to toe and still win the attraction of every man she passed.

As we walked from her doorway to my car, I knew that I had numerous pieces of exciting news to tell her, but I could hardly get out a single word. I hadn't realized how much I missed her until I was walking with my arm around her. To her, my thirst to be as close to her as possible appeared to do little more than appeal to her reciprocated affection toward me. I looked at her with a gaze that suggested there was no world outside the few feet we shared, and she responded with that heart-stopping smile while she gently rested her head on my shoulder. I had more surprises on the tip of my tongue than I could wrap my head around, but the question of where to start halted every word.

We were only able to drive about a block before one of Trish's many intriguing talents began to show itself. Somehow, she always knew when there was something lingering in the forefront of my mind, especially when it was something big.

"All right," she said. "What's going on?"

"There's this big fundraiser the day after tomorrow. Apparently it's this big black-tie shindig for five hundred bucks a plate."

"Are you writing about it for your next column?"

I couldn't help but start laughing, which startled Trish. In all the excitement of getting the invitation and the knowledge that it would be a virtual who's who of Chicago's most wealthy and influential figures, it never once occurred to me that this event could give me inspiration and connections to write at least a couple of juicy stories. This rather obvious suggestion gave me a convenient segue into my first big surprise, "Well, if you want to go with me, maybe you could help me write."

In a quick sleight of hand that punctuated my words, I pulled the invitation from the center console. Trish read it with a quizzical look on her face. "You got invited?"

"Sure did. And as I'm sure you can imagine, I need a date."

"Wait, how did you get an invite to such an exclusive party?"

"Turns out Rick has been bragging about me to some of his wealthier golf buddies." From there, I gave the details about how Rick passed along the invitation and how the event was a large, formal affair. In stressing the formality of this event, I knew that eventually she would ask the question or pose the concern that would set up my next surprise.

"That sounds like fun!" Trish said. "I just need to find a dress that's formal enough."

"Oh, that's no problem. I made a call today to that boutique dress shop you like. I told them that I'd send you in to try on whatever you'd like and that I would pay for whatever you chose."

"Some of those dresses are two or three thousand dollars."

"And I'm sure any one of them would look stunning on you."

"Are you sure you can afford it?"

"Positive." By that point, any question of money made my mind start to swim around the lucrative possibilities that awaited me with my new chamber-enhanced productivity. I had always been good about saving my money, which was what allowed me to have the excess funds for these expenditures. But now, with the ability to do more and accomplish more, I could also earn more, and indulges like this could become more common. "And one other thing, you know that new spa uptown?"

"Yeah, the Royal something." Trish's answer showed me that she hadn't considered a trip to a spa, or even a day to herself, since she took over her father's bookstore.

"It's called the Grand Royale. I gave them a call as well. Figured you could use a massage, mud bath, whatever other witchcraft they do at those places that you may find appealing."

That little joke gave Trish a good laugh, but the look on her face held its astonished, Christmas-morning mysticism. For a moment, I was tempted to divulge the third phone call to the limousine company, but my immediate decision was to hold off that surprise for the evening of the fundraiser. Telling someone about renting a limo doesn't have anywhere near the dramatic appeal that showing up in one does, and I wasn't going to pass up an opportunity to show off. Throughout the stops to the video store and the pizza place, I filled in the details about how I might or might not be considered for a huge biography project, the kind that could enhance my budding career.

Once we returned to the apartment, the next topic of discussion was the expansion of the website. Trish followed every word of my story, even asking those kinds of questions that helped me see my life through her eyes. Her support always made whatever I was doing feel bigger and better than it really was. Even when I was just a dreamer of an undergraduate writing for the university newspaper, she made me feel like my writing would be up for the Pulitzer Prize. At one point, she gave me her special rose-colored perspective on my most recent endeavor.

"Y'know," she began, "I think it's really sweet what you're doing for that PR guy."

"Stephen?"

"Yeah, the one who hardly ever talks."

"Well, he is our PR guy. I mean it's his job to think about our image, so it's only natural that we need his input on the website."

"That's not it. From what you told me, he barely opens his mouth, and you're including him, kinda taking him under your wing."

With this suggestion, a feeling of guilt hit the pit of my stomach. Her notion that I was engaging in some sort of act of kindness toward Stephen wasn't altogether untrue; I really wanted him to come out of his shell. When it came to the website project, however, Marcus and Stephen, two men who I had come to deeply appreciate and respect, were simply being used as pawns for my own power play to gain greater influence at the Falcon office. If Trish knew that, and if she had seen the way I put down Jim Berndstandt after turning in my rewrite, it would have definitely tainted that ever-positive view of me she always had. I didn't really regret berating "Jimbo," but it definitely was an act from a darker side of me that I hoped Trish would never see.

This whole series of events that began with the time chamber virtually being dropped in my lap gave me a larger-than-life view of the man I could become. At the same time, I wondered if the shining, successful version of myself could ever really live up to the potential that Trish saw in me.

Chapter 8

The day of the fundraiser began in a rather uneventful fashion, considering that the evening could evolve into one of the turning points of my professional life. My surprise-wrought evening of pizza and movies was still recent in terms of days on the calendar since it had only happened on Thursday night less than forty-eight hours before. That Saturday morning, Trish was on her way to a dress fitting and several hours of relaxation at the spa. I, on the other hand, intended to have a casual morning, unhindered by to-do lists and occupied by leisure.

I began my morning at the quaint café located between my apartment and the University of Chicago campus, the same one that I stormed by and was doused in coffee by Michael upon our first meeting. After sitting down and placing my order, a familiar voice greeted me.

"Hey there, friend. Mind if I join you?" The voice belonged to Michael. This was the very café where he had spilled his coffee on me before proceeding to give me a gift that would change my life. "I loved your last column."

His voice suggested that we were mere acquaintances, which I guess we were, but what really struck me was his gesture. His hand slid a copy of the Falcon across the table. I noticed a small piece of paper sticking out from between the pages. Answering an unspoken call for discretion, I opened the magazine and read the note sideways without moving this small message from its hiding place. It read, "If we're going to talk in public, we have to be careful." This message immediately triggered my memory toward the rather cryptic code with which we spoke that night at Fritz's bar. Without any pretense, I nodded, and Michael sat down in the seat on the opposite side of the table. The booth-style seats of the diner gave an illusion of privacy that could not be trusted since any of the passersby could easily drop an ear into our conversation.

"So how do you like the new toy?"

"Love it."

"What are you working on right now?"

"Oh, various things, but mostly I'm trying to plan my first of several big projects."

"And those 'projects' are?"

"First, I'm writing a novel, historical fiction. Who knows, if the first one sells I could turn it into a series."

"Brilliant." Michael spoke as if he actually knew the depth of what was going on in my mind. What I was telling him was entirely true. As a matter of fact, I had done several days' worth of research the night before toward a novel featuring a young US marine near the end of World War II. This genre was one that was first introduced to me by Trish's father, and they even had a special section for historical fiction in the bookstore for those books that her father loved so much. Every so often, one of the bookstore employees would catch Trish just sitting in a corner of that section, as she felt closer to her father there than anywhere else.

As Michael and I continued our conversation, I filled him in on the details of that evening's event, telling him about the chance that I might be writing a biography for one of the most well-known, influential figures of our time.

"It seems," he said, "that you've started to set your sights on bigger and better things."

"Definitely."

"Like I said before, I knew you had it in you to make a difference."

"Well, I've certainly been able to get my life back on track."

"What about other people's lives?" he asked.

That question gave me the feeling that you may get in church when the offering plate goes by and you don't put anything in it. "Well, I was thinking that when I had more money I'd—"

"It's not about money!" Michael waved his hand, swatting my suggestion out of the air like it was an annoying house fly.

"What did you have in mind?"

"I chose you because I think your gifts can be put to good use. Start looking for places where you—and only you—can change things. Once you come up with a few ideas you and I will get things done."

I could hardly comprehend what Michael was talking about. He had been so enigmatic in every conversation that the notion of he and I working together on any kind of project became difficult to envision. "Sounds good," I replied.

To be honest, I was unapologetically blithe in my response. Immediately I felt a conflict between my desire to conquer and accomplish and Michael's suggestion that I should go on some sort of goodwill mission for the betterment of those around me. Always trying to please but also trying to rationalize, I concluded that the chamber allowed me both opportunities. I could lead two lives, one of selfish ambition and another of well-intended philanthropy.

As we paid our tabs and made our exit onto the street, Michael continued. "You have a gift for the written word. You also know how to research. No, if you can find a way to—" All at once, Michael stopped dead cold midsentence. His eyes widened as a pallor of absolute terror immediately overcame his posture and facial expressions.

When I looked over my shoulder to see what caught his attention, I noticed a man across the street who had to stand close to seven feet tall. This enormous figure appeared to be in his midtwenties, wearing a hooded sweatshirt and black leather jacket. At first I thought the sheer size of this pedestrian was what caught Michael's attention, but a second glance told me otherwise. This hooded giant's eyes were locked on Michael with a furious, accusatory glare that demanded blood.

"Michael?" I was waving my hand and doing anything I could to get his attention. "Michael!" My second call snapped him out of his terrified trance. "Who was that?"

"Nobody." Michael's gaze continued to shift back and forth between me and the giant figure across the street.

If there was anything I had learned from Michael it was that he was only going to give me as much as information as he wanted to give and only when he was willing to give it. After walking two more blocks, we parted ways, and he gave me a card with his phone number. I told him that I would call him in a few days so we could begin whatever project of goodwill we could decide upon.

The rest of my afternoon was filled with last-minute preparations for the evening to come. Trish, meanwhile, was picking up the dress that I had paid for and was going to the spa to get pampered. At various times throughout the day, I received texts from her that gave me little details while expressing her appreciation for the showering of gifts that I had used to surprise her. At moments I wondered if I could make days like that a more common occurrence so we could punctuate long days of leisure and luxury with glamorous evenings among the wealthy social elites. After a work session in the time chamber, I was able to slowly and comfortably put on my tuxedo and even have a drink in my apartment while waiting for the limousine to come pick me up. Once the stretch Ford Lincoln stopped at Trish's apartment complex, I asked the chauffer to wait with the door open, alluding to the fact that limousine was a surprise to my date.

The moment that Trish opened the door was one of those moments that can permanently and immediately etch itself into one's memory. It would have taken me several hours of reading about modern cosmetics to accurately describe what she did differently with her makeup, but every line and contour of her already beautiful face was allowed to present itself in stunning detail. Her dress, a wine-red backless ball gown, seemed like it was designed with the intent that no woman but her should ever wear it. While I stood speechless, she did a full spin. I knew that Trish took pride in always appearing classy and modest, but her smile showed me a side of her that I didn't even know existed. In that evening, in that moment, I realized that nothing in the world can be more breathtaking than a woman who has all at once realized how beautiful she really is.

When we walked into the grand hall where the event was held, I could almost immediately detect all eyes falling on Trish. I found it rather lamentable that we arrived early, as a fashionably late appearance would have given a larger audience to my arrival with the most stunning date in the room. It didn't take long before the who's who began to present themselves. I counted at least ten people whose pictures I had seen in the *Chicago Tribune* and numerous others who introduced themselves as company presidents, CEOs and law firm partners. As humbling as it was to be in the company of all these wealthy and influential figures, what really astounded me was how Trish could so gracefully work the room. She was charming and funny, and when her social graces combined with her breathtaking appearance, she had anyone we spoke to practically eating out of her hand.

Finally, the dinner was about to begin, and Trish and I took our seats at our designated table. Every seat in the room was specifically assigned, and my stomach began to leap into my throat when I saw the name on the seat to my immediate left. The little placard showed none other than William C. Gastineux, the host of the entire event. Just as I finished reading the placard, Rick and his wife took their seats at our table. I had met Rick's wife before but realized that she had never met Trish. Thus, the two ladies were given their obligatory introduction, and although they were separated by more than twenty years, they immediately hit it off.

Next, Mr. Gastineux made his entrance and, after pulling out the chair for his wife, took a seat to my immediate left. "Good evening," he began. "My name is William Gastineux, and this is my wife, Carla."

Carla smiled and extended her hand to shake mine and then Trish's. Mr. and Mrs. Gastineux's introduction seemed like it had been performed hundreds of times, yet they both had warm and approachable personalities.

"Eric," Mr. Gastineux said, "I can't think of a single golf game where Rick hasn't ranted about you. That is, when he can find his way out of the woods to join me on the fairway."

The whole table laughed. Even Rick was able to manage a hearty chuckle, although he apparently wasn't used to hearing jokes at his expense.

"Well," I quickly retorted, "Rick is definitely a great boss and a huge mentor of mine. Beyond that, I'll assure you that he is completely full of shit."

The laughter then came to a crescendo, and Rick was once again a good sport. Meanwhile, Trish looked at me with her jaw dropped. This kind of flashy, irreverent confidence was inconsistent with my usual demeanor when I was around her. Nonetheless, the life afforded to me by the time chamber carried with it an assertive deportment that sometimes surprised even me.

As the laughter subsided to a low rumble, Mr. Gastineux began his response. "Even if I agree with you about ole Rick here, it appears to me that your columns can speak for themselves."

"Thank you. I'm glad you enjoyed them."

"More than that. Do you know what has gotten me this far, Eric?"

"Persistence?" I wanted to give an answer better than simply admitting that I didn't have the first clue.

"Well, sure, persistence is important, but it took something more than that. You see, most people think that to manage a successful business, you need to spend your life buried in receipts and income statements. There are business students everywhere who could tell you anything you'd like to know about profit and loss or return on investment, but they miss the point."

"And that is?"

"It's people!" he quickly responded. "If I have learned anything, it's that there are certain things you can't simply create by mentoring or management. One is sincerity. The other is passion. I see both of those in your writing. You write as though nobody's reading. You tell stories with no apologies and without an agenda. You make arguments as though you don't care whether the reader is infuriated or inspired. It's what makes your work truly a breath of fresh air."

"Well, thank you, sir."

"Cut the sir. You can call me William. And besides, I'm not telling you all this just to blow smoke up your ass." His slight smirk showed me that he wasn't irritated, despite his blunt choice of words. He continued. "I've turned down several young journalists who wanted to write my biography. They've come into my office stuttering and shaking, hoping that writing my story would make a nice little bullet point on their resumes."

"With all due respect, William," I quickly responded, "your biography wouldn't be just a bullet point. It would be a resume in and of itself. Getting to write a biography for someone of your prominence would be an absolute game changer."

"That's why I want you to do it."

Although Rick had told me that this request might be the very reason I was there that evening, I was shocked. "Wait. Why me?"

"Eric, I've seen all these aspiring young hotshots wander into my office, trying to win me over with all their credentials. I chose you not only because you come highly recommended by someone I trust"—he nodded toward Rick—"but also because your writing simply speaks for itself."

At this moment, I realized that the entire table was listening in to our conversation. I felt Trish's hand slide over my knee. As her eyes met mine, I could see a proud smile flash across her face. Rick's facial expression seemed eager and yet satisfied, knowing that this would be not only a great milestone for me but also a huge step forward for the reputation of our magazine. I quickly felt an awkward form of guilt overcome me, as the word of Rick's sterling recommendation came to me only moments after I told the entire table he was full of shit.

Quickly, I turned back to William, who spoke to me as if we were old friends. "I want you to be the one who writes it for me," he began, "and I can free myself up whenever it works for you."

"I'd be honored." I responded.

"Well, I'll have my assistant get in touch with you. Before we start to iron out the details, I'd love to meet up to hear some of your ideas."

"I can tell you right away, it's going to take a lot of interviews," I responded quickly. My ideas were almost slamming against a dam

I had put up by trying to sound pragmatic. "You see, people don't just read biographies because they want to know how to find similar or comparable successes. They read because they want to know the person. If the subject is a figure that they can relate to on a personal level, and they can almost live vicariously through—"

"Gentlemen," Rick interrupted, "I believe there will be ample time to talk shop later. For now, let's just relax and enjoy the party." He shot William a quick grin and winked an eye at me as some form of congratulations.

As the evening progressed, I rubbed elbows and made conversation as if these older, wealthy social elites were my peers. William was finishing what had to be his sixth glass of scotch, and Rick was dancing with his wife. Both of these occurrences struck me as odd, although I couldn't really determine why. All the while, Trish was on my arm, serving as a more than welcome distraction with her stunning appearance and staggering presence. She made this overwhelming sense of victory feel complete. She was witty, charming, and welcoming to everyone she engaged in conversation.

At one point in the evening, I felt a wave of fatigue coming over me, but Trish was having such a good time that I couldn't bring myself to cut the evening short. While she sat with Carla talking about their favorite books, I excused myself for a moment and exited the grand hall to get a breath of fresh air. I had spent quite some time in the chamber during the previous days and hadn't made the logical prediction that I would grow tired earlier in the evening. So as I stepped out, I started to wrap my mind around ways I could make my transitions in and out of the chamber slightly less taxing.

The grand hall was part of a convention center attached to a large and luxurious hotel. Once outside this grand hall, I couldn't help but notice the small bar area between the convention center and the hotel lobby. This bar was ornate, with a coffee station decked out with the kind of coffee equipment one would expect to see at an upscale coffee shop. I asked the bartender to a make a cup of coffee and throw in a shot of Kahlua. I loved this beverage because it gave me a much-needed shot of caffeine while helping me keep the comfortable buzz I had going.

"Busy night?" I asked the bartender.

"Not too bad," the bartender responded. His hands moved up and down the brass machinery with stunning speed and precision.

"You sure know your way around that coffee machine," I noted.

"Yeah, been savin' up money so someday I can have my own coffee shop. The problem is the startup costs. What do you do for a living?"

"I'm a journalist. I write columns for the Falcon Magazine. Ever read it?"

"Can't say I have."

"Check it out sometime. What do I owe ya?"

"That'll be eleven dollars."

I was in such a good mood from the goings on that evening that I put down a ten and a five and told the young would-be barista to keep the change. I then guzzled down the spiked coffee drink and returned to the grand hall with a fresh dose of booze and caffeine running through my veins. The party was in full swing.

As the evening came to a close, Trish and I rode in the limousine back to my apartment. What Trish didn't know was that I had a bottle of champagne, chocolate-covered strawberries, and a bouquet of lilies waiting for her. I had envisioned that we would come back and relax and enjoy a few glasses together, but I had no idea that we would have so much to celebrate.

Chapter 9

The week and a half between the fundraiser and the Falcon staff meeting was a flurry of progress. The Monday after the event, I called William Gastineux's office to set up a preliminary interview for the biography project. The assistant who answered the phone told me that he would be away for the week, so I set an appointment for the last Wednesday in March. That was the same day of the staff meeting where I would present the ideas for the website expansion. This meant that I had ten days to put together the presentation as well as prepare to begin the biography project. It might as well have been a lifetime. Meanwhile, I was halfway through the first draft of a novel, and I had to get moving on my thesis for grad school.

That Monday morning, I decided to hit the ground running. I drove to Dr. Karzeck's office and, luckily, was able to catch him in between classes. After only a few quick questions, we were able to put together a committee and hammer out a timeline to have my prospectus ready for defense. This timeline meant very little to me, as I had every intention of getting into the time chamber and having that document completed by that very evening. Upon leaving Dr.

Karzeck's office, I immediately headed toward the bookstore to have an early lunch with Trish.

While we ate, Trish alluded to the fact that two floors above the bookstore were completely uninhabited and that their owner had been desperately trying to sell them for the last several months. "You thinking of expanding the bookstore?" I asked.

"Well, I would, but that would take a pretty big investment, plus the cost of expanding my inventory to fill more floors. Getting the space is only half the battle. The next is coming up with something to do with it."

"No risk, no reward." I could hardly believe those words were coming out of my mouth, but it seemed that since I began taking the world by storm, thirsty ambition had all but eradicated my risk averse better-safe-than-sorry outlook.

"Maybe so. The owner sold my dad the space we have now, and I got a promise that I would be given a chance to make an offer before the top floors were sold."

"At least you'll know when you have to decide."

"True."

From there, our conversation began to dwindle into idle banter, but in the back of my mind, I started to dance with ideas about the video store where I had rented the Stallone movie and the bartender from the fundraiser who dreamed of having his own space. I started to think about the larger-scale bookstore chains and how many of them also sold or rented movies and had some sort of attached coffee shop. Michael had implored me to start thinking of ways I could help other people. It was readily apparent that Trish was interested in expanding the bookstore, but she had her reservations. *This may be it!* I thought quietly to myself, hoping that helping those closest to me would be enough of a goodwill mission to satisfy Michael. However, I wanted to think my ideas over before I presented them to Trish, and it wasn't long before she had to get back to work and I had to be on my way.

I stopped at the grocery store on my way back to my apartment to get rations. Trish would be coming to my apartment that evening to watch movies after her yoga class, but the time between that afternoon and that evening was going to be exponentially elongated. I bought coffee and tons of microwaveable meals that would be quick and easy to prepare so as to avoid taking my attention away from all my projects. When I got home, I packed a suitcase with all the clothes I could fit. I was in for the long haul. I walked into the chamber and closed the door behind me. The unloading of the clothes and groceries had to appear as though I was moving into a temporary home.

The first step was to make a to-do list, one that would prioritize my tasks and get me through the questions of where to start. My top priority was to get the prospectus finished. Since I had started this with the research paper, all I had to do was take the thirty or so scholarly articles that I hadn't read yet and use them to add about twenty pages onto what I had already written. Next, I would write a methodology section, upon which I would later conduct my own primary research once the prospectus was approved.

The next priority was to prepare for my first interview with William. The prerequisite work there was going to be lengthy research on similar biographical works to see why some of these kinds of books would flourish while others failed. I would run search after search, printing whatever I found useful and then use what I learned to put together the kinds of questions that I would want to ask. I had been trained in how to properly and professionally conduct an interview, but this project was going to be enormous, and I wanted to be as well-equipped as possible. I would also do extensive research on William, writing out the skeleton of my own storyline that my subject could then bring to life.

Finally, I would revise and edit the writing that I had done on the novel. More importantly, I had to decide how my story was going to end. I felt I had already put together a fairly intriguing plot about a brave young marine, and the first forty thousand words had gripping battle scenes and a fairly dynamic internal and external conflict. This left me with a few decisions. Would my protagonist go down in a blaze of glory or return home to his high school sweetheart to live out the American dream? Who else was going to survive? Most importantly, was I going to leave room in the plot for another book if the first one sold?

With all this planning completed, I had stacks of scholarly articles, biography reviews, and news stories strewn across my desk. Once these stacks were neatly organized, I decided to get some sleep. I wanted to approach these tasks rested, so I gobbled two Tylenol PMs, grabbed a book off the nightstand, and crawled into bed. The plan was to read until my eyes got too heavy to continue. This didn't take long, only ten pages or so, and when I awoke, I felt rested and prepared.

Once I got into something of rhythm, the chamber-induced productivity simply took over. Moving back and forth between tasks and taking breaks to eat, sleep and work out, I was able to completely eliminate all of the tasks on my rather elaborate to-do list. In all those projects, I found the most gratification in the act of hitting the Print button and having page after page of finished product to show for all my efforts. I felt as though I could have kept working in perpetuity, completing an entire life's worth of work while the rest of the world stood frozen, just waiting for me. I missed Trish, so at times, it felt like keeping busy was the only thing that would allow the lovesickness to subside.

Eventually, the rations and clean clothes ran out, so I made my exit from the time chamber and stepped back into the world of the ticking clock. One thing I knew was that the longer I sat in the time chamber, the more disoriented I would feel when the clock would start ticking again. The commonplace sounds of a world in motion were all the more deafening when I had stayed longer in the frozen solitude.

After a while, I was able to readjust, and then the only thing I cared about was Trish's arrival. When she walked into my apartment, the elongated absence from the world took its full effect. I threw my arms around her like a soldier returning from war. To Trish, this had to seem irrational, as we had just eaten lunch together only a few hours before. Oddly enough, it wasn't my behavior that she noticed. When we finally separated, she ran the palm of her hand against my face, exclaiming, "Your five o'clock shadow is out of control!"

I brought my hand to my other cheek to investigate. She had a point. I had stopped to shower on two separate occasions but never got in a shave. Considering that my jawline was completely smooth during our lunch date, this had to have appeared to be the most aggressive facial hair growth the world would ever know. When I bumbled through some explanation that would keep my bigger secret concealed, the utmost surprise came when Trish shrugged off the anomaly, taking me at my word and moving on to the next topic of conversation. After two movies, we retreated back to the bedroom, and I was able to enjoy going to sleep with her head on my shoulder.

When we awoke the next morning, an idea began burning into the front of my skull that could only be alleviated by sharing it with someone else. I kept thinking about Trish's option to buy the top two uninhabited floors above the bookstore. This also triggered my memory toward the young bartender I had met outside the fundraiser. Then it occurred to me that almost all of the larger bookstore chains in existence had some sort of upscale coffee shop inside their establishment. I even remembered having joked about how "those are the places where all the hipsters go to drink coffee and act like they read." Despite my somewhat cynical depiction of these bookstore coffee bars, I was still left with the reality that both Trish and the bartender were at a crossroad and they could possibly both stand to benefit from taking a step forward.

That morning, Trish's sister had watch over the bookstore, so Trish would not actually have to be there until around noon. Thus, we had until that time to simply enjoy each other's company. I got up just moments before she did and gave her the nod to keep snoozing while I started breakfast. Just as the pancakes were ready to flip, the sound of barefoot steps announced her entrance into the kitchen, wearing my button-up shirt from the night before. She sat down at my kitchen table, smiling while I poured her cup of coffee and meekly asked, "Do you need any help?"

"I got it. You just sit there and relax."

"What do you have going on today?"

"Well, I have to finish putting the presentation together for the staff meeting."

"When's that?"

"The meeting is next Wednesday, so I have the rest of the week to finish ironing out the details. I've gotten a lot of input from a lot of people, so now it's just a matter of compressing it into a short spiel and making it sound like I know something."

"I'm sure it'll look great."

"Hope so. Hey I was thinking—"

Trish's proverbial ears seemed to perk up for a moment, "What about?"

"The two floors above your bookstore."

At my very mention of the subject, I could tell that Trish had been struggling with the decision. What I couldn't ascertain was whether or not my input was going to help or just further exacerbate the stress she was feeling.

"I just don't know," she started. "Do you know how much it would cost not only to buy those floors but also to fill them with books? My dad was always very careful about making big changes, and I'd hate to rack up that much debt."

"The cost of buying the extra space is considerable," I responded in a way that I hoped would alleviate her worries. "But who says you have to fill those two floors just with books?"

"What do you mean?"

"Well, you could allow some of that space to be occupied by somebody who could set up their own business while helping yours. How about a coffee shop?" I stated this idea like it had just occurred to me at the spur of the moment, wondering to myself why I was trying to be manipulative.

"You mean like the ones at Barnes & Noble?"

"Yeah, except you can find someone whose coffee tastes good." I don't know what compelled me to take that little shot at Barnes and Noble coffee. I had probably had a bad experience there years before, but what was really behind that little jab was a new competitive streak that I can retrospectively admit wasn't very becoming of me.

Nonetheless, Trish laughed, asking, "Okay, we just need to find somebody who wants to start a coffee shop and pitch the idea to them."

"I know just the guy. Remember the night of the fundraiser when I stepped out for a few minutes?" I waited just a moment, in which Trish gave a very interested nod. "Well, I popped my head into the hotel bar to get a cup of coffee. There was this bartender who could make an excellent cup of coffee and wanted to open his own coffee shop. I know these kinds of small shops have trouble competing with the big chains, but if he's imbedded in your bookstore, maybe he'll have a shot."

I had to admit that I actually knew very little about this would-be barista. Although it was true that he could make a wonderful cup of coffee, I had no idea if he had any clue how to run a coffee shop. I also didn't know whether he was a reputable character that Trish would want to join with in some sort of business partnership. At this point, we were in something of an idea phase. If Ricky the starry-eyed bartender didn't work out, there had to be countless other people who would be able to capitalize on this opportunity. The big opportunities afforded to me by the time chamber had me thinking that anything was possible, and my caution and pragmatism were fading with each passing day.

"That's not a bad idea." Her eyes lit up.

"He told me that his biggest concern was the startup cost, which I'm sure we, I mean you, could help with by offering him some space. It would be a lower cost to him than it would be if he had to go buy a space on his own."

"That would definitely help." I could still detect some reservations as Trish continued, "I'm still worried about what could go wrong. My dad was the one who bought the original space, and I don't really know what I would have to do to get the financing to buy the extra floors."

"If only we knew someone in the finance game who has a background in real estate. Wait a minute…"

"You don't think your new friend would be willing to help do you?"

Trish and I were both thinking about William. Not only was he "a friend in the finance game with a background in real estate" but he was also one of the best business minds walking the planet. We also saw firsthand that he was always willing to talk about new ideas. I even thought for a moment that if I could get him to drink a scotch or two he would tell me anything we wanted to know.

"What could it hurt to ask?" I said. "If anything, I could at least pick his brain a little bit. If it's a terrible risk, I'm sure he'd be able to tell me right away."

Although Trish was trying to be as reserved and pragmatic as possible, I could tell that she was intrigued by the idea. As though she was soothing her concern like a wrinkle in a table cloth, she continued, "Who knows? Maybe when the biography of William

Gastineux becomes a bestseller, I can get the author to do a book signing at my store."

"I don't know," I responded with self-deprecating laughter. "I hear he's a colossal jerk."

At that, Trish punched my arm and the conversation regressed back into idle chatter about what all was going on that day. At around eleven o'clock, I walked Trish to her car, and she was on her way to work. This allowed me once again to proceed into the time chamber with a few large tasks to complete. Surrounded by the frozen solitude of the chamber, I decided that a good workout was in order. I was a pent-up ball of energy, and I knew that a good workout would help me regain my focus. I started on the treadmill, churning my legs and running until I felt too out of breath to continue. Just before I began to lift weights, I decided that I should begin to have a little bit more of a plan to my workouts. Thus, I started to search the internet for workout programs that I thought suited me.

Since I finally had the time to really focus on fitness goals, I started designing a workout split that would challenge me. I decided that I would begin with typical lower-body/upper-body alternating program, and then once I built up some strength, I would follow some of the more intricate workout programs that I found online. With a little bit more guidance, I proceeded to lift weights until muscle fatigue caught up with me, and after a shower and change of clothes, I got to work.

I once again had several tasks to complete, the first of which was to put together the slide show for the website presentation. At first I expected this task to become rather cumbersome, but it didn't take long for a logical organization to present itself. Before I knew it, I was messing around with the formatting and then applying the finishing touches.

Feeling somewhat accomplished, I moved on to the next task, which was reading and revising the work I had done to that point on the novel. The biggest challenge here was trying not to bite off more than I could chew. I found that it took about six pages before I would grow impatient, my eyes would start to drift, and I would overlook rather noticeable errors and inconsistencies. This was where the ever-shifting work style came back into play. I decided that I would only revise about five pages at a time before moving on to something else.

After one good blitz of productivity, I had twenty or so pages of the novel polished and edited, as well as a general outline for my first interview with William. Finally, I wrote a column for the next printing of the Falcon. My next task was to do some research on the idea that I had just presented to Trish. In essence, the idea seemed pretty simple—put a coffee shop in the bookstore. However, I knew that this would entail many different questions about liability and shared ownership. None of these concerns were within my realm of expertise, so I did several Google searches to try to see what I could learn.

Before long, I had a thick stack of printed material about tax issues in joint ventures, ADA compliance, health codes, and anything else I thought would be pertinent. By then, I had two folders that I had to give to Trish. The first folder was the compilation of all the things I found for her business, and the second was the beginning twenty pages of the novel, freshly printed after extensive revision and editing. Since the genre I had selected for this work was her father's favorite, I was practically beaming with excitement to have her read it. Finally, I printed off my most recent column and put it into the courier bag with all my other printed work, and I quietly rejoiced in all the tangible material I had to show for my efforts. When I stepped outside the chamber, the sounds of a world snapping back into motion greeted me, but the sensation was unlike what I had felt before. When I usually stepped into the time chamber, I felt like I was walking into a domain that was mine to be used however I wanted. That day, the feeling went with me both inside the chamber and out.

Chapter 10

After a rather busy week, that turning point of a March Wednesday finally came. For the first time since I received the chamber, I actually felt the kind of nerves that could come from uncertainty. The staff meeting where I would present my ideas for the website expansion was set for ten a.m., and my appointment to interview Mr. Gastineux was scheduled for two that afternoon. I woke up at five thirty in the morning, and I hadn't really slept well the night before because my mind kept wandering about everything that could go right or wrong. When the alarm clock stirred me awake, it took everything I had not to fight the snooze alarm into perpetuity. At around six, I trudged into my apartment's small bathroom to begin my preparations for what would be a more than eventful day. The face that looked back at me from the mirror was that tired, stress-weathered face that I hadn't seen in what felt like ages. My immediate conclusion was that at the moment, I knew I was in no condition to face the challenges that waited for me in the hours to come.

I had benefitted from the chamber up until that moment, but that morning I needed it, and the difference between the two had never been so strikingly apparent. The small press of the blue button brought on a wave of relief, as I knew that it afforded me the precious time I needed not only to regain my rest but to build my confidence. Before I entered the chamber, I gathered some workout clothes, the suit that I would wear for the interview and the presentation, the necessary button-up shirt, the tie, undergarments, and an iron and an ironing board. With these items filling my grasp, I was putting myself in a better position for the preparations to meet the day.

By then, it had become a common practice during every trip into the chamber to have a small planning session before I actually got to work. This instance was somewhat different because I hadn't walked in with any grandiose projects in mind. All I knew was that I wanted to put some more time into preparing for the presentation and to get some rest. The plan from that point became to work until I had built up as much fatigue as humanly possible. The top priority was that I walk out of the chamber with my mind clear, focused, and rested. Thus, I would work until I could no longer keep my eyes open and then lie down and get as much sleep as humanly possible.

First, I pulled open the laptop and began to practice my presentation. I used the wireless mouse as a means to guide the slide show and focused on the specific details that I wanted to accentuate. After I practiced presenting each slide, I gave them each a thorough read and made sure the order of the presentation made sense. Next, I started thinking deeply about any and all questions that might be asked and how I would respond, taking notes and making changes to the presentation until it was beyond reproach. Next, I hit Print and the presentation was printed at three slides per page. I took this rather considerable stack of papers and carried it with me onto the treadmill, where I began to read it over once, twice, and three times while my pace sped up to a rather brisk walk. Finally, I became confident in my ability to present the information, so I put the papers back on the desk, resumed my position on the treadmill, and began to run.

The treadmill was one of those state-of-the-art models that connected to my music player, so I queued up a playlist that helped me lose myself in my run. Next, I lifted weights, focusing on my upper body as my newly devised routine dictated. Finally, I wrote an additional several pages for the novel. A funny thing about working solely for the sake of expending energy is how productive one can become when he's working just for the sake of making himself tired.

Sitting on the bedside table was the printed draft of the first fifty pages of my novel. Trish had no idea that I had even started this project, and for some reason, I perpetually put off the task of giving it to her, meanwhile adding to the number of pages that I was able to write, refine, and polish. Perhaps I was afraid that she wouldn't like it, or maybe I feared that she would question where I was getting all of this time. I knew that eventually people would grow suspicious of how I was able to accomplish so much so quickly, but I had put every diligent effort into ensuring that the chamber device remained well hidden, and I had executed word for word Michael's request that I not tell anyone. I then decided that before I went to the staff meeting, I would stop by the bookstore to see Trish and give her the printed beginning of a manuscript, making that day notable for yet another reason. Trish would be, after all, the first person to see this project since I began writing it.

With everything else I had been working on the week before, I had put the novel endeavor on the backburner, so I realized that I could give it a read with the freshest of eyes. This second reading with a week of removal made just the right details present themselves. As I read those fifty or so pages, there were times where I was impressed with my own writing, thinking, *Man, I was really on that day*. At other times, I grimaced at errors in syntax, gaping holes in plot and character development, and places where the writing seemed completely unimaginative.

Before long, I was sitting at my computer once again, opening the digital copy of this draft, and making change after change until I was once again pleased with what I had accomplished. When I hit Print, I was confronted with a notable milestone in my short but notable history in the chamber. The printer had run out of ink. In this small capsule that had no measurement of time, there was no calendar that could mark how many days, weeks, or even years' worth of time that I had spent inside, so the ink cartridge replacement carried with it the feeling of an anniversary.

Once I had printed the writing, I still felt as though there was much more work left before I would need to lay down for some sleep. My focus began to center on the staff meeting, where I would be presenting the ideas that Stephen, Marcus, and I had worked so hard to gather, organize, and turn into a presentation. I wanted to have something extra. My immediate decision was to put together a professional-looking handout that could supplement the slide show. Within minutes, I was toiling away at a multiple-page packet that contained the highlights of ideas, meanwhile inserting information and nuances that I had pondered in many what-if thought processes on the treadmill.

Once created, I gave this document the same degree of meticulous revision and editing I had the other large brainchildren that sat in ink and paper across my desk. When I was finally satisfied with my creation, I attached it alongside the updated slide show in an email to Marcus and Stephen. The time stamp on the email read 6:03 a.m., the exact moment that I pushed the blue button. The message itself was really simple, "Hey guys, I've made a few slight revisions to the presentation, and I created a handout to go with it. I know we present in only a few hours, but give it a read over if you get the chance."

I had completed all the jobs that I had deemed necessary, as well as a few that I had made up. After putting the long and tedious effort into ironing my shirt, I then started to delve once again into the tasks that I had set out for myself during the first few days in the time chamber. I pulled open the Italian book and began to practice conjugating verbs. I read through the work I had done on my thesis prospectus and introduced small changes to make it sound as intelligent as I could make it. Finally, I got online and took notes from a long lecture on quantum physics.

These little endeavors always made me feel like I was bettering myself and not just my career. Near the end of the video lecture, I noticed that my attention was starting to fade, and the more intricate concepts were becoming more and more difficult to follow. In the back of my mind, I noted that this steady decrease in mental clarity was the beginning of my fatigue. Thus, I kept jumping in between tasks until my eyes grew heavy. I wanted to have a sense of physical exhaustion that would compare well with the immense mental weariness, so I jumped on the treadmill once more and began to run until my legs got heavy. I was out to burn as much energy as I could and collapse in the warm confines of the chamber bed. When the running turned to walking and my legs felt as though they could barely carry me, the next step was to take two Tylenol PM and shower while waiting for them to kick in.

Once the sleep aid began its intended effects and I had fully shaved and showered, I defaulted to my time-honored practice of lulling myself to sleep with my nose in a good book. While crawling into bed, I started trying to calculate how many books I had finally been able to read because of the time afforded to me by the chamber, and with great satisfaction, I lost count. Only moments after cracking the spine of my new read, I felt my head begin to bob, and eventually it reclined back. In those moments, the fits of anxiety about what could happen in the presentation were gone. In their place was nothing but relaxation, and what followed was the kind of long sleep that would end only when I wanted it to.

I can't recall if any dreams came to me, or if any dreams had ever come to me at all inside the chamber, but when I crawled out of bed, I was ready to build the dreams that exist while one is awake. Wearing a bathrobe that I carried with me into the chamber at one point or another, I started to fry bacon and eggs while the coffee brewed. Over breakfast, I sat reading the presentation and handout with the satisfaction of knowing that all of my worries had been replaced with a feeling of preparedness. There was no question that I couldn't answer, and there was no fine point about our new mission that I couldn't articulate with striking clarity. While putting on the suit and tie that I had gotten together for that morning, I took note of the sense of power that dressing this way could give me.

When I stepped out of the time chamber, my courier bag had all of the printed work, as well as my notes for the presentation and the interview with Gastineux. As the world of the ticking clock rushed in around me, one of the "big picture" blessings of the chamber began to present itself. The chamber wasn't just a place to get work done, to read books, or to learn languages. The blessing of the chamber wasn't just that I could get ahead of some schedule or beat some deadline. Instead, the chamber offered a change in perspective. I could step back into the exact same moment, at the exact same second, but could return as a different person. I walked into the chamber worried and deprived of sleep, and in absolutely no time, I was able to return with a newfound assertiveness.

The staff meeting was set to begin approximately four hours from that moment, and I wanted to be there about half an hour early in case I had to fill Marcus or Stephen in on any of the finer details. Even with that in mind, I still had about three hours before I needed to arrive, and I had only one intention as to what I was going to do in that time. I had to see Trish. She wasn't expected to open up the bookstore that morning, so she wouldn't be there until around eight, which meant that I had about two hours to kill. At this time, I gave the presentation one more practice run and then made a small pot of coffee, which I then poured into my travel thermos and doctored to my distinct specifications.

When I finally did drive to the bookstore, the street was still mostly uninhabited, which offered me the luxury of parking next to the curb right in front. I had become a ball of energy, constantly changing the radio stations and waiting for Trish to arrive. When this failed to pass the time, I called Marcus, knowing that he usually arrived at the office fairly early on the day of a staff meeting. In a somewhat startling fashion, he picked up on the first ring.

"Marcus, it's Eric. Did you get my email?"

"Yeah, man. What are you doing getting all this done at six in the morning? You're making me look bad."

"All part of the day's work. Could you do me a favor?"

"Sure thing."

"I hate to ask you this, but could you print off the handout and make a bunch of copies? Try to make one for everyone who comes in."

"Should I make copies for our guests too?"

"Guests?"

"Yeah." His tone suggested that I had missed something obvious. "Oh wait. You didn't come in yesterday. A few of the investors are going to be there for the staff meeting."

"What for?"

"I don't know, but there were all sorts of rumors buzzing around the office yesterday, and I heard your name come up. It sounds like something big."

As soon as he uttered those words, I felt all the anxiety come swarming back as a knot formed at the pit of my stomach. For each of the what-ifs I had laid to rest that very morning, it felt as though new monstrous ones had come out of nowhere to hit me from behind. The immediate instinct was to provide at least an illusion of composure. "Well then, if they're going to be in the meeting, they should get a copy of the materials."

"Sounds good, man. I'll have them ready when you get here."

"Thanks."

Just as I hung up the phone, I saw Trish marching down the sidewalk. She did a quick double take and then saw me approaching to meet her at the door.

"Hey, you. Wow, you look great!" She reached out and ran her thumb down my lapel.

"Thanks. I present the new website ideas today, and this afternoon, I have the first interview."

"I know it's a big day. Are you nervous?"

"I was a little when I woke up this morning."

There were all kinds of ambiguity in that response, as I had actually woken up on multiple occasions that morning, and the nerves had once again taken over despite my attempts to hide them. Without a single word, a look from Trish was all it took for me to once again feel like everything was going to turn out in my favor. Before I could even think about what I was saying, I realized my lips were moving. "Hey, however today turns out, could I see you tonight?" I knew that night was the night she would usually spend with her sisters, but I felt as though no matter what the outcome of that day's events would be, I had to be with her that night.

With a glance that expressed understanding and support beyond my comprehension, she responded, "Of course, I'll tell my sisters that we can move girls' night to tomorrow night."

"Thank you. That means a lot. By the way, I've got something for you." I reached into my courier bag and pulled out the manila folders that contained all the work I had done on the novel and the research for the bookstore renovation. I didn't know if she was going to like what I had written or if she was going to question where I had found all the writing hours, but I knew that giving her the folder took both concerns out of my hands.

"What's this?"

"Oh, it's just something I've been working on."

"Something for the bookstore?"

I had already given her a folder full of materials before about the possible acquisition of the top two floors, so it was a natural assumption that this was another packet of research. "Something like that."

She told me that she would look it over, and with that, we kissed good-bye for the day, and she disappeared behind the bookstore's doors. I wanted to stay longer, but I could tell that she had business on her mind, so I thought it better to leave her to her work. When I arrived at the Falcon, the first thing I noticed was the flurry of activity as people were making all of the last-minute changes before that week's edition would be set to print. I glanced across the office to see if anyone was taking a seat in the conference room. The only inhabitants at that moment were Rick and three suited individuals whom I had never seen before. The immediate assumption was that these three men where the investors, and the uncertainty as to why they were there was causing the knots in the pit of my stomach to grow more excruciating by the minute.

As Marcus had mentioned, rumors were swirling about the office, and for reasons unbeknown to either of us, my name was involved in the chatter. I didn't have any fear as to the safety of my job because the chamber-induced comeback had put me once again in Rick's good graces. The greater fear was that something big was about to happen and there was some opportunity that I would squander if I should happen to walk into the presentation and make a fool of myself. Just at that moment, Marcus and Stephen approached me, carrying large stacks of the handout that I had put together just hours before.

"Hey man," Marcus said, "these look great."

Stephen gave an enthusiastic nod of agreement.

"Thanks," I responded, trying to conceal my anxiety. "I think they add a little something. We should have them ready when everyone goes into the meeting room. There's hardly anyone in there right now, so let's go set them in front of each seat so they'll be there waiting."

I extended my hand to grab a large stack from Marcus, and he pulled them away, saying, "It's okay, man. We got this." I could tell right away that he knew I was nervous. He continued, "Stephen and I will set them out. You just relax and get ready to kill it."

"Thanks man," I responded with a sigh.

As my two compatriots darted toward the large meeting room to start laying out packets, I could detect that other people in the office where starting to make their way to the staff meeting. Meanwhile, I headed for the men's restroom, where I stood over the sink, expecting to vomit at any moment. I had never before been nervous when presenting, but in these circumstances, I was trembling like a man about to walk toward his own execution.

I splashed a few handfuls of cold water into my face and then dried my forehead and cheeks with a paper towel. All at once, a confident surge came over me. I concluded that with everything I had accomplished, if the investors were there to announce something big, it had to be something good. Rick wouldn't have had me present in front of the people who literally keep the business running if he didn't think I could put on a good show. That was all the "Win one for the Gipper" speech I needed to give myself, and finally I whispered, "Game time."

Chapter 11

The staff meeting began roughly five minutes late, as the added guests and the slight adjustments to the agenda led to some minor changes in the starting routine. The room was packed, and the last two to enter were Stephen and Lauren. In an overt act of chivalry, Stephen pulled out a chair for Lauren, only to find out that the seat he offered her was the last available chair in the room. This left the most shy, awkward person I know as the only one left standing, with all eyes in the room on him. With his feet shifting and his face turning red, Stephen started mumbling, "It seems we are one seat short. I'll go get another one." Not moments after Stephen made his exit, Bernsandt, in an act of impatience, reached over and pushed the door closed.

Rick began the meeting with an introduction. "Hello, everyone. As you may have noticed, we have some new faces among us this morning. Our guests are the—"

Just as Rick was about to introduce the investors, the collective attention of the room was diverted to the sound of the door rattling. When Bernstandt closed the door, it locked, and on the other side, Stephen was trying to get back in. Rick gave a somewhat irritated gesture, and someone in the back of the room was gracious enough to pull the door open once again. Stephen reentered, pulling a chair behind him and trying with all his might to make a quiet entrance. The chair loudly clanked against the table and other chairs, which then joined the sound of its carrier stumbling and muttering "Excuse me" toward everyone whose foot he managed to step on. When Stephen finally found a space large enough to place his seat, he sat down red-faced and embarrassed, staring at the floor. Bernstandt snickered and rolled his eyes, and I was convinced that I had never wanted to punch someone more in my entire life.

Finally, Rick continued. "Our guests are the investors who have so generously provided more than enough financial support to make our little endeavor what it is today."

The room gave a unison nod of thanks while each of our guests was introduced individually, and then Rick threw the curveball.

"The reason they are here today is because we are getting ready to announce the expansion of our magazine. In just three short months, with the help of some new distribution channels and a major cash infusion from our generous backers"—he gestured toward our distinguished guests once again—"readers will be able to buy our magazine at every bookstore and newsstand across the country. Of course, in order to do this, we are going to have to expand our staff, and I will be stepping out of the role of editor to serve on a more managerial position."

"Wait a minute," one of the beat writers interrupted. "If you're stepping down as editor, who's going to take your place?"

"Well, from this point on, the role of editor will be assumed by our star columnist and beloved colleague, Mr. Eric McHayden. That is, of course, if he would be willing to accept the position."

I could hardly believe what I was hearing. As I was trying to put together a response, a thunderous objection came from exactly the person I expected would be less than pleased by my sudden promotion.

Bernstandt, the constant thorn in my side, rose from his seat and shouted, "Hold on, Rick. Are we sure we want to put all this on Eric? I mean, this is only his first job in this field out of college."

Just as I was about to stand up and make my case, Marcus, who was sitting next to me, shot up with an almost startling intensity. He was practically barking. "Bernstandt, you were working in the restaurant business before Rick hired you, so don't try to take shots at Eric's credentials. Also, let's call it like it is. Eric's columns have been the reason our issues are flying off the shelves."

At this moment, Stephen, who had been staring at the floor in embarrassment from the little chair episode, rose from his seat to join Marcus, although he carried a much more meek and mild demeanor. "It's true. Most of the good feedback I've seen has been about Eric's writing. It started almost exactly the same time his work picked up."

With these two testimonies, as well as a general indication of agreement from everyone else in the room, Bernstandt sat down with the vein in his forehead on the verge of explosion.

In all the commotion, I almost missed the fiery glare that Rick had fixed directly on Bernstandt. Ole Jimbo had, after all, committed one of the cardinal sins of modern employment, as most people know never to correct or second-guess the boss in front of important people, let alone the entire staff of the business. Once Rick was convinced that Bernstandt had his tail fixed squarely between his legs, he shifted his focus back toward me. "Eric, it seems you have the support of most of your coworkers behind you, so what do you say?"

"I'd be honored." Although my response was intended toward Rick, my eyes began to scan the room to read the reactions of everyone else. All but Bernstandt gave me a general congratulatory response.

I could've stood there basking in the glow for hours, but Rick continued. "Well, since that's settled, we now have a new editor, and his first act in this role will be to tell us about the possible expansion of our website."

For a moment, I had completely forgotten about the presentation that just moments before was making me nauseous with anticipation. I grabbed the presenter and activated the overhead projector, which had my slide show primed and ready for display. I was feeling more assertive than I had at any point in that day. In all the times I had practiced this presentation, the words had never come to me so easily. I looked out on a mostly friendly audience and gave the fine points of everything Marcus, Stephen, and I had put together. The features of the new website, the eye-catching and user friendly home page, the easily searchable archives, and the new and improved writer biographies, all seemed to be music to the ears of the entire staff. Before long, I had reached the last slide, and when I uttered the call for questions, only one hand was raised.

That hand belonged to Jim Bernstandt. He still looked embarrassed by having been shot down by a small group of fellow staff members, and the look on his face toward me made his intentions all too clear. He was out to save face and to do so at my expense. Before I even had the chance to recognize him, he started, "Am I the only one who is seeing the obvious problem here?"

"And that would be?" I responded in a way that suggested I was not going to be easily embarrassed.

"Well, how do we expect people to buy our magazine if our content is easily available online? I mean, how can we ask someone to pay for something they can easily get for free?"

Of all the concerns he could have raised, this was the one I was most prepared to answer. I had thought and researched for hours about how to use the website to sell more subscriptions, and like a godsend, Berstandt had unknowingly given me ammunition. Sitting right in front of him was the bottle of Dasani water that he carried with him into the meeting.

"I see what you're saying," I responded with a tone that I found satisfyingly condescending. "But why don't you take another big gulp of that bottled water, you know, the one you passed the sink to buy from the vending machine. Take a nice big drink, and think about your argument for a second."

Bernstandt's embarrassment was at that point exacerbated beyond all understanding. He started to sneer. "You little—"

Just at that moment, Rick intervened. "Jim, I think you've said enough."

Rick's dismissal led Bernstandt to start backpedaling. "Rick, I was just saying that—"

"Sit down!" Rick snapped. When my mismatched adversary began to take his seat, Rick turned to me. "Eric, I'm sure you've thought of something that can ensure that we aren't simply giving our product away." He was throwing me the proverbial underhand pitch that I could knock out of the park.

"Absolutely," I responded. "There are numerous ways we can make sure that our online presence doesn't take away from our sales."

I then gave several examples of how other news sources have been able to maintain or even boost their subscriptions through a creative interplay between their online and print publications. I focused heavily on the *New York Times*, which allowed users to view a set number of articles online before demanding a subscription. I focused on the *Times*, not only because its method was what I thought to be the most effective, but also because I had seen it on Rick's desk on multiple occasions. I also accentuated how our regular subscribers would be given a password that allowed them free roam of all our online content. At one point, I heard an investor lean in toward Rick and mutter, "This kid is sharp." Eventually, I brought the presentation to a close, and Rick gave some indication that my suggestions would be put into place in the weeks ahead.

As we all filed out of the conference room, everyone began to go back to whatever task consumed them that day. Just as I was pulling out my chair to sit at my desk in the bullpen area, Rick dashed in front of me and rolled the chair away from my hand.

"This isn't your desk anymore." He then nodded toward a door in the corner of the office suite that had been closed, to the best of my knowledge, for as long as I had worked at the Falcon. He then walked me from my former desk to a large office with a desk that seemed enormous compared to what I had grown accustomed to having. Outside the window, there was a terrific view that looked down from our fourteenth floor onto downtown Chicago. "It's a little bare," Rick continued, "but you can fill it with whatever you like." There were a few empty boxes sitting in the corner, one of which I picked up to move my few belongings from my old work station to my new one.

Just before I began to put a few books and other items into the box, I noticed Bernstandt, who was still red in the face from the encounter in the conference room. When I saw him sitting with a noticeable glare, mumbling curses under his breath, I couldn't help but smirk. Bernstandt then pushed a few buttons on his keyboard, and I could hear the printer begin to churn out pages. Just as that happened, Lauren walked by. Bernstandt, condescending as ever, began barking orders. "Hey, my article is almost done printing. I need it over here stapled together so I can look it over."

The moment Bernstandt had finished his sentence, Stephen shot across the room. He immediately shouted at Bernstandt. "Dammit! She's not your secretary. Instead of bossing her around, why don't you waddle your fat ass over to the printer, pick up your own damn article, and go back to sitting there acting like anyone actually reads our food-and-dining section?!"

Stephen almost seemed shocked at the words that were coming out of his own mouth. If he wasn't shocked, I knew I was. Meanwhile,

Lauren stood gazing at him with a look of astonished admiration; the quiet PR guy who never spoke up in his own defense was speaking up for her. Stephen's entire body language changed. His shoulders raised as his hunched, meek demeanor shifted to a strong, assertive posture. Berstandt stormed out of the bullpen, headed God knows where. In his wake stood Stephen and Lauren edging toward each other as I stood watching from a distance.

"Would you like to go out sometime?" Stephen asked with a calm demeanor on his face. Never before had I heard so much confidence in Stephen's voice.

"Yeah." Lauren almost bounced with enthusiasm as she replied. "How about tomorrow night?"

At that point, I decided to no longer stand around as an outsider and quickly retreated to my new office. Once I had fully finished moving my belongings into my new larger workspace, my next task was to head directly to the office of William Gastineux. The drive felt like something of a celebration. I rolled down the windows and played my CD player as loud as I could. The song playing was the Rolling Stones' "Time Is on My Side," I couldn't help but think of how appropriate that song choice really was.

When I arrived, I was immediately dumbstruck by the elegance of Gastineux's office area. It looked something like a grandiose study, with a large mahogany desk and floor to ceiling bookshelves. When his assistant, who I assumed was the same woman I spoke with to arrange the appointment, told me to sit down, the large leather chair left me trying to avoid reclining back to take a nap.

"Comfortable?" Mr. Gastineux asked just as he entered the room.

"These chairs are amazing."

"Glad you like it. By the way, I just got a call from Rick on my way back from lunch. Congratulations on the promotion."

"Thank you, sir."

"Eric, I told you to lay off the 'sir.' If we're going to work together on this, it's important that we get to know each other."

"Sounds good." I tried to appear as casual as he was.

"Would you like a cigar?"

"Sure."

As soon as I accepted his offer, he opened a small humidor box that was resting on his desk, pulled out two large dark cigars, and cut the ends off. We both lit our cigars, and the flavor and aroma almost made my head spin. I had smoked a few cigars before, but I could tell that these were the expensive kind, and that this kind of decadent indulgence was rather commonplace for a man of his stature. He then rose from his seat and gestured toward a door leading to a balcony that I wouldn't have noticed had he not pointed it out, and we both stepped outside.

The balcony wrapped around the entire building and had a magnificent view of the Chicago skyline. As we strolled away from the door to his office, he began chatting as though he and I were close friends. "It's a great view, isn't it?"

"I think I can see my apartment from here."

He laughed. "I often like to come out here. We're on the fortieth floor, and it's amazing how such a busy city can seem so quiet from up here."

I nodded in agreement, and then thought to myself about how I could push a little blue button that had the exact same effect. As much as I would have liked to enjoy the cigar and the idle conversation, I couldn't take my mind off the task at hand. I had put a lot of time and energy into preparing the first interview, and I wanted to get some answers for all the questions I had formulated.

"William, I just want you to know I have already put a lot of work into this project, and you can rest assured that—"

"I know you always do your homework. Rick told me that about you. Before we really get into the interviews, I have put together some materials that I think can help you. I have kept journals since I was about your age, and my assistants have kept a long chronicle of all the press I have received over the years. I'm having all of this sent to your office. Once you read it over, you should be able to put together a pretty interesting story, and once you have that put together, I can help you fill in the blanks."

My mind was racing with how much these materials would help. I was also rather glad that I could get a majority of the information I needed through reading rather than having to pry it step by step out of William in interviews. More reading time and less interview time meant I could do more of this project in the chamber than I had originally intended, and I knew that if I could put one long session in the chamber and get all of the information read and synthesized, I could impress William at how quickly I was able to get the job done.

"That'll definitely help," I responded.

"I thought so, and it should save you a lot of the digging. I've been in this for so long, I think those documents will help iron out the when and where details of my story a lot easier than trying to pull it all from an old man's memory." He grinned and let his joke set in. "That should be enough to get you started."

"I'll admit that I had several questions that I planned to ask."

"Well, why don't you give a look over all the stuff I'm sending you, and then maybe it'll change the kinds of questions you want to ask. For right now, I'm interested in you. Where are you from?"

"Born and raised here in Chicago."

"What about your parents?"

"My mother has moved out of the city and is teaching at an elementary school near Joliet."

"And your father?"

"He was a machinist."

"Was?"

"Yeah. He passed away when I was thirteen."

"Oh, sorry to hear that." I could tell he felt somewhat awkward, but he continued. "I came from a military family, so I moved around a lot. But I guess you will read about that a few times once you get the excerpts from my journals."

From then on, we continued to share a wealth of information about each other's backgrounds, our convictions, and brief insights into our political leanings. He told me about his interests, his hobbies, and gave some anecdotes from his many adventures and misadventures, both professional and personal. What amazed me was how he spoke to me as though we were equals. Although our conversation was nothing like the interview I had imagined, I left feeling as though I could write several chapters based on one discussion alone. Before I knew it, it was 5:00 p.m., time for us to part ways. Trish would be arriving at seven, and once again, I had nothing but big news.

When Trish arrived, I had the table set in my apartment, with spaghetti and meatballs for dinner ready and waiting on the stove. This little surprise gave Trish a slight grin, but she could tell that I had a lot to tell her. After walking across my living floor to kiss me, she began, "All right, lets hear it. How did it go?"

"Well, it started with a little curveball. A bunch of the investors happened to be in the staff meeting when I gave my little presentation."

"What for?"

"Well as it turns out, the Falcon is going to be expanding nationally." I was intentionally downplaying this otherwise huge news for the whopper of an announcement that was to come.

Meanwhile, Trish's eyes widened as she said, "That's awesome! I bet Rick was excited."

"Definitely. He also announced that he would be stepping out of the role of the editor into a more managerial position."

"If he's not the editor, who is?"

"They decided to give the job to some hotshot in the office."

"Do you know him very well?"

"I am him." After playfully delivering the news, I stood back and let it sink in. Trish threw her arms around me in a congratulatory display of affection. After a taking several minutes to just enjoy the embrace, I asked, "By the way, did you read what I gave you this morning?"

"Yes! I loved it."

"Really?"

"Oh, yes. It made me think of all those books my dad used to read. He would have loved it too."

From then on, the rest of our evening was spent exchanging the little details of our day. It was then and there that it occurred to me how much I truly needed her. Had that day gone differently in some devastating way, she would have been the only one who could have consoled me. With every big development, she was the first one I wanted to tell. That night, I knew the chamber waited for me, but I had no work on my mind. I was going to celebrate and then wake up the next morning ready to attack the days and weeks that lay ahead.

Chapter 12

The weeks that followed my promotion saw my life taking leaping steps toward the bevy of conquests that I had envisioned. The day after my first "interview" with William, two large boxes full of journals and binders of news clippings and press releases arrived. With the aid of the time chamber, I sent William an outline that took the information from every single document, synthesized it, and gave a blueprint for how the book would be laid out. "My lord," he commented, "It took you less than a day to learn my whole life story." From there, we made a ritual out of interviewing once a week, and he was always impressed at how I was able have at least one new chapter ready for him to read the next morning. "My story sounds so much better the way you tell it," he would often say.

When I wasn't stunning William with my unheard of level of productivity, I was making a similar impression on my coworkers. The new closed office gave me a unique advantage in my new post as editor. When one of the writers brought a story, I honored Rick's tradition of red-ink revision, but the way I did it made heads turn. As soon as a new story or column was left on my desk, I would tell the writer to step out of my office and close the door. Then I used the chamber to give it extensive care and attention to detail. I would return it to them in less than five minutes, but their work had received hours' worth of attention. Whenever we had a story to assign to one of our many new journalists, I wouldn't just give them a run-down, but instead they would receive folders full of information that could help them write their stories. If the information overload didn't leave them dumbfounded, then at least I knew they would be astounded at how quickly I had gathered the research on a story that I wasn't even assigned to write. One morning, I distinctly heard someone in the office comment, "I don't know how he does it. The man is a machine."

It wasn't just my life that was taking major steps forward. After some consideration, Trish agreed to purchase the top two floors above her small bookstore, and we were able to negotiate a deal with Ricky, the barista from the fundraiser, wherein he left his job and started the process of opening his own shop on the second floor of Trish's new three story establishment. With the guidance of William Gastineux, as well as my newfound ability to gather copious amounts of information on a moment's notice, the details of financing and investment in this expansion almost worked themselves out before our eyes.

Trish and I still had our daily lunch ritual, and we spent as many evenings as possible together. For every update I could give about work or the biography, she had an equally exciting renovation update. However, what thrilled her most was when I brought several new pages of my novel hot off the press and ready for her to read.

I had somehow managed to make the time chamber a routine part of my daily life, trying as best I could to coordinate days and nights so that I kept a regular schedule even though my days were longer than everyone else's. This took a series of processes that came from a wide array of anomalies from life in and out of the chamber. The first anomaly was that I had to become an almost obsessive note-taker. My day planner and a small notebook became my constant companions as I documented even the smallest of tasks and the most commonplace conversations. This came about from a few instances where I found myself unable to remember little jobs I had to do or forgetting details of conversations that had occurred just hours before. Thus, the chamber work sessions would not only begin with a planning session but were also punctuated with a review of my notes to get up to speed with what had happened a day, an hour, or even minutes before I left the world of the ticking clock.

Another anomaly was my newfound respect and use for time-pieces. I purchased a digital clock that I could easily set and reset inside the time chamber. Also, I would take my watch off before entering the chamber and put it back on once resuming life in the real world. I found that although time would freeze without fail once the little blue button was pushed, the internal mechanisms of a watch or clock, just like the ones in the chamber's treadmill and refrigerator, continued quite literally like clockwork. Thus, if I wore my watch into the chamber, it would continue ticking and wouldn't be able to give me an accurate depiction of real world time.

The clock inside the chamber would always be set to match the time of the moment when I pushed the blue button, and this timepiece would serve the specific purpose of helping me keep my bearings. I realized at one point that I lost a great deal of efficiency by having to acclimate myself to the elongated seconds, so this chamber clock could help me keep track of exactly how long I had been awake and how long I had slept. Thus, the amounts of time I spent outside the chamber were no longer hampered by crashing waves of fatigue, as I was able to make sure that I always kept up on my rest.

Just as all of these elements were beginning to create something of a routine, I decided that it was time to meet with Michael. I had to discuss with him my project with Trish and how this was my first step to using the time chamber to help others. We agreed to meet at the diner for lunch to discuss my most recent endeavors, and he was immediately pleased with what Trish and I had accomplished.

"That's excellent," he said. "You're using your gifts and your connections to help people. That kid may never have opened his coffee shop and Trish may not have been able to expand the store had you not put two and two together."

"Not only that." For some reason, I was unapologetically letting my enthusiasm show. "I used the new toy to help me research and figure out the finer details." I was particularly careful to be as cryptic as ever when describing my work with the chamber. I then spoke about all of the intricate planning that went into the expansion of Trish's bookstore. He listened intently as I conversed about the guidance provided by William Gastineux and how I was able to use the chamber to research every possible consideration that went into the endeavor. At one point, I added, "If things go the way we think they will, Trish may even hire at least five new employees."

"That's wonderful, Eric. Five people may get jobs because you were able to make something happen. Incredible."

The more Michael praised this endeavor, the more I just thought about what else I could accomplish. The prospectus was not only complete, but I had defended it and was on the way to finishing my thesis. This meant that the added academic endeavors were beginning to take shape and it wouldn't be long until I was applying for a doctorate program. Nonetheless, I was pleased to have Michael's approval.

Once our lunch meeting was complete, I had the afternoon to myself. The promotion at the Falcon brought with it a considerable increase in salary, and I was resolved that this meant I should upgrade my wardrobe. I took the bus from our diner to a small retail district. Once there, I tried on about a dozen different suits, picking out six that I liked and then purchasing a wide array of shirts and ties of varying colors. I had never before invested in having shirts and suits tailored to fit me specifically, so I allotted the extra time for a sales associate to take my measurements and make the marks to alter my new clothes. The old Eric would have had heart palpitations at the final price calculation, but the new one felt powerful spending such an exorbitant amount of money on this new look. The sales associate said it would take some time to have all of these items altered, so I said I would come back at another time to pick up my new clothes.

I had my courier bag with me that day with the chamber inside, so I decided that I would find a bus route back to the Falcon office. Once there, I would go into my office and start a chamber-aided work session in the middle of the afternoon.

The nearest bus stop was about a block away, and after stopping at a coffee shop to grab a cup of coffee, I decided to cut through a back alley to avoid the longer walk. Once I was halfway across the alley, a voice from behind me called out. "Hey, you! I want a word with you."

When I turned around, I was shocked at the sheer size of the person who was trying to get my attention. This goliath of a human being was the same one whose image alone was enough to stop Michael dead in his tracks. The face, contorted with anger, was now staring directly at me, and once he was nearly within an arm's reach, I saw a knife coming out from one of his enormous clinched fists. He spoke not a word, as his breath came from his nostrils in an incensed hiss. I knew then that I didn't have the luxury of trying to determine his next move, so I instinctively threw my coffee in his face, and I could tell the scalding hot liquid had caught his eyes.

As he roared with pain, I immediately turned and ran as fast as I could. The scalding splash of the hot coffee had stunned my assailant and given me a good head start, but I knew that it was going to take more to than that to get away. Realizing I had about half a block's distance to formulate a plan, I started to reach deep within the courier bag to retrieve the chamber device. In pure survival instinct, I realized that having the chance to freeze that moment might be the only advantage that would help me get away in one piece. Placing the small device on the ground and pushing the blue button, the notion struck me that this was the first time I had ever activated the chamber outdoors in broad daylight. When that moment froze, my hands were shaking and a cold sweat began to roll down my forehead.

My escape route left me in a narrow alley, the kind that one would avoid walking through at night for fear of getting attacked or robbed. Since I was already in the process of getting attacked, this didn't seem like much of a concern. This was such a secluded alley, inhabited only by a rusty blue Dumpster, that I knew no one was going to see the altercation I had just unwittingly gotten myself into. This also meant that I could activate the time chamber without having to explain it to any outside observers.

The behemoth, meanwhile, was frozen in mid stride about twenty feet away. The fog from his breath sat frozen in time. I had to remove myself from the situation, so for a moment, I stepped into the time chamber. Once inside the chamber, it took me longer than I expected to finally catch my breath. I started to formulate some sort of plan that would help me get out of the predicament, but none was readily apparent. At first, I thought I could give myself some sort of crash course in self-defense that would help me thwart my attacker, but I almost grimaced at the idea of stepping back into the altercation armed with little more than a Google search. I then began to scan the chamber in search of some item that could be wielded as a weapon.

What was important was that I could find something that would create distance. My first idea was to grab a knife, and at least that would level the playing field. But that led to the conclusion that two people both armed with knives made my chances only slightly better, if at all. The last item to catch my gaze was the mop that I had carried with me at some point into the chamber to clean up after myself. If detached, the handle was light enough in weight to be wielded as a weapon, and the length of the handle could help me stay away from the business end of the knife. After detaching the mop head and taking a few practice swings with the handle, I stepped out of the chamber door to face my attacker.

Although never before had I found myself in any kind of physical altercation, I actually had some faith in my mop-stick strategy. I stood with a wide stance, clutching the handle as I slammed the door to the chamber behind me. The moment the sound came rushing back, I charged my opponent, stopping a few feet short and swinging the handle with every ounce of strength I could muster. The other end of my newly crafted weapon struck the giant across the temple, disorienting him and knocking him off his feet. As he caught himself on one hand and one knee, I didn't wait to see if he would retaliate. A second swing caught him on the jaw, and blood splattered onto the asphalt beneath us. The third swing struck him squarely on the forehead, sending him sprawling onto his back unconscious.

For a moment, I recognized that I was lucky that this was the knockout blow, as the long handle was now broken into two pieces, and the smaller of the two was what remained in my hands. I paused to make sure this enormous mass of a human being wasn't going to regain consciousness. The broken fiberglass stick in my hand had broken into a jagged, sharp point. This meant that if the weapon was going to be used again, the blunt force would be replaced with a much grizzlier sort of attack. With that in mind, I kicked the knife into some trash in case my opponent turned victim should awake and begin to search for it.

As the monster of a man remained motionless on the ground, I thought for a moment of all of the action movies I had watched as a kid and how the hero usually had some sort of witty one-liner after a victory. Unfortunately, as I stood there with adrenaline pumping through my veins, the best I could come up with was "Dammit! That was a perfectly good mop." I even laughed at how I failed to come up with compelling words, thinking, *Action hero I am not.*

As I returned to my courier bag and the chamber device, it all at once struck me that I had, for the first time, run the risk of exposing my secret. My head began to swivel in every possible direction, checking to see if there were any witnesses. I didn't have to worry about my attacker saying anything; he couldn't retell the story without incriminating himself. Even if he did, if he tried to explain what had occurred, there was a good chance his listener would take him immediately to some sort of asylum. This also led me to the realization that I couldn't go to the authorities for fear that their interrogation would lead to me unveiling the secret of the chamber and breaking my promise to Michael. I knew there was a good reason why he wanted the chamber to be kept a secret, and I didn't even want to calculate the risk of what could occur if other people were to find out about the device.

As I began to put the chamber device back in its hiding place, another voice called out, seeming to be from out of nowhere. "What the hell was that?"

Startled, I began to search the area to determine the origin of this question. My immediate fear was that my large attacker had sprung into consciousness and was going to kill me as soon as I gave him an answer. However, he was still lying motionless on the ground. Instead, what I found was a pair of eyes gazing at me from inside the Dumpster. This inquiry came from a man whose clothes were dirty and ragged, and it appeared as though that Dumpster was his place of residence.

With the adrenaline still coursing through my veins, my gaze immediately shifted toward the jagged half of the mop handle that sat on the ground next to my courier bag. I picked it up and began to walk toward the dumpster. My voice dropped into a low growl, "If you tell anyone about this."

The dumpster-dweller's eyes began to well up with fear, and an immediate remorse took over. It was then and only then that I realized the mop handle that I had been wielding as a weapon of extreme prejudice was a gag gift from Trish. She got it to make a joke about how filthy I used to keep my apartment. And thus, the handle was fluorescent pink. This meant that my moment of manly glory had occurred using a weapon that was nearly lethal—and also "fabulous." In the fight or flight response, the mind typically tends to attach less value to the aesthetic, so it never occurred to me how ridiculous this weapon must have looked. I laughed at the sight of it, and the man in the dumpster uneasily began to laugh with me.

"What would you tell?" I asked with a grin.

"Well, I would say that a man was being chased, and he managed to make a door appear out of nowhere. A second later, he came out of that door with the girly-looking beat stick, and beat the hell out of a man twice his size." The dumpster man's eyes were shifting as he was trying to conceptualize what he just saw.

"I don't think anyone would believe you."

He laughed. "Nope. And besides, living in a dumpster doesn't make me what you'd call a credible witness. I can't even explain it, but your secret's safe with me."

"Thanks, man."

Feeling not only guilty because I had come so close to harming this man but also overcame with appreciation, I pulled out my wallet. I handed the man twenty dollars, telling him to get himself something to eat and expressing my sincerest thanks. The humor of this exchange made me almost forget that a man twice my size seemed like he was ready to kill me and that this was the same man who had Michael looking petrified weeks before. Once I started to think about these two realities, there was no longer any humor to be found. There was something Michael hadn't told me, and I had to know what this enormous man wanted from him and from me.

Once I had gathered my belongings, I pulled out my cell phone and called Michael's number. He picked up after two rings.

"Eric, we just spoke two hours ago. What's going on?"

"We need to talk."

Chapter 13

When I hung up the phone, I backtracked toward the bistro I had just left, where I demanded Michael come to meet me. I knew he would have some trouble finding parking, so I expressed my understanding when it took him about forty-five minutes to get there. The physical altercation left me somewhat paranoid. The little laugh I received from my choice of weapon and the rather pleasant exchange with the homeless man failed to give me any long-lasting comfort.

My mind kept returning to the fact that an enormous human being I didn't know had tried to attack me for reasons I couldn't begin to comprehend. Once I began trying to fathom an explanation, every scenario left me more terrified than the one before. I shuddered every time the door to the building opened, expecting to see my rather massive opponent coming in with a bludgeoned face and ready for round 2. Every noise made me jump. It was so noticeable that one of the waitresses asked, "Are you all right?"

"Yeah. Fine. Just waiting to meet with someone." My tone was not altogether unpleasant, but the concerned inquirer easily got the impression that I wasn't going to satisfy her curiosity.

Eventually, Michael finally arrived, and when he noticed me, he sat down at my table. "Eric," he said, "you look terrible. What happened?"

"I don't think we should talk about this here." Michael's face became about as grave as I imagined mine was. He asked, "Is it about the, you know?"

I nodded. With that, he suggested that we both go to his car so at least we could have doors to close to the rest of the world and no one could listen in to our conversation. Once the doors were closed, and I felt that I could speak freely, I began. "I ran into your friend after we left the diner."

"Who?"

"You know, the big guy. And don't act like you don't know who I'm talking about. I saw the way you looked when you saw him. You were afraid. Who is this guy?"

Michael's jaw dropped, and then he began to stare off through the front windshield. From the look on his face, I couldn't guess for the life of me what he was going to say next. Before speaking, he started the car and began to pull out of his parking space. "Before I tell you about him, there's something I need to show you."

"Where are we going?"

"My home. While we're headed there, tell me what happened."

I began to lay out a long, intricate narrative of what occurred just moments after he and I parted ways. I told him how this massive stranger attacked, or at least seemed intent on attacking me, and how I used the chamber to get myself out of the situation. Since I didn't know anything about my attacker, his connection with Michael, or why we were taking this trip, I had no idea what parts of this story would prove important and which ones wouldn't. With every detail of my story, Michael's face contorted with shock, horror, and what began to look like guilt. Only one time during the entire drive did he even ask a question.

"And you're sure no one saw you use the chamber?"

"No one except the guy in the Dumpster. He told me he wouldn't say anything, and like he said, if he did talk, no one would listen."

"And you're sure there was no one else?"

"Positive."

We arrived at Michael's house, which stood in a large residential district outside of town. When he killed the engine, he began to make his way toward the two-story house and gestured for me to follow him. Once inside his home, I was surprised at how normal it actually looked. Considering that this man had given me such a unique and revolutionary gift, I expected the home to look something like a mad scientist's laboratory out of some old science-fiction movie. Instead, it was just a tastefully furnished home, one that I presumed held a family at one point or another. Without saying a word, Michael led me up the stairs and down a long hallway. He then opened a door at the end of the hallway and walked into what appeared to be a bedroom.

Next to the bed lay a contraption that looked strikingly similar to the one that I had in the courier bag hanging off my shoulder. When I looked at him in disbelief, he gave a nod to suggest that the device was indeed what I thought it was and then pointed a finger at it, indicating that I should activate the device as if it were my own. I pushed the blue button, and time effectively froze, just as it had in every instance when I had activated my own chamber. I knew that whatever Michael had to show me was waiting on the other side of the white door.

When I walked in, I found a bizarre perversion of my own time chamber. The walls were covered in writing. I could detect some numerical symbols, suggesting that these were equations of some sort, but they seemed either so frantic or intricate that they might as well have been cave wall writings in some long-gone archaic language. This inner sanctum was much less equipped than my own, with two rooms breaking off, one appearing to be a bathroom. In the other room, I could see a small workspace and the foot of a bed that, much to my surprise, had someone lying in it. Michael walked toward this bedroom area, gesturing for me to follow him.

Lying in the bed was a man who had to be at least ninety years old. His skin was wrinkled and transparent. His body looked weak and frail. The old man in the bed didn't even respond when Michael and I walked into the room, with his eyes darting, hands shaking, and muttering unintelligible phrases under his breathe.

"He's lost all grasp of reality," Michael said, his words cutting through the silence to the point that he almost startled me.

"Are you telling me that he never leaves this chamber?"

"Hardly ever, and not more than a few hours. I come in here three times a day just to take care of him. I figure it's the least I can do because I'm the one who put him here."

"What do you mean?"

"I was the one who gave him this chamber."

From there, Michael went into a long elaborate story. At one point or another, he and I both ended up sitting down, with me taking a seat at the small workspace while he sat at the foot of the bed. From what Michael told me, this person, who appeared to be on his deathbed, was the first person to receive a time chamber. When Michael met this man, he was a young physicist who had just received a rather prestigious research position at MIT. This man, whose name was Jason, had an immeasurable understanding of physics and was on the verge of becoming the next great scientific mind of his generation.

"Then something went wrong," I asserted.

"Exactly," Michael replied. "Two years after receiving the chamber, he published an article on the flaws of modern thought in the field of quantum mechanics. I read the article—it was absolutely terrible. He was getting work published in highly prestigious volumes left and right, mostly because he was able to do much of the long, tedious work inside this time chamber."

I thought for a moment about how I could relate to that kind of meteoric rise out of obscurity. "What went wrong?" I asked.

"It got to the point that periodicals were willing to put out almost anything with his name on it. Thus, he wrote this absolutely terrible article, and his hypothesis was ripped to shreds by almost all of his peers."

"He had one failure. So what?"

"Those were my sentiments exactly. But he couldn't handle it. He walked in to the chamber one day and began trying to come up with something that was going to prove all his critics wrong. Eventually, this pursuit pushed him over the edge, and he's been lying here like this ever since."

"Wait, how does that work?"

"What do you mean?"

"Time freezes when you walk into this chamber. If he walked in to the chamber never to come out, wouldn't time have remained frozen?"

"Like I told you the night that you received your own chamber device, it's not that time freezes. These chambers are domiciles that exist outside of time, which means that you can move in and out of the exact same moment of the exact same day. For the user and any-one standing close enough to the device when it is activated, it would appear as though time has frozen, and for all intents and purposes, it has. However, the world will go on if this device is allowed to run perpetually."

"What does this have to do with the man who attacked me today?" As I asked that question, I looked at Jason. Through all the wrinkles in his graying, faded flesh, I started to notice a resemblance between him and the man I had rendered unconscious just hours before. Then it occurred to me that if Jason were able to stand, he would more than likely tower to a height equal to my attacker. The similarities in height brought my attention to the similarities in facial features.

"Oh my god!" I trembled. "Jason is that man's father."

"Not exactly," Michael replied, "How old do you think Jason is?"

"If I had to guess, I'd say he was well into his late eighties if not older."

"Actually, he was born December 18, 1988."

"That's impossible. That would make us almost exactly the same age."

"You're right. I gave him his chamber about two years before you received yours, and he's been in here so much that this is how quickly he has aged. I have no idea how long it takes someone to begin aging after a prolonged stay in the chamber, but he never leaves, so he keeps getting older. If I didn't force him to come out every so often, he'd be long dead. I've hoped and waited that he would come out and get a grip on reality, even if it just means that he can enjoy whatever time he has left."

"So Jason isn't the man's father?"

"No. The man who attacked you today was Jason's younger brother, the only one to my knowledge that Jason has ever told about the chamber. That is why I made you promise that you would keep it a secret."

"I understand now."

"The kid's name is Billy. He blames me for everything that happened to Jason, and I can't say that I totally disagree. Odds are, he saw you with me and has since kept tabs on you. You've accomplished quite a lot over the last few months, so I'm sure he's been able to put two and two together. He's so blinded by his anger toward me that I'm sure he's got his eye on you. He's been following me for the last year, and I don't know how or when he intends to do it, but I fully believe that he has plans to kill me and, apparently, to do the same to you."

With that, we walked out of the chamber and stepped back into the natural flow of time. I was astounded at everything I had just heard. I asked him with an overt degree of concern in my voice. "What does this mean? Where should we go from here?"

Michael reached into a desk drawer and pulled out a small snub-nosed revolver. "For the most part, you should go about your life as if nothing happened. Billy is so erratic that I couldn't even pretend to predict what he would do. For now, I'll assert than whenever he acts upon his urge for vengeance, he will probably come for me first. In case I'm wrong, keep this on you."

I had some apprehensions about carrying a firearm with me at all times, but I thought about how unprepared I felt while being chased that afternoon, and all of my concerns quickly subsided. "So you're basically expecting me to carry a gun and otherwise act like today never happened?"

"Precisely. You have too many big things going on to slow them down by living in fear. Besides, Billy was always a problem child even before I gave Jason the chamber. He was a hothead, and he now has a pretty considerable background when it comes to physical altercations and assault charges."

"I believe that."

"This guy is a walking powder keg. For all we know, tomorrow he could be picked up for doing God knows what to God knows who."

"That's reassuring."

"Well, for now, that's the best we can do. Besides, I think he would love to see you lose what you have going for you because you're worried about him. That alone would be satisfying for a guy like him. Like the saying goes, 'The best revenge is living well.'"

Interestingly enough, those words brought me considerable comfort. I agreed that I would continue to work as though nothing had happened, although quietly I knew that I would forever be more vigilant than usual. Michael then drove me back to my apartment, telling me that I could call him if I had any concerns. Sitting in my apartment, I sat for what had to be a few hours trying to wrap my mind around what had occurred that day. I then decided that if I was going to go on living as if nothing had happened, it would be better to start sooner than later.

I had several projects left to finish, so I gathered the materials and clothes that I needed and continued into the time chamber. I started to play some music to help me relax, and I started on the treadmill. Since fighting for my life didn't strike me as enough of a workout, I put myself through some rather vigorous exercise, hoping to lose myself in the endorphin release that usually came with relatively intense physical training. This workout involved upper body exercises, long and meticulous core training, and was bracketed by two good long cardio sessions. At the end of this workout, I stood wiping sweat off my forehead and saying, "I feel better already," as if to convince myself.

The first few moments at the chamber desk were hazy and distracted at best. In those first few scatterbrained moments, the transition of fighting for my life to putting my nose to the grindstone appeared just as troublesome as I thought it would be. It took what felt like hours to put the finishing touches on my opinion piece that would go into the Falcon's next printing. Although I struggled to do what I could often complete in minutes, eventually the words became sentences, sentences built paragraphs, and eventually a column came to fruition. That was progress.

Next, I put together an agenda for the execution and completion of the website's expansion. It then occurred to me that I should draw up a few cost estimations for Trish's bookstore renovations. For that task, I had already gathered price estimations, so putting them together into one itemized list was a job of simple data entry with some semblance of organization. With all the numbers neatly organized, I was able to efficiently add three items to my list of competed tasks.

It was at this point that the image of an ostrich came to mind. When this bird senses danger, it will instinctively bury its head in the sand. What I was doing felt all too similar, as I was burying my head in the sands of my work. A glance at my desk, covered in freshly completed projects, told a completely different story of determination and accomplishment. *No!* I thought to myself. I would not bury my head in cowardice. Just that afternoon I stood, outsmarted, and overcame an opponent much larger than myself. I overcame a knife with a mop handle, and now my new gift from Michael gave me the upper hand. That realization gave me a sense of power, as though nothing stood in my way.

The occurrences of the afternoon, however, continued to replay in my mind. My eyes intermittently drifted back to my courier bag because I continued to ignore the new item that had been added to its contents. I walked over to it and stared down into the open compartment where the small handgun's barrel held a small glimmer of the light. My mind swirled with questions that I imagine arose upon becoming a gun owner for the first time. If I ever had to use it to defend myself, could I bring myself to pull the trigger? Would I shoot to kill? Eventually, as if compelled by a mind of its own, my hand reached down into the bag and wrapped itself around the handgrip. I sat on the foot of the bed, taking note of the surprising weight of the relatively small weapon. I held an instrument of death, and a combined feeling of power and horror overcame me.

I thought for a moment of firing a shot, knowing that in the confines of the chamber, no one would be able to hear it. I thought the better of it immediately. I had no idea if the bullet would enter a chamber wall or ricochet perpetually until it sunk into the bed, the counter, or worse, my body. I would lay shot in my own inner sanctum with no one to come help me or find my corpse. The disappearance of a newly big-time news magazine editor would generate some headlines, and then eventually I would be forgotten by those who didn't know me personally. The risk of that was not worth the appeasement of my curiosity.

I then began to work again, although this time it was different. I wasn't working to keep my mind occupied; I was acting upon a bizarre adrenaline rush. Page after page of William's biography began to materialize. At moments it seemed as though my hands were working on autopilot, and the work was simply completing itself. Within what felt like only a few hours, the biography project was completed, and then I was on to the novel. When I sat down for the work session, I only had a few more chapters to write, and they, much like the biography, began to fly onto the pages. The pile of completing tasks was becoming mountainous, and yet it still wasn't enough, as though through some spontaneous spark of madness, I had developed a hunger for accomplishment with no satiety in sight.

I had, in one sitting, completed the novel, the biography, and about a handful of other projects. In the weeks before that moment, I had used the chamber to get ahead on projects. Being able to return pieces for my writers in less than a few moments was definitely an advantage, but in light of completing entire books, these feats seemed like mere parlor tricks, not much more impressive then the little depreciation lesson I gave to the accounting students. Deep within me, I knew that this hunger, this drive, needed something bigger.

When I stepped out of the chamber, the clock on the cable box told me that it was just after 6:00 p.m. and I had the rest of the evening to accomplish whatever I deemed necessary. It was a Wednesday night, and I had already assigned all the stories for the next week at the Falcon. This thirst to accomplish more still sat unquenched, so

I began to start planning another long work session in the chamber. This was going to equate to working for more than a week, or even two weeks, so I wanted to make sure I could set up a launch pad that would take me to heights I had otherwise deemed inconceivable. This planning involved a long and elaborate grocery list, and I began a few loads of laundry. I would take the next day to complete my preparations, and then I would enter the chamber for one long retreat on Thursday night.

Trish called and asked if we could spend Thursday night together. At first I thought about how this would interact with the plans I was quietly putting into motion, but after a moment's delay, I concluded that this actually worked really well with my agenda. The bookstore was still in the early phases of its renovation and expansion, and I could tell that Trish wanted to get some time away to relax and recharge. I suggested that she stay at my apartment; we could relax together and then even sleep in a little bit the next morning. The possibilities as to how I could coordinate this around my departure and return into the chamber began to become more and more intriguing. As excited as I was to see Trish, all plans began to hinge around my own personal schedule. Meanwhile, every sensation that I experienced was dwarfed by the size of my newfound ambition.

One of the pieces of advice William had given me was, "Always let the work you do today get you ahead of the game tomorrow." With the chamber, it was possible that I would always be ahead of schedule. I no longer wanted to get ahead on projects. I wanted to build, create, and establish something that not only puts my tasks ahead of their deadlines but also puts me ahead of the rest of the world. I had a completed thesis, which I had almost forgotten altogether, a completed biography, and a novel. At the same time, these accomplishments weren't enough. The mountain of progress beneath my feet gave a new view of the world around me, and even though I stood on a mountaintop, my only urge was to keep climbing.

Chapter 14

Thursday morning came after a long restful sleep. My chamber-aided morning routine included its usual workout and long, leisurely breakfast. At one point during this routine, I began to question how I had ever gone through life waking up an hour before I had to be functional only to trudge headlong and half-asleep into my day. As I sat at the small kitchen table in the chamber, reading over my day planner, I began taking little notes of everything I wanted to accomplish in the next twelve hours or so before I would make a return into the chamber and begin another blitz of projects and accomplishments. The logistical considerations included groceries, clothing, and to-do lists. I also had a small agenda of people I needed to call. Building Rome in a day all of sudden seemed much more possible when the day was as long as I needed it to be.

My first call was to Trish, who was seemingly in between numerous tasks regarding the renovation of her bookstore. We finalized the plans for our evening together, and I was pleasantly surprised to find that she would be able to stay with me roughly until nine o'clock the next morning. This meant that if I could plan to start my long chamber work session at just the right time, I would be able to not only see her moments before I left, but also I could get the opportunity to spend time with her when I returned.

As though he knew exactly what I was doing, Marcus called just moments after I finished my phone call with Trish. At that point, he was assigned to do an interview with Travis Jermaine, a young college pitcher who was from the Chicago area and was now playing for the Chicago Cubs' minor-league franchise. I told him to call me as frequently as possible to keep me updated on the progress.

"What's up, man?" I asked.

"Oh, just getting some work done on my next article. I finished the interview with Jermaine last night, and I have my coverage of the Bulls game tonight."

"Awesome, man. When do you think you could have that done?"

"Oh, I could wrap it up tonight, probably an hour or so after the game."

"Well then, I figure you should be the first to know. I'm setting a deadline for all of next week's writing to get to me by 11:00 a.m. tomorrow." I actually hadn't chosen the exact time until that very moment. I had come to know the general work speeds of all the writers in the office. Marcus was pretty quick and efficient when it came to completing his work, although there were some much faster than he was. Really, I wanted to set a deadline that Marcus would have no problem meeting, although I knew it was going to be a crunch for a few of the people at the Falcon. I had to stop myself from asking Marcus if that was okay.

"Why the deadline?"

"I want everything to get to me early. That way, we have the weekend to see what works, see what doesn't, and I can give everyone more time to make my corrections and give their work a second look." I knew Marcus would have no problem with this deadline. We had become a highly efficient weekly news magazine, which meant we didn't have the same kind of time concerns as the daily publications. Part of me wanted to set this new deadline so that I could have more time for face-to-face to work with our newer writers. Another part of me wanted to set this deadline simply because it was a way to assert my newfound authority.

"Makes sense," Marcus said. "Have you run this by Rick?"

"No. He put me in charge, so this was my call."

"All right. Well, I'll have it to you well before then, so no need to worry about me."

"That's what I like to hear."

With that, Marcus and I concluded our conversation, and my next and final correspondence was intended for William. I had completed the biography the night before, so I wanted to start the process of having him read it and push it toward publication. Of course, I had to give this work some revision, but that was just one of the many tasks I had planned for the chamber marathon that evening. I called his office and was greeted by his receptionist, who told me he could not be reached at the moment and offered to take a message. I lamented for a moment that the announcement of the biography's completion was going to be underscored by falling into a myriad of messages and appointments. Nonetheless, I told her to leave a message for William that the biography was completed. She had scheduled all of our interview meetings, and thus, I could detect the shock in her voice at this news. "I'll tell him right away!" she told me before feverishly hanging up the phone.

With all of these small matters of correspondence completed, I began my commute toward the Falcon office. The whole trip there, my mind was clouded by volumes of to-do lists and last-minute preparations that came to mind. My brain was so busy that I almost didn't recognize the Falcon building against the backdrop of the Chicago skyline. This building, which had appeared to me as both a kingdom in my time of triumph and a prison in the days when I was an underachiever, now appeared as just one of many buildings that did little to demand my attention.

The office was abuzz with activity, and I walked in as though the bullpen office area was my own inner sanctum and everyone was there by my allowance. Standing in the middle of the room, I began to pound my fist against the desk trying to get everyone's attention. "Excuse me!" I shouted.

Everyone in the office slowly began to stop whatever they were doing and look at me. I even noticed Rick slowly creeping out of his office to see what was going on.

"I would like to start taking a little more time to work with you on your pieces. I believe I've been able to get your work to you in a timely fashion." With that, I could tell that many were beginning to chuckle at my obvious and deliberate understatement. My turnaround time wasn't timely; it was outright inhuman. "So from here on out, the deadline for all columns and pieces for our weekly printing will be Friday at 11:00 a.m. That is all."

As I began to walk to my office, I noticed that the only empty desk in the room was the workspace of Jim Bernstandt. As I passed his desk, I turned to the nearest employee and barked, "Whenever Jimbo gets here, let him know about the new deadline."

Rick was standing close to my office, giving a gesture that I had come to know meant he wanted to speak with me in private. I patted him on the shoulder and led him into my office, closing the door behind him. I could tell right away that he had his doubts.

"So you're giving them a deadline."

"Yep. I'm allowing more time for them to work with me and implement the changes I make. I've looked at some of the stuff we've put out. We have good writers, but they could be so much better with a little more time and attention."

"I never gave them a deadline, so this may be pretty new to them."

"That's the way you did things. This is the way I do things." I knew immediately that my tone sounded more than defensive; I was outright cavalier.

"I get that, Eric. I'm just wondering what you're thinking here."

"I'm thinking that when you appointed me editor, the arrangement was that you would handle the business end of things and I would handle the day-to-day operations. The deadline is just my way of doing it." As I spoke, I fidgeted around my desk and made it visually apparent that I was too busy for his inquisition.

When I caught Rick out of the corner of my eye, I could tell that he was taken aback by my rather flippant and brazen attitude. He stood to exit my office, and just before opening the door, he turned and, with a fatherly, concerned tone, said, "I'm going to trust your judgment on this one. The people in this office respect you, so you need to think long and hard about what you're going to do if someone doesn't meet your new deadline. I would hate to see them come to resent you, or worse, think you're a pushover."

Rick stepped out and closed the door behind him, and I was left sitting with a blank stare on my face, trying to process what had just occurred in that conversation. Was that last little caveat meant to be taken as a challenge or a warning? I decided to pop my head out the door to get a general reading of the atmosphere in the Falcon office. Despite Rick's objections, it seemed as though the office as a whole was responding well to my new demand. I could tell that a few of them would struggle to meet the deadline, but all in all, they stayed focused and motivated.

Just I was starting to feel proud of myself, in walked Jim Bernstand.

I watched quietly from a distance as good ole Jimbo waddled his way toward his desk. His head began to pivot back and forth as though the intensified buzz of activity was catching his attention. He began a conversation with one of our field reporters who worked near his desk, presumably asking why everyone looked so busy. I could only make presumptions about the conversation I was witnessing based on the body language, but moments after the reporter gestured toward my office, I could immediately ascertain ole Jimbo's reaction. He slammed his fist down on his desk, yelling "Bullshit!" and glaring directly at me. In the weeks following my promotion, Jim had managed to slowly but surely alienate himself from everyone in the office, so his objection was of little concern to me. As a matter of fact, I almost reveled in the fact that my new change in policy was having this adverse effect on him. Watching a few of the other writers roll their eyes at Jim's objection only vindicated me even further.

I was fully prepared for a standoff with Jim, but just as I was about to approach him, Stephen stepped into my line of vision. Perhaps Stephen's motivation was to stop any confrontation, but his immediate and explicit concern was to pass me his weekly report about the Falcon. Thus, I chose to forego the stare down with Jim and meet with Stephen.

"How are we doing?" I asked as I invited Stephen into my office.

"Very well," he exclaimed with a considerable degree of enthusiasm.

This newfound energy and liveliness was a welcome change from our once solemn and silent PR guy. He laid out for me the buzz that we were creating on social media, as well as the projected new traffic to our expanded website. I made sure that I asked on regular intervals for him to provide his input. I did this for two reasons. The first was that I knew Stephen's resurgent confidence was only further enhanced when I sincerely asked for his input. My other less magnanimous reason was that I knew the news was going to be good, and hearing that the Falcon was flourishing under my direction served as a means to simply stroke my ego.

After a brief conversation, I excused him, and he was back to work. In the quiet confines of my office, I finished writing out to-do lists and grocery lists, planning for one long work session inside the chamber. The many large tasks I had to complete would have once appeared to me as so daunting that I would have been quickly overwhelmed. Instead, I looked at this list with a sense of ambition.

Before long, I was able to leave the Falcon building, do my grocery shopping, and prepare for a long absence from the world of the ticking clock. I bought my rations in bulk, and when I returned to my apartment, the numerous bags of groceries were soon joined by many piles of clothes to get me through the long haul. With the satisfaction that I had completed the preparations, my next immediate concern was Trish's arrival. I started thinking about how I was going to depart for a long work session and how, if I planned it just right, I would be able to punctuate both my departure and arrival with some good, quiet alone time with Trish.

When Trish arrived at my door, suddenly everything that had demanded my attention all day long seemed altogether insignificant. In the days leading up to that evening, we had only gotten to see each other coming and going, and absence truly had made the hearts grow fonder. Our conversation was what any outside observer would have written off as small talk, but her words sounded like poetry, and I hung on every one. Normally, I preferred that our evenings together would take place in the private and peaceful confines of my apartment, but that evening, I was feeling more like getting out, so I suggested that we go to a movie and then eat at the little diner down the street. I didn't mention the fact that this was the same diner where I would normally see Michael and discuss how I was going to bend time to get things done. For the purposes of our date, the diner was just a local eatery that would provide an easy and convenient meal.

Trish and I finally decided on some comedy at the movie theater. While the on-screen antics of Will Ferrell were fairly entertaining, I could have been watching two hours of someone reading the phonebook and would have been just as happy, because in the dark escape of the movie theater, I found my own personal nirvana sitting with one arm around Trish. She always knew that my favorite indulgence was movie-theater popcorn and Coca Cola, so she insisted that we get the large couple's combo. When the movie was over, we walked hand in hand to the small diner.

Over dinner, Trish and I discussed the bookstore renovations and my daily work at the Falcon. We laughed as we celebrated each other's successes, and I felt the warmth of her always unconditional support. She asked if I was enjoying the new role of editor, and I responded with an overwhelming yes and then divulged to her about the decision to set a deadline that I had made that very morning.

"The Falcon has never had a deadline like that, right?" she asked.

"Nope. It's a new policy that I have put in place."

"I had no idea I was dating a slave driver," she joked.

"No, nothing like that," I responded with a grin. "I set the deadline days before we put to print so that we can have more time to fine-tune the work that comes to my desk. It gives me a little more oversight, and I can give each writer more of my attention."

"Did they take well to the deadline?"

"For the most part. I think they respect me, so while it may take some getting used to for the next couple of weeks, they'll get used to it." I completely avoided how Bernstandt almost blew a vein when he heard the news. I was having too good a time to let that fat, annoying pain in the ass kill my mood. As far as I was concerned, he wasn't going to get the privilege of being brought up or even thought of in my conversations outside the office.

"Well, I hope they don't give you any problems." Trish always had a way of expressing her support in a way that let me know she cared. She may have thought my decision was foolish, but I always knew she was behind me.

After finishing our dinner and paying the bill, we walked hand in hand under the lights of the city back toward my apartment building. Right next to the doorway into the building, in a covered alcove that was still accessible to the outside world, sat the vending machines. I gave Trish the key and told her to go ahead up to the apartment, and I would get us some sodas. I fumbled with the money and fought with the often sluggish dollar slot that would malevolently kick a dollar back to me. It seemed as though the machine would take my money on the first attempt when I was by myself and had nowhere to be, but when I had the love of my life waiting for me upstairs, and I wanted nothing more than to just get the drinks and move on, the machine would toy with me, stealing minutes away that I could have been spending with her.

With two sodas in my hands, I was about to turn and go back inside when something caught my eye from the far outskirts of my periphery. I don't know how I almost overlooked him, but across the street, I saw a man walking deliberately out of the shadows and toward my building. With each passing step, it became obvious that it wasn't just my building he was walking toward, but instead, it was me who was his immediate target, as I was standing directly in his path.

As the streetlights shone on this dark and shadowy figure, not just his path presented itself, but also his size. That was a figure I couldn't mistake. It was one I had seen before and one I had irrationally hoped that I wouldn't see again. A chill ran up my spine as my jaw dropped. In a shocked and terrified gasp, all I could do was say his name.

"Billy."

Chapter 15

I stood petrified for only a moment. The gun that Michael gave me was sitting in my courier bag upstairs, making it of virtually no use to me. During our first run-in, I had the benefit of the chamber to give me some space and time to plan an attack. This time, however, I had no chamber, no gun, and no immediate advantage. It then occurred to me that if I could just get inside the building, the door would lock behind me, leaving him unable to get in.

Although getting inside the building seemed to be the most painless and viable option, I couldn't bring myself to run away from him again. I had overcome Billy once before, and since then, a resolve had overcome me that I would overpower anything or anyone that stood in my path. The likelihood that he had a knife or worse hidden from my view never crossed my mind as I clinched my hands into fists and stepped out of the alcove and toward him. In retrospect, I know that I was not only stepping out of that small covered area in front of my apartment but I was also stepping over that fine line that separates courage from stupidity.

Just before he got to the curb, he stopped dead in his tracks. For a second, my ego told me that it was my approach that staggered him, but down the block, I saw a police car come gliding to a stop just twenty or so feet away, and the officer sauntered toward the small newsstand that I often frequented when I needed my morning cup of substandard coffee. Within the thousands of messages that were firing in my brain, somewhere in between the survival instincts and the compulsion to hide my fear, a random thought crossed my mind about whether or not that newsstand served donuts.

Billy's gaze shifted back and forth between me and the officer. Billy always carried a furious glare on his face, but now that anger was met with what appeared to be frustrated indecision. I stopped my determined gait in his direction and held my arms wide, as if to ask what he was going to do next. He stepped back, growling with frustration, then began to walk away from my apartment building.

"Hey, jackass!" I yelled in his direction. He turned with an incensed look on his face to see me standing in the outskirts of the alcove with my middle finger waved high above my head. At this point, I was brazenly standing unafraid of him or any threat he may have posed to me. Flippantly brushing off our meeting, I walked inside and climbed the stairs back to my apartment.

When I stepped through the doorway into my apartment, Trish was sitting on my couch with a somewhat perplexed look on her face as she asked, "What took you so long?"

To even suggest that I had been in a small confrontation would have meant that I would have to divulge many more details than I would want. I felt it better to act as though I had not come across anyone at all. "Oh, just fumbling with the machine. It tried to eat my dollar, so I had to tell it who's the boss around here." I handed her the soda as though absolutely nothing had happened at all, then sat on the couch. We sat together, almost drifting off while watching one of the often interchangeable late night talk shows.

Although she was on the verge of dozing off, I sat taking in every detail, from even the smallest facial feature to the smell of her hair. I was about to go into the chamber for a long haul, and these would have to be the images to get me through when the work proved lonely. I had enough food and clothing prepared for the equivalent of two continuous weeks. Although this wasn't an unbearable amount of time when measured by the clock or calendar, I knew from experience that it would feel much longer. This time would feel elongated, not only because of the amount of work I wanted to do, but also by the maddening and lonely silence of the chamber.

When I could tell that she would be unable to stay awake much longer, I gently woke her up, and we retreated back to the bedroom. As she lay there next to me, I continued to focus solely on her for as long as I could. Once she drifted off into a deep sleep, I quietly rose from the bed. Just before stepping out of the bedroom, I looked over my shoulder to see her lying there one more time. The small streak of light from the window was shining down on her face, and the empty space next to her called out to me. After the long session in the chamber, when all the work was completed, that was exactly where I wanted to return, and when the work grew tedious or difficult, that image would pull me through.

When I stepped into the time chamber, I took yet another inventory of all the food rations and clothing that I had prepared. Usually, my first instinct was to sit down at the chamber desk and immediately start working, but I felt so tired from that day that the easy decision was to get as much sleep as possible and then get to work later feeling rested. I set the digital clock on the wall to the exact time that I had left behind when I pushed the blue button. Without some reference point to mark days and nights, the stillness of the chamber would prove enough to drive me insane. I took two sleep-aid capsules and tried to rest my head against the pillow. Usually, the chamber bed was where I could immediately drift off into sleep, but I wanted nothing more than to be back in my bed in the real world, where Trish could be lying there with me.

Eventually, after quite a bit of tossing and turning, I was able to fall asleep. The clock, when I awoke, said that I had gotten about nine hours of sleep, and I felt alert and ready to face the day. I opened my email knowing that all emails sent to me up until the time I hit the blue button would be waiting in my inbox. I was pleased to see that a striking majority of the writers for the Falcon had been able to send me drafts before the day was over, well before the deadline. I printed them off one by one and then placed the printed copies next to the finished manuscripts of my novel and the biography. I had plenty of editing to do, and I knew that my stick-and-move technique would be the best way to make my work most efficient. If I was going to endure missing Trish and cutting myself off from the world for such a long period of time, then I was resolved that I was going to get as much out of this time as possible.

I started with a sizable workout consisting of running on the treadmill and weightlifting. The food I used to stock the chamber was relatively healthy, so I figured that I should keep a stable exercise regimen, because doing so always seemed to keep me more awake and alert. After toweling off the sweat and starting a fresh pot of coffee, I was off to the races. I would edit a chapter of the novel, then a chapter of the biography, and then I would review one of the submissions from my writers. Occasionally, all the reading and reviewing would give me an idea of my own, which would either get jotted down in my notebook, or would immediately begin its evolution into a new column. I made sure to write five or six of these columns so that I could publish online every day once I got back into the world of the ticking clock. This process repeated itself over and over, and when I felt as though I could no longer focus, I stopped to eat or to get on the treadmill and move a little bit.

I checked the clock after several cycles of editing and revision. The fatigue had begun to catch up with me, and so I began another race against exhaustion. I accomplished as much as I could until I was simply too tired to keep going. I wanted to be so exhausted that even my longing to be with Trish wouldn't keep me awake. I focused myself. I kept reading through page after page of my novel and William's biography, making changes to whatever error my weary eyes could catch. I then did a random search on the internet for independent editors who I could hire to give a review of my work before publication. If I could find an editor I trusted, that person would stand to benefit from many more projects in the future. I generated a list of about ten or so candidates. I would review them later on when my mind was less tired and more able to make such a potentially critical decision.

Finally, the exhaustion brought me to a screeching halt, and so I trudged wearily toward my bed to get a good night's rest. Although missing Trish didn't cause me to lose sleep, I remember dreaming about her. To the best of my knowledge, that was the only time I can remember dreaming when I was asleep in the chamber. That dream, along with the feeling of accomplishment from everything that I had done the day before, allowed me to rise the next morning with high spirits and large ambitions.

Several days went by just like the first inside the chamber, cycling from one project to another. Although I had a clock to tell me how long I had slept and how long I had worked, there was still the disorienting feeling of having no sunrise or sunset to tell me that a day had passed. Although I had almost grown to take the benefits of the chamber for granted, I often reveled in the fact that when this self-imposed indenture met its end, I would step out to find Trish waiting for me in the night just as I had left her. At some point, I began counting the artificial days and nights by the sets of clothes I had gone through or the food I had eaten.

At one point, I felt all of the cycles of editing come to a complete stop. I didn't believe it at first, but it was all finished. I had edited both books, made revisions on every piece that I had received, and written enough columns to get me through at least a week in the real world. It occurred to me at that point that I could simply stop and I would have enough work done to live comfortably for the foreseeable future. A quick check of my rations told me that I had several more days' worth of clothing and food, and that intrigued my newfound ambition. As though it was screaming my name, the manuscript of my novel caught my attention.

The first novel was a project that I began simply to see if I could finish it. However, I started getting an idea for a new project. I could have told myself that this novel would be one that was just as personally and artistically meaningful as the first, but to hell with that. I wanted to write something that would sell. I wanted to write a story about sex, greed, corruption, and betrayal. As quickly as the idea began to swirl around in my head, I was filling page after page of a small notebook with outlines and character notes. I went in to my last creative project somewhat blindly, and because of this, I often had to rewrite or make sweeping changes. On this project, however, I knew more what I was doing and intended to attack the rather large endeavor with lethal precision.

After completing all of the planning and outlining for my new novel, I retired to the chamber bed for yet another long, restful sleep. I awoke nine hours later feeling energized and alert. My first task was to determine how much longer my rations and clothes could be stretched. The chamber allowed me the luxury of eating every two hours, which, according to all the fitness magazines, was the best way to maintain a healthy metabolism, and this ritual could be modified based on whether I wanted to build some muscle or get rid of some extra body fat. At that rate of consumption, I would be able to last another week or so, and my clothes could feasibly stretch over that period, although doing so would be less than hygienic.

For the next six artificial days inside the chamber, I worked and exercised like a man consumed by some uncontrollable obsession. I woke up every morning hungry to accomplish something and went to sleep feeling exhausted with nothing left to give. My clothing and food calculations were slightly off. I was left with two more days of food, but all my clothes were now well-worn, and most of them were soaked with sweat from my workouts. That was when I began to go through the same routines, only naked, thinking at times that nothing in the world would stop me.

It was uncomfortable at first, but then I realized that in the climate-controlled and isolated solace of the time chamber, there was really no reason why clothing was necessary for my survival. I subsequently realized that although I had been able to build a somewhat impressive physique, a naked man on the treadmill is never a pleasant sight to see. My bob-and-weave approach to finishing tasks had been whittled down to four simple activities—exercise, write, sleep, and eat. The more I wrote, the more the other tasks began to fall by the wayside. Eventually, I became so focused on writing that I lost all grasp of time and grew into disequilibrium. I only stopped to eat when I could no longer stand the grumblings from my stomach; I only stopped to sleep when I was so exhausted that I could no longer put a sentence together.

After what could have been days of writing, I realized that I was within ten thousand words or so of completing my second novel. Next to the kitchen counter sat half a dozen bags of trash that I would have to remove from the chamber, and all that remained from my once enormous supply of rations was a single can of chicken noodle soup. This meal, although far from glamorous, would be my own quiet celebration when this project was completed. The realization that I was within hours of finishing invigorated me and my fingers began to fly across the keyboard. The sentences that I would often have to fight to create began to present themselves on the screen, and I became a bystander. The story that I created in a fit of productivity began to hurdle toward a gripping conclusion (if I do say so myself), and I felt an astounded zeal come over me. I wrote the last sentence like I was savoring the end of a bottle of fine wine.

As I rose from my desk, I looked over all I had completed. The biography and first novel were clean and freshly edited, as were all of the articles that were sent to me from the writers at the Falcon. I had written enough columns that I was ahead for weeks to come. Most notably, I had written a whole new novel. While the soup was heating up in the microwave, I thought about what waited for me outside the chamber. Trish would still be lying there, just as I had left her, and that was going to be as great a celebration as I could imagine, even if she didn't know she was celebrating with me. After devouring the soup, I took a shower and shaved, trying my best to make my appearance match what it was when I stepped into the chamber. My hair had grown slightly, but not enough to make me believe Trish would notice.

I stepped out of the chamber door, and I knew that when the door was pulled closed, the world, with all of its otherwise unnoticeable sounds, would come crashing into me. That feeling of having the world suddenly come back to life was what I began to refer to as the wave. Of course, no one would ever hear me talk about the wave because I had promised never to mention the chamber to anyone. But when I stepped daringly back into the world of the ticking clock and that sensation came over me, the wave was the name I had for it. I had come to know from experience that the longer the time session in the chamber, the larger and more overwhelming the wave would feel. The door was just inches away from its freestanding frame as I clinched every muscle in body in anticipation of the oncoming wave. This would be the kind of wave that could level entire cities, amplified by the longest absence I had ever had away from the world of the ticking clock. Luckily, I chose to begin this work session at a relatively quiet time of night, so it didn't take long for me to acclimate myself to the seemingly foreign world of commonplace sounds and sensations.

Feeling tired and satisfied, I put on the sweatpants and the shirt that were waiting for me by the bathroom door, still chuckling at the many naked days I spent completely absorbed by the task of finishing my book. I was so tired and ready to get back into bed with Trish that I didn't know or care if I had put these clothes on backwards or inside out. When I stepped back into the bedroom, there she was, as beautiful and peaceful as she was the moment I left. It is a fact that baffles me to this day, because no woman will ever believe that she is beautiful when asleep. I knew that fact to be true in that moment, standing there in my bedroom doorway. As badly as I wanted to wake her up just to hear her voice, I couldn't bring myself to disturb her. As the smell of her hair became the only thing worthy of my attention, I realized the single greatest irony of living with the time chamber. I could freeze any moment I wanted and stay as long as I wanted while working and moving toward any aspiration I deemed worth my effort. But she was my greatest aspiration, and I wanted to freeze that moment and let the rest of the world go by without me.

Chapter 16

When Trish and I awoke the next morning tangled in each other's arms, I took in every iota of her attention like I was drowning and she was my oxygen. Our idle conversations began as soon as we awoke, continued through breakfast, and carried through into our preparations to meet the day. Although our hands were busied with gathering our belongings and changing clothes, our minds were fixed solely on each other. Trish told me everything she needed to accomplish that day at the bookstore, and I was spouting out random details about meetings and deadlines. I was putting on my shirt when I noticed Trish eyeballing my day planner.

"You've started to keep a lot of notes," she said.

I knew that I had to be careful with my response. I was never really a note-taker before, and I seldom wrote out lists of any kind, so the day planner was definitely a deviation from my usual tendencies. "Yeah," I replied. "I've been trying to be more organized. I've got a lot of stuff to remember nowadays."

Almost simultaneously our eyes shifted to what I had to do on that particular day. "Oh, yeah," she said. "Today is the day you set the deadline for all the writers."

"Yes, it is," I responded. The long absence in the chamber almost allowed me to forget the deadline altogether. I had edited all of the writing that was sent to me the evening before, and there were only a few pieces left to be submitted, some of which I knew would come right down to the last minute.

"You think it's going to work?" Trish asked, making a deliberate effort to take an interest in my daily work.

"We'll see how it goes." The assertive, audacious me that was born in the time chamber hated that answer. I knew exactly what I was going to do if my deadline wasn't met, and that meek, uncertain answer almost made me cringe.

"You'd better be ready to lay down the law."

I chuckled at this, but her retort was something of a turn on. Trish was never really afraid to be blunt, but this sort of take-charge attitude intrigued my newfound brazenness. She then gave me this sort of half-serious, half-joking smile that was just too flirtatious for me to ignore. I leaned in toward her, hoping for the kind of physical exchange that we usually would have in the back room of her bookstore. But just as I leaned in, she kissed me on the cheek and then pulled away.

"Never took you for a tease." I didn't want to show it, but she could have had me eating out of her hand.

"I'm just full of surprises."

These kinds of playful and coquettish interplays overcame the rest of the morning routine until finally we were wrapped around each other just before making it to the door out of my apartment. Although it didn't feel like it lasted long, our little make out was long enough to put me a few minutes behind schedule in getting to work. I certainly didn't mind, as that kind of romantic interaction gave even more bounce to my step as I entered the office.

The first thing I had to do when I got into the bullpen-style atrium was distribute all the work I had edited. All but three desks received a printed copy of one article or another, each of which were covered with my red-ink revisions. It was eight thirty, which meant the last three submissions had little time to either land on my desk or arrive in my email. The first arrived at 8:35 a.m. It was Marcus's piece for our sports section. I knew this one would come right down to the wire because Marcus was covering a basketball game that ended late the night before. The second submission came at 8:50 a.m. This submission was from Eddie, a new staff writer whose hiring came from my personal recommendation, and I knew that this article would come in at the last minute because he was the kind of writer who would take as much time as humanly possible to perfect even the slightest detail of his work. I was somewhat surprised that he was able to submit his work almost two hours before the eleven o'clock deadline. These two submissions meant that there was only one person who would inevitably fail to meet my demands.

I printed and began to revise the last two columns with my red pen. Usually, I would reserve this sort of task for a quick stint in the time chamber. However, in this case I was more focused on watching each passing minute on the clock, seeing how long it would take my one problem child to get his work on my desk. While my red pen made its marks on every page of the new printed material, my eyes constantly shifted up toward the clock. Fifteen minutes came to pass after the deadline. Then it was forty-five minutes. At roughly eleven thirty, just as I was filling out some paperwork at my desk, in walked Jim Bernstandt, the one and only writer at the Falcon who had failed to meet my deadline. As he was taking a seat at his desk, I marched directly toward him.

I knew that he was going to try to brush off the new policy I was putting in place. Although I would have felt justified in immediately reprimanding him, I wanted to at least appear cordial in front of the other writers in the office. I began with the most diplomatic tone I could muster.

"Hello, Jim. I was just looking through all the articles that were sent to me, and I realized that I hadn't gotten one from you. The deadline was eleven o'clock. Do you have something for me?"

There was a pause, and I could tell that Jim was trying to read me. Finally, he snickered. "Yeah, I know about your deadline. Rick never set one, and so you know what? You can play boss all you want, but I'll get you my work whenever I damn well please."

I could have responded to Bernstandt man to man; I could have taken the higher road and told him to speak with me in my office. I wasn't willing to do that. His retort to my simple inquiry was just loud enough to come across as some sort of grandstanding, and I was not about to be upstaged.

"Everyone," I shouted, while pounding on good ole Jimbo's desk, "I'd like to start off by thanking all of you for responding so well to the new deadline. I'm pleased to announce that almost everyone in the office was able to get their work to me well in time, and because of this, all but one of you have received your work back with some suggestions from me, and we now have until next Wednesday to make our work better than ever."

Most of the office apparently didn't hear Jim's act of defiance, but I was speaking loud enough to make every single one of them my audience. "Now I say 'most of you' because there was only one person who couldn't pull his head out of his ass long enough to meet the deadline. That man was our own food-and-dining contributor." I gestured toward Bernstandt's desk and made it deliberately clear I was going to make an example out of him. "Now I've wondered for a long time why this magazine, which has reached national syndication, even needs a food-and-dining section. I mean, why on earth would someone in Tampa Bay want to read Chicago restaurant reviews? Nonetheless, Rick made the decision to keep him here, and since I respect Rick, we will continue to carry his deadweight. We are only as strong as our weakest link, and now we know who that is. I mean, for God's sake, how hard can it be to write about *food*?!"

By then, my tone of voice had reached a full, domineering shout. Not only was I speaking to a roomful of wide eyes and dropped jaws, but I even noticed Rick coming out of his private office with a horrified look on his face. That was when I upped the ante. "Jim, you either get your submission to me today, or you can pack up your desk."

"You son of a—" Bernstandt was so flabbergasted that he could hardly put a sentence together. "Rick, he can't do this."

For a moment, every eye in the room shifted to Rick. Normally, a behind-the-scenes kind of leader, Rick hated this direct attention. He looked back and forth between Bernstandt and me, and I could see the conflict begin to contort his face. Finally, I shrugged in his direction, as though there was only one way he could respond. Deep within me, I was unsure which way he would go. He had expressed concern about my new deadline, and now he was being stuck with helping me to enforce it. Had I not been so incensed with Bernstandt, I would have felt more remorse for putting him in this position.

Rick noticeably shifted his position away from me and faced Bernstandt as he said, "Jim, Eric's the editor now. It's his place to make these decisions, and I will stand by them. Submit your writing by the end of the day."

As Jimbo sat down grumbling at his desk, I walked back to my office feeling satisfied. I could hear footsteps behind me but felt the need to act as though I didn't notice them. Just seconds after I sat down in my office, Rick followed me in and closed the door.

"What the hell was that?" He was visibly frustrated, and yet I sat looking almost cold and lifeless in my responses.

"Jim is deadweight, and I want him to know it."

"So that's how you're going to assert authority around here—by loudly berating anyone who questions you?"

"Since you've put me in this position, it seems the only one who has questioned me has been Jim, so I doubt it will be a problem." Although the old Eric McHayden would have shuddered at this kind of confrontation, the new one seemed perfectly calm and confident, as the responses rolled off my tongue in a matter-of-fact sort of tone.

"Eric, I have every confidence that you can run this magazine, but I must say I don't like the way you're doing things."

"Really?" My cold, emotionless responses were becoming more and more pompous with each and every word. "Did you like the way I did things when my columns were what made this magazine take off? Did you like the way I did things when I hired four new writers that have come to be four of the most productive workers in this office?"

"Hold on a minute." Rick was obviously taken aback.

"No, Rick, this is the way I go about business. Now I get that you started this, but I've become the brains of the operation. I'm going to take this little magazine and make it something bigger, and I'm going to do it one way or the other. And Bernstandt, well, he's just learned not to get in my way."

At this, Rick was shocked, and he knew that he couldn't exactly reprimand me, having just backed me up in front of the entire office. He also knew that I was right. My columns were what helped the Falcon get the recognition, and with the Gastineux biography on its way toward publication, letting me go would cost the Falcon its biggest name. I was his discovery, and he knew that. I hated sounding so ungrateful, but at the same time, my ambitions to build my own success story had become my sole focus.

It pained me a little to have this sort of abrasive dialogue with Rick, but at the time, it seemed like the ends would eventually justify the means. Mercifully, my phone began to ring, which gave us a chance to end the conversation without any more unpleasantness.

"I'm sorry Rick, I have to take this," I said. Rick nodded, and then I was alone in my office.

The voice at the other end of the line was William, who seemed to be elated with the news that I had completed the biography. I then gave him the news that I had also given the work a long and thorough edit, to which William responded, "Good lord, boy, do you ever sleep?"

With this, I responded, "Not if I can help it."

We began to make plans to push this work along the road to publication. William had already contacted an agent who would be more than willing to promote the manuscript, and we agreed that the three of us would meet on Monday morning. After some idle small talk, William and I exchanged a mutual feeling of excitement, and I suddenly had yet another big milestone waiting just on the horizon.

With the benefit of the chamber, I made the following weekend as productive as possible. I chose to do as much work as possible in the world of the ticking clock because I was so excited for the meeting on Monday that I didn't want to prolong the wait any longer than I absolutely had to. I spent most of the weekend giving ample editing and revision time to my second novel. If I had a good feeling about this agent that William found, there was a great chance I would be dropping a little bit more than just one biography on his desk. It was that weekend that I found the best use of the chamber. I would use it not for long marathons of productivity, but instead I utilized it in a way that would add just a few good hours of work to each day. Thus, I was able to wake up rested, refreshed, and ambitious, and I was able to go to bed with such a sense of pride that I drifted off to sleep with a smile on my face.

Trish spent Sunday night at my apartment, and I was able to surprise her with the fully written and revised first novel. I wanted to show her the second, but I felt like having that much work done would only provoke suspicion. I had never mentioned the second novel, and it seemed too farfetched that I would be able to fit a whole other book into my already busy schedule without some sort of trickery or deceit. I enjoyed every moment of having Trish with me that night. She seemed more than intrigued by the next morning's meeting with William and the literary agent, and I found that I was spending most of that evening answering her questions.

The next morning, I awoke just minutes before Trish and used the time chamber to get in a full morning routine. This took some preparation, as I made sure that my suit was ready and waiting for me, hanging on a valet that I bought for the chamber for these sorts of occasions. I did just enough of a workout to get my blood pumping and then showered and made sure I looked my absolute best. After I left the chamber, I started breakfast, and soon after, Trish came out of the bedroom to join me.

"I swear," she said, "you've developed this habit of getting your whole day started while I'm still asleep. I'm starting to feel lazy."

"I like getting a head start so I can have your coffee ready."

"And I love going to work and bragging about a boyfriend who makes me coffee."

I could tell that Trish was doing everything in her power to boost my confidence. I wasn't particularly nervous about this meeting, even though it meant that as many as three of my rather large projects would either see acceptance or denial. Trish, on the other hand, was a ball of anxiety. While she was putting on her clothes, she stopped dead to look over her shoulder and tell me, "I'm so excited. Aren't you? This is a big day for you."

"It's a big day for us," I responded.

Through everything I had accomplished, Trish was the only one with whom I wanted to share my victories. She smiled at me to show she understood, and I checked my courier bag. The chamber sat in its usual hiding place, and the other compartment had three bulky printed documents. I was excited to get these to the agent, if only just to no longer have to bear their weight. Trish and I walked down the stairs and exited the apartment building, and I accompanied her to her car. She had somehow managed to get the ideal parking space right next to the curb in front of my building, and at the last minute, she offered, "Do you need a ride somewhere?"

It was amazing timing, the kind I knew I would enjoy only a few times in my entire life, but just as she made this offer, a long stretch limousine turned the corner and stopped right in front of us. William had told me that he would be picking me up, and he said that he had arranged this rather luxurious means of travel, but I never thought it would give me such a chance to show off. "It's okay." I grinned. "I have a ride of my own."

With a rather impressed smile, Trish called out to me as I got into the limo, "Good luck, rock star."

William, who was sitting in the car waiting for me, threw a wave to Trish, and we were off. Much like Trish had been all morning, William was almost twitching with excitement.

"Relax, William." I was almost surprised at the fact that I was the only one who didn't appear to be on the verge of explosion. "They're going to love it."

"I sure hope so." William chuckled. "I must say, I'm a little nervous about having my story put out there for everyone to see."

"You're one of the greatest minds of our time. This book is going to fly off the racks."

"Well, I must say, it's written really well." William was nobody's cheerleader, so I took his compliments seriously. "I enjoyed reading it so much I almost forgot that I was the one who lived it."

The ride to the agent's office was pleasant. The entire meeting felt like something of a blur, and before I knew it, my bag was three manuscripts lighter than it was an hour before, and I had what could be years' worth of writing potentially on its way toward publication. When the whirlwind of activity finally slowed down, I was sitting back in William's limousine once again, and William was ranting and raving about the "overwhelming success" that I was supposedly on my way to becoming.

As much as William's encouragement meant to me, I could only halfway pay attention. I had just put three books on the path to publication, and my mind was racing with plans for what I was going to do next. I had been working in sprints, and now it was time to plan the marathon. As I was texting Trish the details of the meeting, I had to drop the bomb about getting not only the biography but also two novels in the hands of the literary agent. She was as supportive and encouraging as ever, and I took a moment to note that the success didn't feel complete until I got to speak with her. I knew I would eventually have to spin some sort of fiction about the origin of the second novel, so in the back of my mind, I started to conjure up a story about this project being started years before and completed on a whim in little fits and starts.

When we arrived at my apartment, I realized that the small one-bedroom home, although comfortable, was no longer anywhere near the proportions of the life I wanted to live. I had already upgraded my wardrobe, and the time chamber allowed me to upgrade my physical appearance. Thus, I decided that a change in habitat would be enough to complete my transformation. I took a moment to quietly appraise all I had accomplished and decided that every facet of my life still needed to get bigger.

Chapter 17

About a year came and went after that meeting with the literary agent, and in every way, my life began to hurtle forward. The publication of the biography gave me a marketable name, which added even more attention to the two novels. My new agent was able to brilliantly market these works, and the release dates came to pass like small holidays. By going into the chamber once a week and writing for the equivalent of one day, I was able to quickly complete, edit, and prepare yet another book for publication. Meanwhile, the proceeds from the first three books filled my bank account to the extent that I could live like modern-day royalty.

I moved out of my small one bedroom home and into a palatial three-bedroom penthouse apartment that the overlooked the city. I carefully chose the location of this new place, as it sat almost equidistant between the Falcon building and Trish's bookstore. The sheer convenience of having a place to rest her head closer to work made it commonplace for Trish to stay at my place. Eventually, my home became our home, and we loved coming back to each other every night. Of course, our cohabitation made my concealment of the time chamber all the more difficult. I constructed a small, imperceptible compartment in the bathroom underneath the counter, and I kept my courier bag in places that Trish would seldom look. It became difficult to plan long work sessions in the chamber because I had to find a time to conceal the rations. At the same time, I loved using the chamber even more when I knew Trish would be right there when I returned. The more I had to make a deliberate effort to hide the chamber, however, the more guilt I often felt to keep such a huge part of my life hidden from her.

It was a warm April Friday morning when I walked into the Falcon office for just another day's work. I had come to make a routine out of using Friday mornings to edit all of the articles in one chamber work session. The eleven o'clock deadline became a commonly accepted policy around the office, and the one tirade was all it took to get Bernstandt to acquiesce to my demands. Although he followed my orders rather predictably, ole Jimbo always looked at me with absolute disdain, as if he was waiting for me to commit one big screwup, and then he would be the one to make sure I'd get driven out of my job. It was an almost common occurrence for me to find him eavesdropping outside my office or asking the other writers questions about me, hoping to find that I was stealing money or sleeping with one of the interns. Of course, I never committed any of these offenses, and I almost cruelly let him go on with hopes that he could be the one to bring me down.

Meanwhile, Rick had become the human equivalent of the mission statement we kept hanging on the back office wall. He always had been and always would be a revered and respected part of the business, but his role in the day-to-day business had been mitigated down to where he just sat in his office looking over financial statements and was often ignored as though he was a potted plant or underutilized piece of furniture. Rick's first and biggest mistake was showing me that I could easily overpower him, and this became the new modus operandi whenever I wanted to make changes in the way we did business.

I often regretted how I would so frequently manipulate Rick, but he made such a habit out of deferring to me that it got to the point that I spoke more than he did at staff and investor meetings. The Falcon's newly expanded staff involved five more writers that I handpicked, and Rick barely spoke a word, even though personnel decisions were the one area where he took the most pride as a manager. I also made almost every decision regarding resource allocation and distribution channels. All the while, my two closest compatriots were Marcus and Steven, and the three of us had developed something of a brotherhood. Whenever I made decisions, no matter how potentially disagreeable they may have been, their support heightened my already enormous sense of confidence and resolve.

That particular Friday morning was like almost any other, as I did my usual time-chamber revision and then spoke directly with any writer whom I felt needed some direct guidance. For the rest of the afternoon, I sat at my desk attending to regular tasks and answering any questions from the writers who were making my recommended changes. One writer, Eddie, was one of my handpicked writers and had written yet another column that managed to pique my interest. He had done some research on a new ammunition manufacturer that was developing a bullet that improved on the decades-old hollow-point munitions. The science itself was intriguing, but the problem was that the article was written in such scientific language that I was afraid the average reader wouldn't be able to understand it.

When Eddie walked into my office, he carried that same pensive demeanor that I once had when I walked into Rick's office to talk over a submission.

"Sit down," I said with as welcoming a tone as I could.

Eddie clumsily took a seat at my desk and struggled to put together the wording of his question. "Was there something wrong with what I wrote?"

"The science is fascinating," I retorted, "but the writing could be simplified a little bit."

"How so?"

"Well, let's try it this way. What is a hollow-point bullet?"

"It's a round of ammunition that is designed to have a gap in its tip so that it basically collapses when it collides with its target."

"Why should I care?"

"Well, considering that guns have become somewhat common in our society, it is important to know what kind of ammunition is being used."

"Because?" My inquiries were becoming somewhat combative, but I really wanted Eddie to find where I was going on his own.

"Because..." Eddie seemed puzzled at why he was finding himself explaining this to me. "The major difference between a hollow point and basic full-metal jacket is that it usually stops dead once it hits its target. This is arguably better because it doesn't penetrate or ricochet, which means the person firing the gun has less reason to worry about stray bullets."

"But the problem is?"

"Well, the problem is that although hollow-point bullets are attractive because they won't go through their target and hit someone or something else, they do much more damage to whatever, or whoever, they hit."

"So now, tell me about this new technology."

Eddie's confidence began to show. He had researched this topic extensively, and I could tell he knew every detail inside and out. "Well, AGR, the ammunition company in my column, makes nothing but hollow-point bullets and is trying to develop a new bullet that is designed to have the stopping power of a hollow-point round but will do less damage."

"Basically these new bullets would be able to stop when they hit a target without blowing it to pieces."

"Yeah. That's essentially how it works."

I could tell that the intended light bulb had been set off in Eddie's mind. "You see, that was simple. This article tells a great story, but you make it sound much more complicated than it really is. I've made a couple of comments on your work. Dumb it down, and I think it will really get people interested."

"Did you like the part about the inscription on the bullets?"

"To be honest, I really didn't see where you were going with that."

"I just found it interesting that a company would want to so easily create an identifier for the bullets they manufacture. For instance, if a gang or something got their hands on a bunch of AGR bullets, that would only create a PR nightmare."

Although my first instinct was not to show it, I was truly impressed. "I like the angle," I said. "Try to write a little more about that sort of stuff, and leave the crazy science to other publications."

"All right. Thanks, Eric." Eddie left and was immediately back to work.

I liked giving that kind of guidance to my writers; it felt like an exercise of power and helped me put my own fingerprint on every article that we printed. Feeling like I had truly accomplished something, I began to pack my bag and make my departure from the Falcon office. Trish and I were throwing a party that night for some of our new high-society friends. I wanted to invite Marcus and Stephen to the party, but Stephen was nowhere to be found.

After accepting my invitation, Marcus told me that Stephen had some sort of family function and would be working late that evening. I wanted to call Stephen and tell him that he was more than welcome to put the work off and join in the festivities, but I knew that he would be terrified of going to this sort of social function. Although he and Lauren were several months into becoming a well-matched couple, Stephen still carried with him a considerable number of social phobias.

With the day's work behind me, my next focus was to prepare for the party that evening. Trish had left the bookstore to one of her sisters that day and had organized most of the details for that evening. Between the overwhelming success of her expanded bookstore and my literary endeavors, we suddenly seemed to have more money and influence than we knew how to use, and we began doing things like throwing parties and having dinner guests because "that just seems like something successful people do." When I arrived, Trish was opening bottles of wine and laying out cheese trays, wearing a dress that guaranteed no matter what occurred that evening, my eyes would always be on her.

I offered to provide assistance, but when it became readily apparent that I was just going to get in the way, I assumed a position on the couch with an open beer and found a basketball game on TV. When Trish was finished with all the preparations, her focus shifted directly to me.

"Our guests should be getting here soon," she said.

I could tell by her tone that she meant that some sort of action was required on my part, but since I didn't know what that was, I relied on the kind of obliviousness that only men can get away with. "Awesome," I replied. "Everything looks great."

"Is that what you're wearing?"

"Apparently not." I chuckled as I retreated from the enormous front room into the bedroom. I swapped the wrinkled clothes from a day of work for a pair of jeans and a black sweater. This attire was dressy enough to appease our group of friends, yet not so formal as to appear pretentious. As I returned to the front room, I asked, "Does this look okay?"

"Looks great," Trish said.

"We're like a married couple." I chuckled.

With her usual half playful grin, she looked over her shoulder as she approached the front door. "Not yet," she replied with a tone that was wrought with subtext.

Before I could question where she was going with that response, the door opened, and our ostentatious home was soon full of party guests. Marcus arrived right on schedule, and the party was in full swing.

At one point in the evening, I asked Marcus to step away from the party so that I could speak with him. He agreed, and when we were having a beer behind closed doors, the conversation immediately shifted to Trish. "So I know we've talked about this," I started, "but what do you think about me and Trish?"

"I think you two are a power couple. What, with her bookstore and you kicking ass at the Falcon, you're like the new Kennedys."

"I'm glad you think so because I'm trying to find the time to give her this." I pulled a small box with an engagement ring out of a drawer that I knew Trish never opened. "You think this is a good call?"

"I think it's about damn time!" Marcus replied.

We raised our beers as he congratulated me, and I added that caveat that congratulations should be held off until Trish said yes. We then returned to the party, acting as though our little exit was just for purposes of talking shop. I spent the rest of the night carousing with Marcus and my new friends, knowing that because of the chamber, I could easily sleep off the hangover the next day.

The next morning, I arose to a screeching hangover, just as I had expected and trudged headlong into the chamber, where I would sleep off the effects of such a good night of drinking. I was able to get some writing done and then get a good shower before stepping back into the world of the ticking clock. When Trish awoke, she made some amazed comment at my ability to drink so much without spending the next day on my deathbed. I decided to let her sleep in, and when she awoke, she had a cup of coffee waiting for her on the bedside table.

At one point or another, it occurred to me that I had left my phone on the bedside table before the party and hadn't checked it since. All that waited for me were a bunch of work-related emails and one missed call from Stephen, the latter of which I assumed was just a call to check on some mundane, work-related task. I sent him a text to say that I would be available in the office on Monday morning and that I hoped he was having a good weekend. After that, I put the phone away and dedicated my entire weekend to nothing but quality time with Trish.

We spent most of the day in the quiet confines of our new palatial home, but we did go out for dinner and a movie. It was weekends like that where I could return to work and feel more energized than ever. The hazy memory of showing the ring to Marcus made me start thinking about when I would ask Trish to take the next step, but I remained steadfast in my resolution that I would do more to build my own personal empire before I asked that question. With every task, and with every accomplishment, I was getting myself one step closer to becoming the ideal man with whom Trish would want to spend the rest of her life.

Although the weekend came to a close too quickly, as most weekends tend to do, I felt ready to meet the week that lay ahead. When I arrived at work on Monday morning, there was a general nervous buzz that permeated the entire office. I could hear what seemed like hundreds of whispered frantic conversations, and when I started fishing for an explanation, Lauren was the only one who came to speak with me.

"Eric, we've been trying all weekend to get in touch with you." She seemed as though distress was wrapping a strangling hand over every word.

"What's wrong?"

"Stephen. He was leaving the Falcon office Friday night when someone attacked him. The police are saying it was an attempted robbery, but all that was taken was his cell phone."

"Where is he?"

"He's at Mercy Hospital. They released him from the ICU and into his own room yesterday."

Just as I was trying to put a few words together to console Lauren, Rick got my attention. He pulled me aside to discuss how we should respond to this incident, and I assured him that I knew exactly what we needed to do.

"Everyone!" I shouted. "I'm sure you've all heard about what happened to Stephen. I know that we have plenty of work to get done today, but Stephen is a friend to all of us, so if you'd like to take some time to process this whole thing, or even go see him, Rick and I will understand."

Rick looked at me with a look of relieved approval. I knew Rick well enough to know that this is how he would have handled the situation, but I had become the de facto leader of the organization, and it was my word that counted.

A few members of the Falcon left at various times throughout the day to go visit Stephen, and I sat in my office tending to my usual tasks. It took me until almost sundown to go visit Stephen myself, and I was horrified to see my friend lying broken and battered in a hospital bed. Stephen didn't wake up, so I decided to leave and let him get his rest. Only as I was leaving the hospital did it cross my mind that maybe what happened to Stephen had something to do with me. In most instances, the idea of these crimes being completely random can compromise the average person's sense of security, making him think, *If this could happen to anyone, why can't it happen to me?* I, on the other hand, began to shudder at the thought that I had been targeted by one violent individual, and I had no way to tell if that had anything to do with why Stephen was lying in a hospital bed.

It was that thought that demanded the entirety of my attention as I scuffled out of the hospital and toward my car. The sky outside the parking structure was growing dark, and my vehicle was one of the few within sight. Just as I opened my car door, my phone began to ring. I had to look twice at my phone to make sure my eyes weren't deceiving me. It was Stephen's name that appeared on the small touchscreen. *That can't be right*, I thought. Stephen was unconscious in his bed when I left him.

When I answered the phone, I heard, "I'm sorry your friend had to get hurt." I knew immediately that the voice on the other end of the line wasn't Stephen's. I also knew that the tone of this voice was so maniacal and malevolent that the expression of remorse was empty to the point of sarcasm. I heard that voice not only from the cell phone but also from a figure that was approaching me from twenty paces away.

"It was you," I said, doing everything I could to conceal even the slightest emotional reaction. I then lowered the phone and turned toward the caller, who was approaching me with a deliberate and resolved stride. Although I had only actually heard that voice one time, I knew that walk and I recognized the figure. There was Billy, approaching me with the same knife that I had seen once before.

"I was looking for you Friday night, and I happened to overhear your friend trying to get ahold of you. He was just in the wrong place at the wrong time."

"If you have an issue with me, that's fine." I could tell from where he was standing, he couldn't see my hand that hung between my torso and the car. That hand was beginning to drift slowly into the courier bag and wrap around the handle of the small snub-nosed pistol. "What did Stephen do to deserve that?"

"I asked him where to find you. I think he knew what I had in mind, and he wouldn't give you up!" Billy shouted. "By the way, I really enjoyed reading the texts between you and Stephen. That scrawny little shit looks up to you, you know, like a brother?"

With those words, I couldn't help but think of Jason, Billy's own brother, who lay decaying in a time chamber not unlike my own. It was that image that revealed to me exactly what Billy had in mind. Michael took his brother, and Billy was going to make him pay. But first, he was going to punish anyone who benefited from Michael's chamber, and Stephen got in his way. As Billy was about to continue his tirade, I was able to get the handle of the gun out from the courier bag. I had questioned whether or not I would be able to actually pull the trigger if this situation ever occurred. I might not have had it not been for the next words to come out of Billy's mouth.

"You see, I was going to find you one way or another. Since that sniveling little prick wasn't willing to give you up, my next step was going to be that blonde I always see you with. She looks like a great piece of—"

That was too much. I would later want to tell myself that I was enraged at Billy for hurting my friend or that even the suggestion of hurting Trish was enough to make me pull the trigger. In reality, while those two things did make me feel justified in what I did next, the real reason was that I couldn't handle Billy acting like he had won something. Right until the minute I put a bullet in his forehead, he was acting like he had the better of me, and the one impetus that got from thinking about shooting him to actually pulling the trigger was that I just couldn't stand being taunted.

No matter what my motivation was, just a moment later, Billy was lying lifeless on the concrete.

Chapter 18

After the echo of the gunshot subsided, I began to move with what would have appeared to be a frantic sense of urgency. The thought that I had just killed a human being—although I wasn't quite ready to call myself a murderer—should have stunted my ability to think clearly and recognize important details. Instead, I immediately realized that the time chamber could give me a unique advantage in the concealment of what I had just done. Only mere seconds had elapsed from the sound of the gunshot, so I knew that I could easily survey the surrounding area to see if there was any chance of getting caught.

I began to sprint from one end of the parking structure to another, looking to see if there was anyone responding to the sound of the gun. When no such bystander could be found, I then returned to what I could only describe as the scene of the crime to begin covering my tracks. First, I scanned the area to see if any security cameras were present. When none were apparent, I began to a haul Billy's enormous body toward my car and then proceeded to stuff him in my trunk. I knew there was nothing I could do about the rather large puddle of blood in the parking lot, and even if I could, the top priority was to get away from the scene as quickly as possible. Once Billy was in the trunk, it then occurred to me that I had at least water that could be used to clear the bloodstain.

I found a mop bucket in the time chamber and filled it with water, then stepped back into the world of the ticking clock to dump the bucket over the stain. The remaining result was a wide puddle that could be much more easily overlooked. Not perfect, but it would have to do, so I deactivated the chamber and placed the device back inside the courier bag. As I drove away, a sense of relief began to come over me with every block I covered without seeing blue and red lights in my rearview mirror.

The only logical destination I could decide upon was Michael's home. He was the only one who could help, or even understand, the predicament that I had found myself in. As I began to turn and weave through the quiet neighborhoods, an odd mix of panic and guilt began to overcome me. My heart began racing, and sweat began to roll down my forehead. I tried my best not to think about Billy as a person who may or may not have had a family, instead trying to frame him as a rabid animal that had to be put down. Knowing that I was taking him to the same house where his brother was decaying in a lonely bed only made Billy's human nature more undeniable.

When Michael came to the door, he made some comment about how pale I was, but I was in no state to take in words, let alone intelligently answer questions. "Billy!" I gasped, having to sound like some wild animal in fight-flight response.

"What about him?"

"He's in my trunk. I killed him!"

I couldn't tell if the moisture running down my face was sweat, tears, or some panicked combination of the two. Michael pulled me inside and forced me to sit down. He told me to breathe and then compose myself. Eventually I was able to put sentences together, and after that, the whole narrative of my run-in with Billy in the parking lot was laid out in details that I was in no mood to conceal.

"Okay, give me your keys, and I'll pull your car into the garage." With those words, Michael's soothing demeanor turned cold and deliberate.

"What are we going to do?"

"You just wait here."

With my keys in hand, Michael stepped outside. I could hear the garage door open and the sound of my car being driven into the two-car garage. I then heard some rumblings, and in a matter of minutes, I could see Michael dragging Billy's corpse across the kitchen floor.

"Help me with this," he said in a hushed tone.

Without asking a question, I took hold of Billy's feet so that Michael could take the head. We hauled his rather cumbersome body up the stairs until Michael gave the order to leave him on the floor of the upstairs hallway. Michael then brought his version of the time-chamber device out of a bedroom and placed it on the floor right next to Billy's torso. He pushed the little blue button, and the world of the ticking clock, the world in which I had just become a murderer, came to a screeching halt.

In a startling break of the silence and stillness, Michael spoke for what felt like the first time in ages. "Jason has been asking me to do what I'm about to do for the last few weeks. I never thought I would have to do it like this."

Michael gestured for me to follow him into Jason's own time chamber. In the much smaller space, I could see Jason's feet just around the doorframe. Michael stepped into that bedroom, pulled the pillow out from beneath Jason's head, and then, with a pained, apologetic look in his eyes, shut the bedroom door. He and Jason were now alone in a room within a room where time stood still, where I would be the only one who would hear or see what was about to happen. Through the door, I could hear a muffled yell and then absolute silence. The bedroom door opened just moments later, and

Michael stepped out while wiping a tear from beneath his eye. He then cleared his throat as though to collect himself, and we were both back to work.

At first, I blindly followed Michael's lead, not knowing what our next move was going to be, but soon it all became gruesomely clear. The time chamber existed outside the normal parameters of time and space. Only living beings had the power to pull themselves in and out of this sanctum, and thus, this original time chamber was about to become the tomb for both Jason and his brother. We pulled Billy's body into the chamber and sat it on the floor next to Jason's bed. We then stepped outside the chamber, and Michael reached out to grab the door. He closed it most of the way, and then there was a pause. In a movement that could only be compared to throwing a handful of soil at a burial, he pressed the door against its frame. The wavelike feeling came over me as it always did, but in the dark, lonely hours of the night, the world of the ticking clock seemed just as unsettlingly still.

"It's done, Eric," he said. I couldn't tell if Michael was trying to convince me or himself. "You just go on home, and I'll bury the chamber." He handed me the keys to my car and gave an assurance that he would take care of all the gruesome details from then on out. I didn't know what to say, so I just turned away and began to walk down the stairs and out the front door. Just before I could make my exit, Michael said one more thing. "This had to be done. I'm just sorry you had to do it."

"I..." Unable to complete even the simplest of thoughts, I pulled the small snub-nosed revolver out of my pocket and placed it on the end table.

"Good thinking, Eric. He's gone now. You don't need it anymore."

"You don't get it, do you? I killed someone tonight! That's not who I am." My voice was cracking with hysteria, and my words came out in frenzied barks.

"It's not what I intended for either of us. But you have to understand. It was either going to be you or him. You did what you had to do."

Realizing that no words were going to make the situation any better, I gave a halfhearted nod and then proceeded outside. The garage door opened, and I could see Michael watching from the door that led into the house. The drive home was eerily quiet, but all the sounds and sights from that evening were playing on repeat in my mind. As I rode the elevator up to my apartment, I realized that I had three missed calls from Trish. The issues of what to divulge and what to conceal began to swirl around in my head. When I opened the apartment door, Trish came rushing toward me.

"Oh, thank God!" she said. "I was getting worried about you. Are you okay? You look terrible!"

"Stephen was attacked Friday night." I couldn't muster any kind of elaborate narrative to conceal what I had been doing for the last few hours. The only thing I could do was sputter out little details that would hopefully put together a plausible story.

"I know," she said with a caring voice. "I called Marcus when you didn't come home. Is he okay?"

"They've got him under observation. I didn't really get to talk to him."

"Well, I'm sure they'll take care of him." Much like me but for entirely better reasons, Trish didn't know what to say. It seemed as though her caretaking instincts had begun to set in. "Why don't you go take a shower? Would you like a drink? Are you hungry?"

"No, I'm okay, but the shower sounds great." I smiled at her and then retreated to the bathroom.

When I peeled off my jacket, I noticed a bloodstain on my right sleeve that ran from my wrist to my elbow. I was immediately relieved that Trish hadn't noticed it, and I forced myself to take a deep breath while I started the shower. When I was done, I bundled the clothes in a way that would conceal the bloodstained shirt. I placed the rest of the clothes, which I made sure were unmarked, in the laundry and took great care to make sure that the shirt was hidden at the bottom of the trashcan in our kitchen.

I then crawled into bed, and Trish rolled over and wrapped her arms around me. Her embrace could do more to ease my troubled soul than any words, gift, or action from anyone else in the world. Across the room, in a drawer filled with notebooks and mismatched remote controls, sat the ring that I was waiting to give to her. Just a few hours ago, I was busying myself with building my own personal empire, and when it was finished, then and only then would I feel okay about asking her to marry me. I wanted to offer her the best version of myself, and I couldn't let what had occurred in the last few hours distract me from that ultimate goal.

That was when the justifications for my actions started to flood my thoughts. Billy had it coming, that sadistic maniac. Michael was right; I didn't choose to put myself in that position. I was acting in self-defense, and maybe someday when I told Trish this story, she would understand. And Jason, why was I feeling so sorry for him? He and I were both given the same opportunity; one of us made a huge success of himself, and the other lost his mind. I was on my way to big things, and this wasn't going to slow me down. Between my ability to rationalize just about anything and the warmth of Trish's presence, I was able to drift off to sleep, knowing that it would only take time for me to feel normal again.

The next day came way too fast for my liking, and that was a time where the chamber-aided morning definitely came in handy. I was able to get in a good workout to make sure I was caught up on my work and then took a long hot shower. There were no dead brothers in that chamber. No, this was a winner's inner sanctum, and although I was still a little shaky from the night before, I started feeling better with every single move. I then proceeded out of the time chamber and into the bathroom of my spacious apartment in the world of the ticking clock. I put on my favorite shirt and tie and even set aside a few more minutes to make my hair look just right. "Look at that guy," I said to myself. "He wouldn't kill anyone that didn't deserve it."

The rest of the morning was almost morbidly pleasant, considering the horrendous evening before. Trish had started making breakfast, and on our way to the ground floor, we put on something of a risqué show for the elevator security camera. I marched into the Falcon office ready to take on any foreseeable challenge. I expected at first that the horrific images from the night before would come crashing forward in numerous flashbacks, but to my surprise, I was able to remain focused and efficient. Of course, there was the worry that I had left some sort of evidence in the parking structure, and this worry was accompanied by the concern that at any given moment, the police could come walking into my office. However, I was able to think myself out of this worry. I left nothing there that could directly identify me, there were no security cameras watching the parking lot, and it would be rather difficult for the police to prove any violence occurred when the victim was in a time chamber buried in Michael's backyard.

One day went by, and then another, and soon the days blended into a week. I noticed after about five days that I hadn't seen Jim. He was my one sole adversary in that office, and his absence made the days feel all the more pleasant and free of distraction. I decided that I wouldn't even bother to ask where he was or why he wasn't working. I wasn't going to waste a moment of my concern on him; I had too much to accomplish. If he didn't get an article in by the deadline, then the Falcon would print without a food-and-dining section, and the fault would lie solely on him.

When the deadline came to pass, Rick worriedly stumbled into my office. "Eric," he mumbled, "you're going to have to leave Jim alone this week. He's having a—"

"It's all right, Rick," I said with as calm and confident a voice as I ever had. "The Falcon can run one week without a food-and-dining section. I doubt anyone will notice."

There was a feeling of revenge in this decision. At first, I made ole Jimbo pay by loudly and angrily berating him in front of the entire office. While that got my message through loud and clear, I knew what would really get under Bernstandt's skin whenever he decided to come back to work was that I was slowly but surely making him irrelevant.

Meanwhile, I started making decisions that were growing the Falcon into an absolute powerhouse. In one day's work, I started talking with some of our writers about making small video columns, which we would broadcast on the Falcon's website. When Rick asked me about why I was doing this, I mentioned the possibility that our blockbuster news magazine might start branching out into other mediums, like radio and television. Rick was concerned, and justifiably so, because these were the sort of decisions that he believed were subject to his discretion.

"This isn't what I had in mind, Eric. I started the Falcon because I believed in good, honest, print journalism, and I hired you because I thought you believed in that too."

"I do, Rick," I responded in a tone that was both calm and dismissive. "And that's not changing, but you've got to stop thinking small."

As Rick stormed flabbergasted out of my office, I knew then more than ever that I was going to have to build up the Falcon with or without his support. Using the chamber had turned me into something bigger and better than I could have ever imagined, and the rest of the world could either go along or get out of my way. After a week of absence, I received word from Rick that Jim had quit his job at the Falcon. When I responded in a blithe, dismissive remark, that was when Rick dropped the bombshell.

"I'm leaving too, Eric."

"What? Rick, you started this place. Who's going to manage the place with you gone?"

"You! Who else? You seem to be the one who makes all the decisions around here." Rick could tell that a pang of guilt was beginning to come over me. "I get it now," he said. "I'm a relic. You, on the other hand, are taking this business to new heights. You're made to run this place, and I'm sure you'll do great things with it."

Although I could tell it was killing Rick to let go and leave the Falcon behind, I couldn't ignore the fact that the Falcon was suddenly under my control. In a whirlwind of events, obstacles were being knocked one by one out of my path. Although I cared about Rick, he was too conservative in his vision for the business. Jim was outright defiant, and he was on his way out the door. Billy wanted to take everything from me, and he was dead and buried. There was nothing that could stand in my way.

My biggest fear was that the guilt from having killed Billy would be enough to ruin me. Within less than a month, my new, zealous persona, the power-hungry dynamo that could only be born in the chamber, was back and bigger than ever. This fearless figure felt a morbid sense of pride for having killed Billy. The idea that my victim was a living, breathing person no longer bothered me. In fact, it was in that moment that it occurred to me that I hardly knew anything about Billy other than the fact that he was undoubtedly insane.

Although the moment was bittersweet, I helped Rick pack up his office. He slowly and affectionately said good-bye to everyone working in the office, even the new hires that he barely knew. The whole office wished him well, and at one point, I could've sworn he had a tear in his eye as he told them the Falcon would be better off under my direction. Just before walking out the door, he turned to give a somewhat unceremonious impromptu retirement speech.

"Everyone, I know this is sudden, but now is the time I leave the Falcon and ride off into the sunset. Eric will be taking over for me, and I can honestly say that I couldn't be leaving it in better hands. I now have a long retirement to look forward to and know that I'll still be reading your work every week." Rick then departed with a warm applause and well wishes from everyone in the office. I walked him to the elevator and then out the building's front door.

"Look," I said just as he began to load his car, "I'm sorry if I'm the reason you—"

Rick cut me off midsentence. "Don't worry about it. I may not have always agreed with you, but just know that I'm proud of what you've been able to accomplish."

After that, all we needed was a warm yet bittersweet handshake, and Rick drove off. I was almost shaking with excitement, as I used the elevator ride to call Trish and tell her that Rick was retiring and now the Falcon was mine. I could tell that not everyone was pleased Rick was gone, but all in all, the energy in the room still felt overwhelmingly positive. My next call was to Michael, and that call would take place in my office behind closed doors.

"That's wonderful!" Michael said upon hearing the news. "Sounds like things are really shaping up in your favor."

"They sure are." I then felt an awkward silence take over our conversation; there was still a proverbial elephant in the room. "By the way," I added, as though my next question was some minor detail, "what was Billy's last name?"

"Come on, what does that matter? He's gone."

"No, dammit!" I hissed. "Consider everything that happened, I think I should at least know this man's name." There wasn't one iota of guilt or remorse that was driving that question. By then, I was resolved that Billy deserved what he got, and these questions were sheer morbid curiosity.

"Are you sure you want to know?"

"Positive. Now for the love of God, this guy had to have a last name, and I want know what it was."

"Fine. The kid's name was *Bernstandt*."

Chapter 19

It didn't take much investigative work for me to find out that the two men Michael and I had laid to rest were none other than the two sons of Jim Bernstandt, the man with whom I'd been butting heads for more than a year. It had taken a lot of persuading to convince myself that the police would never come for me, and all at once those concerns came crashing back into my mind. It wasn't just the worry that began to torment me, but with it came a bizarre form of guilt. At one time, I thought there was no misfortune that could befall Jim Bernstandt that I wouldn't welcome. At the same time, the guilt that came from ending a human life became all the more palpable upon learning that the man indeed had a family, and part of that man's family was a person who worked in my office.

Once the initial shock subsided, I then began the process of rationalization all over again. I scanned my memory to recall if there were any security cameras overlooking the parking lot. I even violated everything the movies had told me about murder and returned to the scene of the crime to verify this fact. I also knew that without a body, it would be highly improbable for anyone, Bernstandt or police included, to prove that I had done anything. Of course, there were still the remnants of a considerable yet watered-down bloodstain on the ground where I shot Billy, but there on the filthy asphalt, it was difficult for anyone to discern the blood from the large overlapping oil spot that I hadn't even noticed. It was the combination of these facts that assured me that the odds of my getting caught were near astronomical. Those facts were enough to let the worry subside, but they did very little to mitigate the guilt.

It was then that I decided staying busy was going to be the only thing that that was going to keep my racing mind at bay. I spoke with my literary agent and arranged another battery of book signings and promotional events. I began to bury myself in tasks that would help the Falcon take the next step in its evolution from a small regional news magazine to a major media powerhouse. I started scheduling meetings with investors and then worked with our newly hired web developers, who helped me set up podcasts for a few of our key journalists and staff writers. Between steering the Falcon and promoting my independent work, I was keeping my mind active enough to avoid gravitating to the feelings of guilt for any longer than the few moments of silence between meetings.

The major problem was that all these endeavors demanded that I spend most of my time interacting with other people. The chamber had helped me make the most of my time, but I couldn't use it when the work required the input of others. Thus, if there was any task that I could perform alone, even if it made the workload enormous, I elected to do that task by myself. This only furthered the perception that I was a workhorse who was bound and determined to make sure the Falcon took off, even if it meant doing alone the work of ten people.

Two weeks went by in an absolute blur. I would often find myself spending ten hours in the Falcon office just to get in all the meetings necessary to address everything that I had to accomplish. The chamber at least gave me the chance to finish my work and have the evenings to spend with Trish, but my mind was always spinning with people I needed to call and tasks that I had to complete. It got to the point that one Wednesday morning, I found myself sleeping through the alarms and waking up only twenty minutes before I had to be at the office.

That particular morning, I used the chamber to ready myself for work just as I had almost every day before. The problem was that even though I could use the chamber to collect myself and take a shower, I still was going to arrive to the Falcon office at least five minutes late. Trish was getting ready in the next room when I concealed the chamber in the courier bag, and I was in such a rush that all I could do was give her a quick kiss, and then I was hurrying out the door. It always seems that on the mornings where one is running late, every foreseeable delay would present itself, and after unusual traffic and countless red lights, I finally arrived at the Falcon to a room full of employees waiting for a staff meeting to begin.

That Wednesday, as per our routine, was the day that we set the Falcon to print. However, our national expansion added hundreds of additional concerns that made the printing days feel like endless montages of setbacks and small crises that needed my immediate attention. With the added details of trying to coordinate the online broadcasts and various other projects, I noticed the sun going down just as I was stopping to catch my breath. That was when I realized that a text message from Trish had been waiting for me for the last two hours. This brief message was a simple question about when I would be coming home, and I responded saying that I should be finished at work and back with her within the hour. In a turn of events that led me to believe that the universe had its own sense of irony, the moment I sent that text message, one of the staff writers came storming into my office.

Our normal process, which functioned like a well-oiled machine until that very day, saw its first snag. This panicked staff writer pulled up the digital copy that we used to check the layout of that week's printing. There was some glitch in the transmittal of that copy, which completely threw off the formatting of the printing. Some two thousand copies of the Falcon had already been printed with pages and pages of offset text, poorly formatted layouts, and three blank pages. A back-of-the-napkin calculation of the cost of this mix-up was enough to make my stomach hurt, but I had to act immediately to get our product ready for distribution. Thus, I spent the next three hours working with the designers and layout guys, making sure that our digital copy was back to our standards and could be passed off to print without any further disruption.

After every detail had been checked and double-checked, and I could rest assured that I had done everything in my power to correct the error, I was still left with a few more tasks that I needed to complete before I returned home. Although the chamber was a much needed aid for many of these tasks, there were two more concerns that I needed to address with two staff writers. When all was said and done, the clock was just past 11:00 p.m. before I began my commute home. When I arrived at the apartment, all the lights were turned off except for the small lamplight that shone from the back bedroom.

Although I almost overlooked it completely, I noticed a full table setting with two small candles that burned most of the way down to their holders. In the refrigerator, I found a rather large serving of cashew chicken, my favorite, sitting in Tupperware containers. It didn't take much conjecture for me to conclude that Trish had put together what would have been a quiet, unapologetically romantic dinner for two and that I had unwittingly managed to stay at work until she eventually gave up and went to bed. When I took off my clothes and crawled into bed with her, it pained me as I mumbled an apology through my fatigued voice.

"It's okay," she said. "There's always next time."

If she had yelled at me or given me the cold shoulder, perhaps I would've been able to deal with that, but her unwavering understanding was enough to send a long blade of remorse deep into my very being. I began muttering on about everything that had gone wrong at the Falcon, and all the while, she just lay listening to me with a look in her eye that told me she understood and was there to support me no matter what had happened. In an odd way, I wanted her to lash out at me. I would carry the burden of what I had done to Billy, and that burden was only made heavier by the fact that the only repercussions I could face would be the way I felt. But hurting Trish was worse, for as much as she understood, and as much as she told me I had every reason to stay late and work, I could tell that she was disappointed.

The next morning, I sent an email to everyone saying that I would not be in the Falcon office until a little bit later and used one of my classic chamber-aided morning routines to get me a jump-start on the day. I made Trish breakfast and used the rest of the morning to thank her for being so forgiving about the night before. She told me that I had no reason to apologize, but nothing she said was going to make me feel better about having let her down. That day at work was just as jam-packed with meetings as the one that came before it, and when I went home that evening, I was too tired to even put together a sentence. Trish was also fighting fatigue from a long day at the bookstore, so we just sat quietly together on the couch watching TV.

Days and weeks went on just like that, with me spending every day getting buried in work and coming home ready to do nothing more than simply collapse. Although our home life was relatively peaceful, at one point I realized that I hadn't said more than a few sentences to Trish in several days. One evening, at around 6:00 p.m., I realized that I could feasibly go home for the day and get back to the apartment just as Trish was arriving home from work. I would have to use the chamber the next morning to get myself on schedule with my work, but that wasn't what was important. All I cared about was going home and spending time with her.

When I arrived back at the apartment, Trish greeted me with a look of what struck me as suspicion. Before even saying a word, she placed the small black jewelry box on the table and asked, "What's this?"

I immediately realized that the little box held the engagement ring that I had shown to Marcus long before. I bought that ring before Stephen was attacked, before I ran Rick out of his job, and most importantly, before I became a murderer. Of all the secrets that I wanted to just let go, this was the one that I wanted most to keep hidden from her. Everything else would have been a relief to simply get off my chest, but this was one of the few good surprises that I wished could have just been given the right moment.

"It's an engagement ring. I was going to give it to you when I—"

"When what, Eric? When you finally spoke to me? You've been so focused on work that I've just gotten what's left of you when you come home."

"I know." I wanted to tell her everything, the chamber, Billy, all of it, but the best I could put together was a sorry rationale for why I was waiting to ask her to marry me. "I wanted to wait for the books to sell, for the Falcon to really take off, and then, when I was a success, I was going to ask you to marry me."

"Why does any of that matter?"

"I wanted you to know I was going to be able to give you anything you wanted."

"What do you mean? You think it was this place? The money? You think that's what you needed to get me to say yes?"

"You can't say it doesn't matter. I mean, think back. Do you remember when I couldn't even get a column done? I was in that little slum apartment and couldn't get myself through grad school.

Yeah, there's a sales pitch, asking you to spend the rest of your life with an absolute nobody."

"You were never a nobody to me."

"That's sweet," I retorted while waving my hands in a dismissive gesture. "But that wasn't good enough."

"The only person who ever thought you weren't good enough was you. I would've taken the slum apartment and to hell with grad school! If you really think that you needed anything more than who you are, then you don't know me anywhere near as well as I thought."

She stopped as tears began to well up in her eyes, and I just stood in front of her, not knowing what to say. I knew that I needed to say something. My words were being printed and sold all over the world, words that had filled entire books, but in that moment, when I tried to speak, there were no words to be found. When the silence proved too much to bear, Trish continued, "I'm going to stay with my sister for a while. Next time we speak, I don't want to hear from some big shot who thinks all this stuff matters. I want you. Until then, don't call."

Trish gathered a few of her belongings, and I stood waiting for the words to come. When they never did, Trish was gone, and I was standing alone in our apartment. That palace of a home was now as still and quiet as the chamber, and the loneliness was there waiting for me. I spent the rest of that night trying to think through what I should do next, even practicing what I would say to Trish. I must have talked myself through countless apologies and explanations, but whenever I picked up the phone to speak to her, either pride or shame stopped me from making the call. Eventually, I retired to the bedroom, hoping that sleep would bring me the promise of a brand-new day. I tossed and turned until eventually I was so exhausted that I simply gave in to a few short hours of sleep.

Only hours later, I awoke and put myself through the old debate of whether the few hours had done more harm than good. The alarm clock chimed and put me into a hell that I had all but forgotten. My almost habitual decision was to head immediately toward the chamber to get more sleep and prepare myself for the workday ahead, but the thought of freezing time was enough to make me nauseous. I realized in that moment that Trish would not be there when I got home, she wasn't going to be just a text message away to discuss even the smallest details, and I wouldn't go home to wrap my arms around her until we fell asleep. I had ruined that, and why would I want to elongate any day where I didn't have her?

Instead of using my go-to methods of giving myself a head start, I threw on the first thing I found in my closet and began my commute to the Falcon office. When I arrived, I was greeted with an onslaught of questions and concerns from the writers, but instead of my usual attentive, detail oriented responses, I gave them grunted one-word answers that left them baffled and unsatisfied. If I couldn't answer in this truncated fashion, I ignored them altogether, walking straight past them and into my office. I tried getting some work done, but my fatigued mind was nowhere near my work.

Eventually, Marcus stepped into my office and closed the door. "Are you all right, man?" he asked.

"She's gone," I sighed, and Marcus knew immediately what I meant.

"What happened?"

"It's all the work, man. I should've paid attention to her. I was so focused on my work that I managed to let her fall by the wayside."

"That's a common problem. I'm sure you guys could work it out."

"Oh, come on. Look at her and look at me. I couldn't afford to screw this up, and that's exactly what I did." I almost had to check for a moment to make sure that there were no tears rolling down my face.

"Eric, she loves you." Marcus was speaking slowly and deliberately, making sure I took in every word. "You just think long and hard about why she does and give her that guy."

I nodded to affirm what he just told me, and he began to leave my office. Just before closing the door behind him, he said, "Just give her some time to cool off, and then talk to her. In the meantime, keep running the show around here, and everything will be back to normal in no time."

When Marcus left, I immediately began taking his advice. I knew that if I called Trish that day, it would just seem as though I was trying to say the right things. I was going to wait to take my shot at getting her back, and then I was going to make it count. In the interim, I started doing little tasks to give myself momentum. First I answered emails, and then I returned phone calls that I had missed from the day before. Next, I began reviewing columns and articles one by one until I had managed to knock every item off my to-do list without even considering the use of the chamber. With an honest day's work behind me, it all started to seem possible once again. I would get the job done and go home, give it a day or two, and then I would start mending my relationship with Trish.

As though some higher force was making sure my optimism would be short-lived, just as I began to shut down my computer and back up my belongings, the door to the Falcon office opened, and in walked Jim Bernstandt. At first my heart skipped a beat, and then it occurred to me that he still needed to clean out his desk. Just as expected, he began to empty his desk into boxes, but then, he walked away from his desk and toward my office. He had an attaché case in one hand, and a look in his eye that suggested he and I both knew something that no one else in the office did. He stepped into my office and pulled the door shut behind him. "I'm on to you," he growled.

At first, I thought I should show some sort of look of surprise or bewilderment, but instead I gave him a cold, stone-faced glare. On the inside, however, I was trembling at the thought of what was going to happen next. He opened the attaché case and pulled out a red notebook, the pages of which were blacked with notes that seemed to have no order or reason.

"My youngest son kept this notebook. At first I didn't think it was anything, and then I read through it, page by page. I know about you, this time chamber thing, and I've finally found out what happened to my older son, Jason. I don't know where Billy is now, but I'm sure you know what happened."

"What are you trying to suggest, Jim?"

"What I'm suggesting is that either you tell me what happened to my sons, or I'll expose you and this little secret you have—this secret that has put you on top of the world. Well, let's just say the rest of the world isn't going to take too kindly to knowing you've basically cheated your way to the top."

In all the time I had the chamber, and with everything I had kept secret from the people closest to me, I had never before thought that the use of the chamber could be construed as cheating. "You'll expose me?" I snickered. "Who's going to believe you? I mean, the only evidence you have are the scribbled notes in your kid's note-book, and let's face it, he wasn't exactly an overachiever."

Jim was about to fire back some response when the fact that I referred to his son in the past tense really sunk in. At that moment, a combination of grief and fury began to contort his face. I could tell that he knew I had gotten the best of him. The good feeling of an honest day's work, the feeling of getting things back to normal, of being the lovable, humble person that Trish loved, and everything just and normal that I had imagined myself to be began to fade away like a sunny horizon quickly disappearing into a dark and cloudy storm. The arrogant, brazen version of my persona that was built in the chamber began to speak for me in a cold and manipulative tone.

"Walk me through this." I began to twist the proverbial knife. "You're going to tell the world that the person who has turned this magazine into a success, someone who has published three books in the last few months, got all of this success because of some magic that could freeze time? Who would believe you and how could you explain it? I mean, are you telling me that somewhere in between your knowledge of steak houses and soufflé recipes, you're going to be able to explain some sort of rift in a space-time continuum? And based on what evidence? Your deadbeat, criminal son has a notebook?"

He knew I was right, that nothing he could say to anyone was going to affect me, not with the evidence he had. Finally, he stood up and shouted, "Everything you've built, everything you care about, you're going to lose all of it."

"Not likely," I responded. "As you said yourself, I've put myself on top of the world, and there's nothing you can do about that. Now get the hell out. You're not welcome at the Falcon anymore." I stood and locked eyes with him, and when he knew that my will would not be broken, he turned and stormed out of the office for the last time.

Everyone in the office suite stood dumbfounded, trying to put together some explanation for what had just occurred. I, on the other hand, dashed toward Rick's office and unlocked the door. In Rick's desk, I found an office directory and jotted down Bernstandt's number on a Post-It note. I didn't even look a coworker in the eye as I gathered my belongings and began to head home.

When I arrived back at the apartment, I was faced by the realization that I would be spending the night completely and utterly alone. In a few moments, I began to think my way through all the emotions that I had buried with work. I wasn't going to stay busy and avoid these feelings anymore, I was going to stand and face them head-on. Eventually, the loneliness, remorse, and shame all blended together into a vindictive sentiment that could only be understood by the brash persona that I had built in the time chamber. This vindictiveness was meant for only one person, as I pulled out the Post-It note and began to dial Bernstandt's number. The phone only rang once, and I could hear his voice crack with anger as he answered the phone.

"What do you want?" Jim answered.

"Both your sons are dead."

"What are you telling me?" In his voice, I could tell he was horrified. "Are you telling me that—?"

"I'm telling you not to cross me."

Chapter 20

I woke up the next morning feeling as though there were two people within me debating in a furious attempt to make sense of what I had done only the night before. The brazen, ambitious persona that was born in the time chamber was pleased. In that figure's mind, Bernstandt was just another obstacle that could be obliterated, another victory, and proof that no one could stop the success story that was beginning to unfold. However, the old me sat in anguish, submerged not only in guilt for happened to both Billy and Jason, but also because of the turmoil that I had inflicted on Bernstandt's very being.

I decided that there was only one person who could help me make sense of all this. He was the only one who knew about how ugly my connection with Jim Bernstandt had become. He was also, at least I thought, the designer and builder of the time chamber device. Perhaps every ethical calculation that left me at war with myself was one he had already conquered. A phone call was all it took to set up a meeting. I immediately established that this meeting needed to take place at his home, a place where we could speak freely and candidly without the cryptic language we used in public places.

His front door was enough to make me shudder. The last time I was there, we were concealing the death of another human being. He invited me in rather cordially, and his lack of reverence to the ugly truth that sat between us was enough to make my skin crawl. "What did you want to talk about?" he asked.

"I called Bernstandt last night."

"My god! Why?"

"That's what's bothering me. While the phone was ringing, I didn't know why I was doing it. When he answered, I realized that I was gloating."

"Eric, you're dealing with a set of circumstances that no one could have predicted. Thus, there's no way to predict the way you would react."

Michael's explanation was cold, matter-of-fact, and almost eerie. It had always struck me as odd, even though I never missed an opportunity to express my gratitude for the chamber. The way he dealt with the disposal of Jason and Billy had the same cold, calculated demeanor made him almost frightening. Nonetheless, I decided to trust him. What other choice did I have?

"Yeah, you have a point there. The problem is that I don't know enough about these circumstances to truly understand them."

"What do you mean?"

"I mean that I don't know enough. Where did the chamber come from? Why did you choose me?"

Michael then began to lay out an elaborate narrative that was enough to make my head spin. Apparently, he had been researching time-space continuum lapses while working on his doctorate at some high-end research institution that, for some reason, he chose not to disclose. He was working on this during the late 1970s, and he was a young scientist with a dream of changing the world. Days before he was set to make his discoveries known to the world, he found other men in his department using the time-chamber prototype. When he asked what they were doing, they wouldn't tell him their intentions. That was when he saw two researchers exit the time chamber, two men whom he didn't recognize. That was all he needed to see. He destroyed all of the notes and data from his experiments and said that he would never share his findings with anyone.

"That doesn't make sense," I protested.

"Eric, I had no idea who those men were. They could have been nuclear physicists, and my chamber could have been a closed-door testing site for God knows what kind of monstrosity. I had hoped that my work would make a difference in the world, but I wasn't going to let someone use it to get a head's start in an arm's race or… I don't even want to think of the other possibilities. Perhaps my reaction was a little excessive. But it was then and there that I started to think of what could happen if just anybody could use this technology."

"So you decided to use it on people you didn't know?"

"Not exactly. My intention was to find talented young minds that could use the time chamber to live out a life's worth of progress in a much-shorter time frame. I would save my invention for an elite group that would only use the chamber for noble purposes. I saw you one day, read a few of your columns, and thought you could use the chamber to enhance and capitalize on your natural ability to research and write. You and Jason were the only two I've shared this with."

"So how did you know so much about me?"

"Well, that's not something I'm particularly proud to tell, but I used the chamber to get to know as much about you as I possibly could. When you can effectively make time stand still, you can get really close to someone without them knowing. That first night we met was not the first time I had been in your apartment."

My jaw hung wide with disgust. I couldn't believe that my life as I knew it, my privacy and my most personal life, had been invaded under a guise of frozen time. "You did what?"

"You have to understand that I did it for the best reasons. I was never going to use any of the knowledge for anything other than to evaluate whether you were a fitting candidate to use the chamber. If I was going to entrust you with such a valuable secret, I had to know everything about you. I had to do so even if resorting to measures that were less than ethical."

"To what end?"

"To be honest, I'm not really sure anymore. I had hoped that while your career was taking off, I could build more duplicates of the chamber device. I would then find even more enthusiastic, innovative minds to use them, and then I'd form an elite group of innovators and world-changers. My goal was noble at the start, and now all I've done is shatter lives and create heartbreak."

"So where do we go from here?"

"I don't know, Eric. I'm out of ideas. I guess we can push on as usual, try to see what we can make of all this."

"I'm not sure how that would work."

My mind was delving into what I had done to myself by using the chamber. I had gained everything and lost sight of who I had become. I simply couldn't imagine any semblance of a normal life in a world where the time chamber existed. Of course, I could always give the chamber back, but the secrets would always sit between Trish and I, and that was enough to make my stomach turn.

"How about this," Michael responded. "Hold on to the chamber for a while longer. Try to see what you can fix. No more getting ahead of the world. Only use the chamber when you feel like you absolutely need it. If you can't get your life back in order, then it might be time to consider a more drastic change."

I could only imagine what the words "drastic change" were intended to mean. At that point, I didn't want to ask. I could tell he was demanding that I find a way to sort the whole thing out. Up to that conversation, I had always trusted his wisdom. He had given me the chamber, so I naturally assumed that he would have all the answers I needed. What bothered me about that evening was seeing him completely lost. He was out of ideas and just as unsure about how to fix this mess as I was. So with that being said, I hung my head and left his house.

Just as I was leaving, a reminder rang on my phone. Apparently, I had a long-standing engagement to have drinks with William at his palatial office. I wanted nothing more than to simply go home and hide from the world, but something within me compelled me to make that meeting. The long drive across town left me alone with my thoughts, and the mess my life had become was more confusing with every attempt at trying to find reason or meaning. From a material standpoint, I had everything that anyone could ever want. I had a luxurious home, an oversized bank account, and a career that could be the envy of almost anyone. Some might have even thought I was spoiled for feeling so empty while having so much. None of it, however, was what I wanted. There would always be a void that only Trish could fill, and I knew that. Thus, no possession, no matter how shiny or expensive, could glimmer enough to make me see the bright side.

When I arrived at William's office, he could tell right away that I was not my old self. After he poured me two fingers of what tasted like expensive bourbon from a crystal decanter, he was immediately shocked at how quickly I downed the drink, hoping something, anything, could get my mind to stop racing. Or perhaps he was taken aback at how I was willing to chugalug such expensive whiskey without even blinking an eye.

"All right, young man, what's wrong."

The fatherly tone was all I needed. I normally kept at least some degree of propriety with William, as our relationship had always been at least somewhat professional. In that moment, I was done pretending like I had all the answers, like I could take the world on by myself. I was reaching out for someone who could explain things to me. I needed someone who could give me comfort, or at least some sense of direction.

"Trish left me."

"What? That doesn't make sense. You two seemed inseparable."

"We were, but at some point along the way, I got so focused on everything else, the books, the Falcon, and I didn't even know I was taking her for granted until she was gone."

William began to lean back as he took a sip of his whiskey. He then sat down next to me and began to talk in a way so candid I could hardly believe. I knew this man very well from having listened to countless stories and writing down every detail. When you write a book about somebody, you can't help but get to know them. This, however, was like some sort of deeper wisdom that he kept in a back pocket of his memory only to be taken out on special occasion.

"Eric, I'm going to tell you something that I learned a long time ago." William leaned back as his eyes seemed to search through a long volume of memories. "I've had ventures that thrived and others that failed. I've loved, I've lost. But at every phase in my life, I made sure that I took the time to focus on what was most important in my life. When you know what comes first, everything else sorts itself out."

"Well, I've always been a good worker, priorities where never a problem."

"You see, that's what I'm talking about. You've done what most people have told you to do. You got a job right out of college. You've climbed the ladder and made a success of yourself. But now it's time to ask what's really most important in your life. You see, you've measured yourself by what the world thinks of you. So now it's time to do what you want, focus on what's important to you."

"It's her. It's definitely her. I mean, I've spent so much time trying to build my career and my reputation. But what good is it if I don't have her?"

"Would she still love you if you didn't have all these things?"

"She's proven it. I mean, we started dating when I was an undergrad living on cheap beer and Little Ceasar's pizza."

He laughed. "See! If she doesn't think all that you've built is what makes you, and if you would choose her over all of it, then your decisions become pretty simple."

"I don't know if she'll take me back. I don't even know what to say to her."

"Of course, you don't. Any man who thinks he knows what to say in situations like this is either full of himself or stupid. But what you say isn't what matters. You just know that you want her back. And you know what you'd give to make that happen."

"Anything."

"In that case, it's time to get moving. Do you know who said 'Time cures all wounds?'"

"No, I don't know where that saying comes from."

"It was some lazy moron. Don't wait for time to go by. Go out there and fix things yourself. You're a smart kid. You know what to do."

When I left William's office, my first desire was to get out my phone and call Trish, but I knew that wasn't the right move. I wanted to make a change. I didn't just want to tell her that things would be different—I wanted to show her. I would make the changes in my life first, showing her that I was only going to pursue that which truly made life better for the both of us and leave the building of empires to other people. I didn't want to have a castle of a home without her to share it with. I didn't want the accolades if she wasn't there with me to share the recognition. I thought back to everything I had accomplished since I received the time chamber, all the wealth, status, and recognition. There were a few things I was proud of, but in comparison to the thought of losing Trish, they all seemed insignificant. So they had to be torn down. That moment, I walked down the street knowing that the arrogant, brazen Eric was no more, and the humble and hard-working one was here to stay.

I would spend the next several days evaluating everything. I was preparing for a rapid downsizing. I would no longer be the superhuman. Instead, I would have to be content being the workhorse that Rick had hired. If I needed to use the time chamber, I would only do so in a pinch when I really needed the advantage. Other than that, I would live the life of a normal human with normal limitations. I had to remember that the chamber gave me a time advantage, but the abilities and ideas were all my own. All at once, everything seemed possible again.

Chapter 21

Only a few days after my little grandstanding act with Jim Bernstandt, I went in to the Falcon office ready to take on the world once more. I aimed to complete every task with my office door wide open, wanting everyone in the office to see just how much of a workhorse I really was. Although I had used the chamber to elongate my morning routine, for some reason, I didn't want to use it while I was at the office. I had a newfound faith in what I could accomplish, and no one, not Bernstandt, not Rick, was going to hold me back. When five o'clock came and the rest of the staff began their commute home, I was still sitting there in my office, barreling through mounds of paperwork and firing off emails. Just as I thought I was alone in the office, in walked Eddie with a few mundane questions about his next article.

Eddie's writing had really begun to flourish, and his work was starting to be compared to the pieces I had submitted back when I was the hotshot columnist under Rick's command. With every question, I could that see he was working on his next piece like it was going to make or break his promise of a career, and I remembered how I felt my first few months working at the Falcon. What was obscure about Eddie was that he had an almost phobic aversion to printing his work and submitting it to me in paper form. At one point, the conversation turned toward the podcasts that were preparing to launch within the next few weeks.

"I'm hoping that if you like what I write," he said, "maybe I can have a segment of my own."

"I don't see why not," I responded.

"Are the rumors true that you're hoping to expand into television?"

"The thought has crossed my mind." When I said that, Eddie's eyes lit up as if he was hanging on my every word.

"Well, I for one, think that's awesome," he said. I couldn't tell if this unsolicited opinion had much of a point other than simple cajolery, but nonetheless, having a little bit of affirmation never hurt. "I mean, we're not just a magazine anymore," he added.

"What do you mean 'just a magazine'?"

"Well, you know, we're branching out. Before long, when nobody's buying printed magazines anymore, we'll have gone on to TV and who knows what else."

All at once, I began my bombastic defense of print journalism. I started making arguments about how the printed word would never die and that the Falcon was founded on the traditions of sound journalistic integrity. At some point, it occurred to me that everything I was saying was something Rick had said to me before in similar circumstances. And then, my entire narrative of the last few months began to change. I had always told myself that my work at the Falcon was taking Rick's dream and turning it into something bigger and better. That moment, when Eddie was being transparent enough that I could see the future of our business the way he saw it, I knew that my story of the Falcon was only a fiction I had spun to make myself feel better. In reality, I had molded the Falcon based on *my* aspirations, strong-arming Rick at every turn, and when the Falcon no longer looked anything like the dream he had, Rick had no choice but to bow out.

Eddie left my office with a somewhat confused look on his face, and suddenly my mind was too occupied to concern myself with setting him straight. When I could no longer make sense of the two competing narratives that were presenting themselves in my mind, I decided that I would just ignore them and get back to work on various tasks. The first of these was to answer my email. When I was just a columnist, answering emails was something of an afterthought, a quick task that I could complete when I was bored or in between projects. When I started running the Falcon, the number of emails grew to the point that it felt like I had taken on another part-time job.

When that task was completed, I realized that I could've stopped for the day, but this odd surge of creative energy was flowing through my veins. I pulled open my laptop and started to write. At first, I didn't know what I was writing, but then it occurred to me that this new impromptu project could be the beginnings of another novel. Next, I took out a legal pad and started to jot down notes about characters and themes. Before long, I had the outline of a plot and the first few pages written and saved on my laptop. I thought that I had been working for hours, but when I checked the clock, I found the hands winding toward midnight. Much to my surprise, only two hours or so had elapsed. If I wrote like this, I thought to myself, I could have another book completed in a matter of months. Of course, I could use the chamber and have it done the next day if I so desired, but why?

The plot of this story started to crystalize in my head, and the characters seemed more intriguing and delightfully human with every ounce of thought I put into them. It was going to be a story about an underachiever who was given a second chance at his childhood. He would be allowed to put his mind in his eight-year-old self and redo every day of his life over again. It would be a story unlike anything I had written before, and the more thought I put into this story, the more deeply meaningful it became. A few of the writers came by my office to ask questions, but I shooed them away with a dismissive hand as I poured myself into this new story. At one point, I said to myself, *Hmm, this is what it feels like to find your true calling.*

It was then that I realized that the benefit of the chamber was one I enjoyed, but no longer one that I needed. That evening, working there in my office, I began what was the first honest appraisal of everything I had accomplished. At some point, the chamber went from being a useful tool to a device that I used to manipulate everything about my daily life. I became power hungry and went on a campaign that affected not just me but everyone I cared about. Of course, I had managed to change my life to something of a legendary rise to fame and success, but I did so at the expense of my relationship with Trish and the career of one of my closest mentors. Not to mention Jim Bernstandt, the man from whom I had taken a livelihood and two sons.

I had a weekend lying just before me, with two days where the Falcon office would be closed and so would be my efforts to build my own personal dominion. In that weekend, I took a lot of time to reflect on my life. By the middle of the day on Sunday, I had plan. This plan was nothing like the plans I had that involved using the chamber to finish some project or chase some accomplishment. Those kinds of plans had lost all their luster to me. Instead, I was thinking about how I wanted to go about getting my life back.

I called Trish on Sunday afternoon, not setting my hopes on any big breakthroughs with one phone call. Instead, we just talked about little things, and the sound of her voice brought me the same sustenance it always had, and I knew that I had to get her back. As I looked through her jewelry box, the one item that didn't seem to be there was the necklace I had bought her when we were still in college. As this little oddity was just part of our idle small talk, I threw in, "Oh, by the way, did you take any of your jewelry with you?"

Reading my mind the way only Trish could, she responded, "Just the necklace you gave me."

"You mean the old one?"

"That's the one."

I started to chuckle. "I've bought you all these other necklaces, bracelets, and"—I paused, stopping myself from mentioning the engagement ring that I never actually got a chance to give to her—"and you take that one?" The point I was trying to make was that I bought that necklace when I was just a broke undergraduate. That small silver necklace looked like tinfoil compared the dazzling diamond-clad pieces that lined her jewelry box."

"That one means the most to me."

My heart sank. I couldn't even put together a response, and the conversation had just taken a turn away from the safe, comfortable small talk that we had started. Eventually, one of us managed to mercifully change the subject before we agreed we would talk again soon, and once again, I was alone. After our phone call, just to keep my mind occupied, I started writing. The novel project that I started to conceive in the office was enough to keep me entertained for the evening. Before long, I had the first draft of a chapter written for my new book. This accomplishment was small, considering that I did it with my less-dazzling, more-human time constraints, but I felt more proud of that chapter than I did the two books that came before it.

All at once, the chapter and the necklace, two items that otherwise had no similarity to one another, combined to make a definitive statement about my life and the chamber. The necklace I gave Trish was not expensive, nor was it made of the most precious metals, but I gave it to her at a time when making such an expenditure was truly a sacrifice. All the other pieces of jewelry in her box were much more luxurious and had the price tag to show it, but I purchased them when I had more money than I knew how to spend, so none of them were anywhere near as meaningful.

Then there was this chapter. Of course, it was only a handful of pages, and on its own, without the chapters that would follow, wouldn't accomplish anything. Yet at the same time, I took pride in it more so than I had on any other work that came before it. That was because I completed this chapter in the world of the ticking clock, where my time was inherently finite, and thus giving time to this chapter meant I was giving it a piece of my life, and that was where it drew its value. Other chapters may have been more entertaining to the reader, but they didn't have the claim to the time in my life that I had invested to that chapter.

My eyes then began to scan the apartment and take in all the possessions that I had begun to accumulate. I had awards that hung on the wall, and my home, with its luxurious amenities, would have told the outside world that I was a success. But what did that matter? Without Trish there to share in my successes, anything I could accomplish and any possession that I could acquire would fail to have any value to me whatsoever. As these conclusions began to coalesce and paint a new picture of my identity and the world in which I lived, I stepped out on to the balcony to get a breath of fresh air. The chilling wind of the city blew through my hair, and I felt more alert and aware than I had ever felt before.

I thought about the persona that had been born in the chamber, the one that was power hungry and willing to step over anyone and anything that got between me and my goals. This twisted, vindictive version of my own identity had no problem pulling the trigger and ending Billy's life. This persona not only caused Jim Bernstandt the most egregious of losses, but then also used those losses to taunt him in some hollow-victory quip over the phone. This character was not a man worthy of Trish's love, not worthy of the successes that it helped me accumulate, and I would not let it define me. When that became my resolution, the questions of what to do next became obvious. The downsizing of my life needed to be much larger than I had envisioned.

My first phone call was to Trish, asking her to meet me at the apartment at 7:00 p.m. the next evening. She seemed somewhat confused at my calling her again so abruptly, but nonetheless, she agreed. My next call was to Michael, telling him to come to the apartment the next evening as well, only I told him to come a little bit earlier. "I don't really want to explain it right now," I said, "but we need to talk about our little secret." He agreed despite the suspicion that was more than noticeable in his tone of voice. My next phone call was to Rick, asking him if he could meet me the next morning so that we could talk over breakfast. "Sure thing, Eric. I mean, it's not like I have anywhere to be." He also seemed somewhat confused. Even I only had a subconscious understanding of the decisions that I was putting into action, but I was acting on what felt like some basic animal instinct, with every move pushing myself toward one inevitable conclusion.

My next task was to return to the Falcon office. I made sure to make this trip in the later hours of the evening when I would have the entire office suite to myself with no one to watch what I was doing. I began to empty my desk and back my office into several large boxes, and within an hour, it was as empty and as barren as it was when I moved in from my more humble workstation in the atrium bullpen. This was the office where I had conducted hundreds of meetings, where I took on my new role as editor and then helped the Falcon grow into something larger than anyone could have predicted. However, in one evening, with not a soul other than me to witness it, it reverted to being just another empty office. "It was a good run while it lasted," I said to the newly vacant walls.

Walking away, a bizarre impulse struck me as I looked over my shoulder at the office building. This building was once my prison and then became my kingdom. That evening, I looked at that building the way one would at an old high school or vacated house. Some of the memories I took from that building were ones I would cherish, others were ones I'd lament. As the lights of the Chicago skyline began to illuminate, I stood with a new sense of what I wanted out of my life and what I wanted to become, and the Falcon office was not where I was going to find it.

The apartment was just as empty as it had been when I left, and although I tricked myself into thinking that maybe I would hear Trish's voice from one of the other rooms, only silence came to greet me. I started doing things just to pass the time, to make the evening end sooner so that I could get on to what would become the rest of my life. I opened a bottle of wine, played some music, and tried to find a movie on TV that would entertain me. None of these things could retain my attention, and before long, I was staring square into the face of the loneliness that I had tried so hard to elude.

When the midnight hour was upon me, and I sat in the quiet confines of the home I had built for myself, an odd whim sent me into the chamber for what would be the last time. I sat for a moment at the desk, thinking that the focus that led me to tackle enormous projects would come back as it always had, and I would once again be sprinting through new endeavors. This focus was nowhere to be found, and all I felt was the still solitude that came from being closed away from the world of the ticking clock. I looked in the bathroom mirror, and my memory showed me the image of my long-lost haggard and weary face from the first time I walked into the chamber. That overworked and overwhelmed person would've foolishly envied the man I had become, but I missed being that person in a way I never could have predicted.

Just like the long good-bye I gave to my office in the Falcon building, I gave my frozen inner sanctum one last appraisal. I the pulled the door shut, bracing myself for the continuation of the world of the ticking clock that I had grown to call the wave. This wave came upon me just like the others before it, but instead of the unsettling feeling of a world crashing back into motion, it felt entirely different. I was coming home.

Chapter 22

"Are you sure you want to do this, Eric?" I could tell that our conversation was leaving Rick stunned. He had agreed to meet me at the small diner that was close to my old apartment. That was the same diner where Michael spilled coffee all over me, where I would go to discuss what had occurred in the time chamber, and that day, the diner became the place where I would go to begin the undoing of my own empire.

"Yes, Rick. And I'll say again, I'm sorry things went the way they did. I appreciate all the opportunities you've given me, and I hope we can still have a friendship."

"If that's how you want it, then I'm happy to respect your wishes."

Rick had every reason to be elated at this conversation, as I was giving him back something that was very near and dear to him. As a small token of my respect and appreciation, I picked up the bill for our little meeting, and Rick began to gather his belongings.

"I can't wait to tell my wife," he chuckled. "I haven't been out of the game long, but I can tell I'm already starting to drive her crazy." We laughed, and it felt good to laugh this way with him for the first time in far too long.

"Well, I know your work habits, so I give it two weeks before she's calling you asking when you'll be home."

"Actually it won't be a phone call anymore. We've taken up texting."

"Texting? Mr. Old School? I'm shocked."

"Just changing with the times," he replied. "Oh, and there's one other thing I forgot to do." Rick reached into the bag that he carried in with him and pulled out a copy of the Gastineux book. "I never got a chance to ask you if you'd sign a copy." He then reached for his shirt pocket and withdrew his classic red pen, the one that he had used to put his revisions on numerous columns that I wrote for him.

As I scribbled a brief message on the inside cover of the book, I felt deep within me the same spirit of the aspiring young journalist who longed so deeply for his approval. "To my friend and mentor, Rick," I wrote, "without whom this accomplishment would not have been possible."

As we left the diner, Rick walked away with a bounce in his step that suggested he had just regained his reason for waking up in the morning. I left with an equal sense of purpose, but with entirely different designs on how my future was going to look. That night, Trish was coming over, and with Michael as my witness, I was going to tell her everything. No longer was I going to keep anything about the last year and a half a secret. She was going to know everything, and regardless of whether or not she decided to take me back, I was going to give her the chance to accept me with knowledge of every conceivable detail.

With each and every action I took that morning, I was stepping back into the life of a normal person, one who had to live with the exact same time restraints as everyone else. My next step was to call the people who worked directly under me at the Falcon, telling them that I wouldn't be coming into the office that day, and that they should proceed in the interim period as if I had been otherwise incapacitated. I gave them an assurance that they would be told the details when the time was right, and that they should have no worries about the future of the Falcon or their livelihoods.

My next step was to go back to the old gym where I had been a member before the time chamber gave me my own place to exercise. One of the employees at the gym, whom I hadn't seen in what felt like ages, inquired, "I haven't seen you in a long time. What have you been up to?"

"Well, I published a few books, finished grad school, and moved into a new apartment uptown. What about you?"

"I, um, well I moved into a new job here as the day manager."

"Oh, that's cool. What were you before?"

"Night manager."

"Well, I'm sure that's a nice change of pace."

That conversation was significantly awkward, and in all honesty, I was trying to one-up the poor guy. When I managed to clumsily put that conversation out of its misery, I changed clothes in the locker room and started my workout. Sharing the weight room with other people was going to take some getting used to, but I still managed to break a good sweat. Another thing I had all but forgotten was the feeling that comes from sharing the gym with members of the opposite sex. For the first time in what felt ages, I had to go through the feeling of possibly having female eyes on me, which could either make a guy endlessly second-guess himself or have a testosterone driven boost of self-confidence. I couldn't decide what would occur if a girl did notice me, and I didn't care. While I did notice one exceptionally attractive girl who seemed to look over at me while I was on the bench press, I didn't give it a second thought. Any girl who would walk by there or anywhere shared the same limitation that would deny my attention. None of them was Trish, and that was all that mattered to me.

Going to the gym was just the first of many processes that I was going to have to get used to doing like a regular person. When I got home, I took a shower, shaved, and put myself through the basic morning routine, timing it to relearn how I would fit these commonplace practices into a morning where I had places to be while time remained unfrozen. I also prepared a breakfast and measured how long that would take, knowing that I would no longer be able to make that a long, relaxed indulgence. At times, I had to remind myself that I had lived with a normal person's schedule for my entire life before receiving the chamber and had to give myself reassurances that I could again function like a normal human being.

I decided then that although I was prepared to never again set foot in the time chamber, I would let Trish decide if we would keep it. I was going to leave our future entirely up to her, and if she could accept the risks involved with keeping the chamber, then I was going to trust her judgment. That would occur, of course, if she was willing to stay with me after knowing the whole story of the last year and a half. Either way, my most sincere hope was that she would be willing to restart and rebuild our relationship. If I took everything I had built with the help of the chamber, burned it all to the ground, and still salvaged my relationship with her, I would have truly counted myself fortunate.

My next step was to plan our finances. I did so based on a best-case scenario hope that Trish and I would still be together from that day forward. I gathered a few bank statements from both of our accounts, as we had always been transparent on matters of money. I was able to easily calculate that with her take-home pay and the proceeds from the average monthly revenue of my book sales, we could still live in the new apartment, could still afford our current standard of living, and could still do so quite comfortably, even with the subtraction of my monthly salary from working at the Falcon. If Trish decided that we should part ways, I could live off the money from my books. Independent of the financial feasibility of this option, it still felt like an existence, but without Trish, it would be a poor excuse for what one would call a life.

With that, I had planned and established a contingency for what I thought would be any foreseeable scenario, and I still had hours before I could set my plan to come into motion. It was just past the noon hour; Michael would be coming over at six thirty, and then Trish would arrive a half hour later. I spent the rest of the afternoon working on my new book, in part because it was a way to pass the time and keep my mind occupied and also simply because it was something that brought me great pleasure. All at once, time had a meaning and value to me again, and I began thinking in terms of, "This is how I'd like to spend my time," or "If I'm going to put my time into something, this feels worth it." When I had the chamber, I haphazardly started any conceivable project because I didn't worry about how long it would take. With this newfound worldview, I became resolved to focus only on tasks or concerns that were worthy of my time or, more importantly, worthy of my passion.

When six thirty rolled around, Michael arrived, and I invited him into the apartment. He sat down on the couch, expressing concern as to why I had him come over that evening. I told him, step by step, how I planned to tell Trish every detail. I realized that the breadth of this narrative was also the entire length of his and my connection to one another.

He definitely had his concerns. "Okay, Eric, you promised me that you would keep this a secret."

"And I have kept that promise, but I can't go on like this. I'm trying to share my life with her, and I can't do that keeping something this big just between you and me." This kind of clear, cathartic transparency was almost euphoric. "I promise, whatever is said here tonight will stay between Trish and me, and I'm going to let her decide if, knowing everything I've done, she still wants us to keep the chamber. If she wants to keep it, then it will stay a secret between her and me, and if she doesn't, then I'm giving it back to you, and then the secret becomes much easier for you to keep."

After some considerable hesitation, he responded, "Okay, Eric, but I'll just say out front that I have my doubts about it. But if this is what you want, then I'm willing to go with it."

"I don't like that it's come to this, but this is the best way."

Just as I was about to give a long oratory about honesty and how I can't blur the lines between right and wrong, the door opened, and Trish stepped into my apartment. I gave an awkward version of an introduction to the two of them and then recalled that they had met before on one passing occasion.

Then the floodgates opened, and I just spoke to Trish in a way that was honest and transparent. I pulled the chamber device out from my courier bag and placed it on the floor. After giving her a basic explanation of the device and how it worked, I told her everything, the whole story, how the chamber helped in every conceivable way and that everything I had changed in my life for the better came in some way because of the chamber. I clearly and openly admitted that every major step forward I had taken was a result not of my own personal strength, but by the ability to freeze any moment I wanted and used it to give myself a head start.

She seemed to accept most of it, as though she was pleased to have her curiosity satisfied, until she spoke up to ask one simple question. "You killed somebody?"

"Yes, I did, but you have to understand. He was going to kill me, and he even mentioned that he was going to hurt you."

Eventually, when all the confessions came to an end, Trish excused herself for a moment, saying, "I need a minute alone. I have to think this through." She stepped out on to the balcony and pulled the sliding glass door closed behind her.

There are moments in a person's life when they know the entire story is going to hinge on one decision. That moment, my whole life, my one chance at the future I wanted for myself, depended on one choice, and that choice was hers, not mine.

"Well, what do you think she's going to say?" Michael asked.

"I don't know," I responded. "But whatever she chooses, I'm just glad to know that she knows the whole story. Who knows, maybe she'll—"

Before I could finish my thought, I heard a loud crash. I spun around and saw my door swing open and in walked Jim Bernstandt, with a pistol in his hand. I staggered for a moment, not knowing what he was going to do next. Trish had turned around and was standing there in the doorway leading out onto the balcony. The room was so large that more than twenty feet separated Michael and me from Bernstandt, and an even greater distance separated him from Trish.

"You took my family!" he shouted while pointing his gun at me.

A feverish heat began to rush up the back of my neck, and I tried to put together a coherent plea that would help me reason with him. Despite all the confessions that I had just offered up moments before, I knew that there was going to be one wrong that I would never be able to reconcile. Just as I raised my hands to show I meant him no harm, Bernstandt spoke up once again.

"I told you, you were going to lose everything, and this where it starts." He then turned the gun away from me and pointed it at Trish.

"No!" I shouted, but my cry fell on deaf ears. I watched his pointer finger begin to contract, and then I heard a loud crack from the front of his gun. The next moment, I was overcame with a staggering silence that was enough to make me tremble. Michael had activated the chamber, and thus that one terrifying moment stood frozen in time.

In the staggering silence, I let out a deep gasp, as the shock of the moment had forced me to hold my breath. I then walked over to Bernstandt; he sat suspended in that moment, standing frozen like a statue. Trish also stood motionless, and I knew that the two them were not close enough to the chamber to avoid its grasp the way Michael and I were. This meant that as soon as the door to the chamber was pulled shut, the world would go on, and the horrors that Michael had momentarily stopped could commence as though nothing had happened. I then noticed that approximately six inches away from the barrel of the gun sat a bullet, which was motionless as it sat in midair.

First, I tried to move Jim Bernstandt. He was like a statue; I couldn't even move the jacket that hung lifelessly from his frame. Next, I tried to move Trish out of the path of the bullet, but she, just like Bernstandt, was frozen in time and could not be moved. Finally I wrapped my fist around the bullet, hoping to pull it out of its path and keep it from hitting Trish. Just like everything else, the bullet could not be moved, and I knew then that I was completely and utterly powerless.

"It won't work, Eric," Michael said with a full understanding of what I was trying to do. "We can't manipulate anything outside the chamber. They weren't in close enough proximity, and thus, they are frozen just like everything else." His words perfectly described the cruel irony of the way the chamber worked and how I was left with limited options. As I was trying to think of something that could bend the situation in my favor, my gaze shifted toward the bullet that sat like it was hanging on string. Around the base of the small round, I was able to read an inscription: "ACR."

"This is a hollow-point bullet." I said, as though I was thinking aloud.

"So what?" Michael responded.

"A hollow-point bullet is designed to avoid going through its target and hitting something or someone else." The little details of Eddie's column began to bounce back into my memory. "This means that if someone stands in the way, it will hit them and then collapse. The kinetic energy will be dispersed in this target, given that it's massive enough to stop it. This means it will do more damage to whatever it hits, but it won't keep going."

"Eric, you can't be thinking about—"

"Michael, this is the way it has to be. The chamber has built one life out of nothing, and it will make nothing out of one life. That's how it works—there's no way around it. Did you bring your gun?"

"Yes."

"Okay, then. When I give you the signal, I want you to pull the chamber door shut"—I gestured toward Bernstandt—"then start shooting at him, and don't stop until you know he can't do any damage."

"What about you?"

"The chamber gave me a new life, and it means nothing without Trish."

"So you know what this means?"

"Yes, Michael. This is how all this needs to end."

"Okay."

Michael pulled his gun and positioned himself where he could get a clean shot at Bernstandt. Meanwhile, I was looking down the path of the bullet, predicting its trajectory and trying to figure out where I should stand.

Interrupting my planning, Michael said, "Do you remember the night I gave you the chamber?"

"Yeah, I do." I couldn't help but let a little note of affection float into my words as I recalled that evening.

"I said that a guy like you could do amazing things if you could bend the time to your will." Michael's eyes began to wander. "I never knew that you would come to understand time in ways that I could never comprehend."

I nodded, knowing that this little conclusion was the best sub-stitute that Michael could get to simply saying good-bye. I gave him a silent but meaningful nod of affirmation, and when Michael recip-rocated, I knew that the plan I had just conjured would soon be put into place. I walked over toward the walkway out onto the bal-cony where Trish was frozen in time. Although the look on her face expressed horror, confusion, and dismay, the only thing that caught my attention was how stunningly beautiful she was even in the worst of circumstances.

I placed myself in just the right position, where behind me stood the love of my life and in front of me sat a bullet that needed a target. When I knew that I was that bullet's new target, I planted my feet, took a deep breath, and gave Michael the nod. With one hand, he raised his gun toward Jim Bernstandt, and with the other, he reached toward the chamber door and began to pull it shut. After a second or two, I felt the wave come over me, as the world of the ticking clock recommenced for the last time that I would witness. I looked over my shoulder and saw Trish with the late-night breeze blowing through her hair. Under my breath, I whispered "I love you." As the bullet cracked through the air and into my chest, those words were the last thing that came through my mind. After that, there was only silence.

The whole world became a blur, with a corresponding deafening hum of otherwise commonplace sounds, punctuated by loud claps of gunfire that quickly faded into the periphery. I didn't feel my body hit the floor, but I immediately noticed Trish rushing to my side to clasp her hand beneath my head. I didn't know if she was going to agree to be with me or if she was going to decide whether or not the chamber had reached the end of its role in my story. All I knew was that for the last year and a half, I could have frozen any moment that I wanted. That moment, my last moment, I got to spend with her, and that was a moment I wish I could have left frozen forever.

About the Author

Adam Blood is a debate coach and graduate assistant teacher at the University of Nebraska Lincoln. Working in the department of Communication Studies, he researches Rhetoric and Public Culture, and teaches business and professional communication, public speaking, and rhetoric. He completed his undergraduate and Master's degree at the University of Central Missouri. *The Time Chamber* is his first novel.